Destiny Awaits

By Michelle Bennett and

Craig Simmons

Library of Congress Control Number: TXU001676981

ISBN: 978-0-578-06021-7

Acknowledgements

We would like to thank our readers Amber Hughes, Keith Hill, Kelli King, Shatima Taylor and Tommy Lipkins, Jr. Your time and input were invaluable.
Tommy, you're a great artist and we look forward to working with you on our future projects.

Prologue

Camille Jacobs stood at the baggage claim in Chicago's O'Hare Airport. She dreaded having to go out into the oppressive summer heat. She waited for her twenty-dollar Target suitcase, which she had managed to get for ten because they had placed it on the wrong shelf, to come around on the conveyer belt. She stood in a large group of people, most of them also waiting for their own luggage. The nice looking guy that she had first noticed when he got on the plane was standing a few people to her right. He looked over at her and smiled.

Nice teeth, she thought, tucking her braids behind her ear with her index finger. *The better to bite you with*. The thought and the accompanying smile came unbidden to her mind and lips.

The nice looking guy took that as an invitation.

"Hi," he said as he excused himself passing the few people that were separating them. He was about six feet tall, and well dressed. He was wearing a short sleeved blue dress shirt with the top two buttons undone, giving a glimpse of a well-defined chest. He was wearing black Armani dress slacks and a pair of black Gucci wingtips.

He had money or at least wanted people to think he did.

"I couldn't help but notice you on the plane," he said foregoing an introduction.

"Oh really? Why's that?" Camille asked. Guys approached her often, though she never really understood why. She thought of herself as nice looking, but nothing spectacular. She was about five and a half feet tall with a medium brown complexion. She had a nice and very feminine build. She was wearing her traveling clothes, a pair of denim Capri, a light blue tank top and her glasses instead of her contacts.

"I don't often see attractive unmarried women flying by themselves. Ya'll usually travel in packs," he flashed his nice teeth again.

"Well, I'm actually here to meet my boyfriend," she lied. In actuality she recently had a bad break up.

"Oh, I'm sorry. Well, is this boyfriend of yours coming to pick you up? 'Cause if not we could share a taxi."

"That's okay, he'll be here shortly," Camille said as her bag finally came around on the belt. She grabbed it and placed it on the floor. She extended the handle and began rolling it back past the man with the nice teeth.

"Hey," he said as she started to walk by. "Here's my card. If you ever make it down to VA and find yourself in need of a friend, give me a call."

"I'll do that," Camille said, taking the card and reading it. She could have used the fact that she was also from Virginia to continue the conversation but decided against it. "It was nice meeting you, Derek Ballard."

"You too, but I didn't catch your name," he was calling after her because she kept walking as he spoke.

"I didn't throw it," she said over her shoulder with a smile to match his.

Chapter 1

Camille Jacobs stood on the scale pushing the little metal slide along the bar. 135...138...141...146. One hundred and forty six pounds, was by no means fat, but it was more than the former high school track star had ever weighed.

She stepped off of the scale, which was located just inside the door of the women's locker room and exited out into the workout area of The Gym Downtown, in Norfolk, Virginia. The windows of the gym displayed the bright lights of the cold February morning. The first floor of the gym was the cardio area with treadmills, stair stepper machines, spinner bikes, and a myriad of other modern day torture devices.

The wall to her right was covered with mirrors, another of the sadistic humiliations with which the gym tormented their clients. She admired her figure in one of the mirrors. Most of the weight she had gained over the last year was concentrated on the lower portion of her 5'5" frame, which wasn't a bad place for it, judging by the approving glances she was receiving from many of the male customers. But she wasn't happy with the present state of her body.

"Girl, you got work to do," she sighed as she found an unoccupied treadmill. A tall bald man was doing a cool down walk on the treadmill next to the one she chose. Camille noticed the sweat glistening on his scalp and the sheen it created on his well-defined arms. She was pleased to see that his legs were equally as defined as his arms. She hated the grape-ape affect many men achieved by ignoring their lower bodies.

Camille could tell that he noticed her too, because he was obviously trying very hard to not to let her see him looking.

Good, she thought. I'm here to get in shape, not find a date.

Unfortunately the man was not on the same mission. As his treadmill came to a stop he ended his forced ignoring of her.

"How ya doin'?" he asked.

She smiled in response quickly turning her attention back to her own still unmoving treadmill.

"You need some help getting started?"

"No, I got it, thank you," Camille answered, finally finding the setting she wanted and starting the belt in motion.

She began walking briskly and turned her attention to one of the several televisions that were bolted to the walls of the gym. He seemed to get the hint. He cleaned off his treadmill with the disinfectant and cloth the gym provided, mumbled a goodbye and made his way upstairs to the weight room.

Camille warmed up with a two-minute walk before speeding up to a moderate pace for a twenty-minute, two mile run. She ended with a five minute cool down walk. She was disappointed at how winded she was when she stepped off of the treadmill. During her first two years of college she ran two miles before breakfast and would feel energized the rest of the day. Now she just felt tired. She had spent too long focusing on her career and not enough time taking care of herself, and now she was paying for it.

She went to the water fountain under the televisions to quench her thirst. She decided to go up to the weight training area on the second floor in order to find out how far she had regressed strength wise. There were machines along the outer walls and free weights in the center of the room. Most of the people upstairs were men, and most, Camille was sad to see, were of the Grape Ape variety. She noticed that the man who had spoken to her earlier was among the grunting sweaty masses. She made her way to the butterfly machine. She sat down and set the weight to about half of what she was doing when she was in great shape. She made a mental note that it was too light and decided that next time she'd increase the weight.

The man who was apparently more persistent than she had given him credit for, came over from where he had been bench pressing and sat down on the overhead press machine located next to the machine Camille was using.

"Hi again," he said as he pressed the weight above his head.

She gave him a quick smile between her own repetitions.

"Haven't seen you here before," he said.

"Neither have I," Camille stated flatly.

Unfazed by her coldness, the man continued his flirtation. "That's cute. Seriously though, my name's Rashad Lancer. What's yours?"

Camille finished her set and stood up from the machine. Rashad followed suit.

"Camille Jacobs," she said as she began wiping down the machine.

"That's a very pretty name, Camille," he said standing up from his own machine. "It's a pleasure to meet you." He extended his hand for a handshake.

"Nice to meet you, too," she said handing him the disinfectant and cloth. She started walking toward the stairs.

"Wait," he called after her. He placed the cleaning supplies down and walked quickly after her.

Camille, out of curiosity, stopped and turned towards him.

"You think I could call you sometime?" he asked.

"No, I don't think so," she said. *But maybe we can talk next time*, she thought to herself. "Maybe after we get to know each other a little better."

"Well, I look forward to it."

It was 3:30 in the afternoon and Camille was still feeling the effects of her early morning workout. She sat in her office on the fifth floor of the Suntrust building in downtown Norfolk. This was her second full week in the office and it was hard to believe that this was the office of Camille Jacobs, marketing and public relations.

Camille was very good at her job and felt as though she was not getting the recognition she deserved at her old firm. She had been passed over twice for promotion. Many of her ideas were being used by the company and she did not feel she was being compensated accordingly. She decided not to leave bitter however, and made sure not to damage relationships with any of her former colleagues. This, she hoped, would mean that perhaps they would throw some business her way. The phone rang.

"Camille Jacobs, how may I help you?" *I can't wait to start interviewing for an assistant.*

"Hi, my name is Thomas Lyons from Lyons Electronics. I wanted to inquire about your services."

"Well Mr. Lyons I can assure you I offer many services to fit your business's needs. As a matter of fact, I feel as though with the one on one attention I can provide, we can maximize our results."

"Well Ms. Jacobs, you sound very confident, I like that. When can we set up a meeting?"

"Is tomorrow too soon?" Camille asked excited about the prospect of a new client.

"Not at all. How about around ten?"

"That would be perfect. We can meet at my office. Do you know where I am located?" she asked.

"Yes, I do."

"All right, then. I'll see you tomorrow."

Camille felt energized after she hung up the phone. It would be her first meeting with a potential client, since going out on her own. Mr. Lyons told her that he had gotten her name and number from one of her former colleagues. She was glad to see that her old friends had kept their promise of forwarding her some of their smaller clients.

She had already done tons of research on local advertising possibilities, including local publications, social media, production companies, television and radio stations. Now she needed to do some research on Lyons Electronics and package all this in to several proposals for Mr. Lyons. It was going to be a long night.

Nearly twelve hours later, around 2am Camille put the finishing touches on her proposals for her meeting. She decided to stop for the night and finish up in the morning after the gym. She sat on her couch in the middle of her apartment in the Ghent section of Norfolk. There wasn't a lot of room in the place, which was fine because she didn't have very much stuff. What she did have still remained in boxes stacked against the walls. She sat with a bag of microwave popcorn watching her DVD copy of *Boomerang*. She didn't get all the way through it. She fell asleep on the couch, as she had done every night since she had moved back to Norfolk.

The next morning Camille arrived at the office at quarter after eight. She had spent an hour at the gym, and she was actually glad because she didn't feel as bad as she had the day before. The meeting with Mr. Lyons wasn't for another two hours, so she decided to use that time to put the finishing touches on her presentation and to make any last second changes. She received several calls from people inquiring about the assistant job and set up interviews for the following day.

The meeting with Mr. Lyons went perfectly. He loved nearly all of Camille's ideas and wanted her to begin implementing them as soon as possible. Lyons Electronics was a local chain and had begun to take quite a hit to their business because of the big box stores that had begun to corner the market on most big electronic sales. Camille suggested that Mr. Lyons begin focusing on a specific customer niche and accept that there was a certain group he would never get back. Her hope was that by focusing on those people who preferred a more intimate and personal approach to their buying experience he would be able to stay profitable. She knew the ideas weren't new or innovative, but her presentation skills and her marketing ideas, excited Mr. Lyons.

"Well, Ms. Jacobs, I have to say I am extremely impressed and very excited to get started on this," Mr. Lyons said as he stood and shook Camille's hand.

"As am I, Mr. Lyons. I know you'll be even more excited when the ideas aren't just ideas anymore. I think we can get these things off the ground in less than a month," Camille said as they made their way to the door.

"That sounds great. I look forward to talking to you again."

They said their goodbyes and after Camille closed the door behind him, she did a happy dance. She stopped in mid-dance as there was a knock at the door. Camille wasn't expecting anyone. She opened the door. There was a young African-American woman standing before her with an attractive short haircut like Halle Berry from *Die Another Day*. She had the good stuff too...natural curls. She appeared to be in her early twenties. She was wearing a black business skirt suit and heels and a beautiful blue top, and she had a body to do die for.

"Yes, may I help you?"

"Yes, my name is Sydney Mitchell. I am here for the administrative assistant position that was advertised in the paper."

"Oh yes, please come in."

She hadn't set up any interviews this early in the day so she was surprised to see the young lady. She had to gather herself from the high she was on from the meeting with Mr. Lyons.

"You can have a seat right here." Camille pointed her in the direction of a chair she had placed in front of her desk.

"Ms. Mitchell, thank you for coming by. However, I did instruct applicants to fax or email their resumes. Trying to find parking in the downtown area at this time of day can be next to impossible."

"Oh, I know," Sydney agreed, "but I was in the area doing some shopping and decided to stop over. I hope this is all right."

"Yes, it's quite all right. So tell me about yourself Ms. Mitchell."

"Well, I am a senior about to graduate from college in May with a degree in marketing. I was looking for a position where I could gain some entry-level experience. Since your ad indicated that you needed a motivated, recent college grad interested in an opportunity for growth, I didn't think I should waste any time."

"Do you have a resume?"

"Yes, I do." Sydney removed her resume from the leather portfolio she purchased earlier in the semester and handed it to Camille. She knew it would be much needed while pounding the pavement trying to attend all of those job interviews. Camille looked over her resume and was very impressed.

"I see you have been busy during your college career. Three internships, creating flyers for organizations on campus, member of a business fraternity and honor society. Do you have any samples of the flyers you created?"

"Funny you should ask. I happen to have some right here." Sydney wasn't trying to be overly confident but she came prepared. She handed some of the flyers she had done for some fraternities, sororities, multi-cultural student services, and other organizations. She was very skilled with Photoshop, Dreamweaver, Illustrator and knew her way around a computer when it came to graphic design.

"Wow!" Camille was impressed. "I am blown away by your skills. These look great. I must say you are very creative."

"Well, thank you. Thank you very much."

Camille had received some resumes via fax and email but couldn't help but feel like Sydney was the right person for the position. She was confident and had a sense of humor. Camille didn't have the budget to hire her full-time right away. Hopefully this would not turn her off.

"Let me ask you a question. Are you looking for employment out of the area as well? I only ask because you will soon be a graduate and with your graphic design skills, you could do something that might be more lucrative."

"Well, my boyfriend is here. Both of us are from the area and we have decided to stay here for a while."

"The job is only part-time for now but I plan to make it full-time when business starts to pick up. I really need someone with your skills and who can be flexible with their working hours. How does this sound to you?"

Sydney was ecstatic. "It sounds great. I assure you I will do my best."

Camille was excited to have a young and vibrant person on board. "Can you start next Monday?"

"Yes, what time should I be here?"

"How about 9 am? I usually get here at eight o'clock but this will give me some time to get settled in before you arrive."

"Okay great and thank you so much Ms. Jacobs," said Sydney.

Sydney stood up from the chair smiling as they exchanged

handshakes while Camille said, “How about Sydney and Camille?” They both smiled in agreement.

Chapter 2

Derek Ballard stepped out of the airport's sliding doors into the crisp early February, Hampton Roads air. Before he had a chance to look around for his brother's car, he heard a honk and the thumping bass. The 1998 Midnight Blue Volkswagen Passat sat in the passenger pickup zone with Jay-z's the Blue Print I turned up well pass the sensible level. The young man in the driver's seat bobbed his head to the beat, ignoring the glares and sideways glances he was receiving from passengers exiting the Norfolk International Airport. Derek walked up to the passenger side window and knocked on it.

"Pop the trunk D.J. Clueless," he said.

His younger brother, Sean flicked him off before pulling the lever to unlock the trunk. Derek wheeled his bag to the back of the car. Before he was able to put it inside, he first had to make room by pushing aside two baseball bat bags, three baseball gloves, and several empty motor oil bottles. He shook his head as he placed his luggage in his brother's already overcrowded trunk. He closed the trunk and made his way back to the passenger side door. It squeaked loudly as he opened and closed it.

"You really need get some WD-40 for this door and clean out your trunk," he said putting on his seatbelt.

"It's good to see you too," Sean said sarcastically. He pulled the car away from the curb making his way back to the main road.

"Yea, whatever," Derek said with a smile. "So how was your weekend?"

"Good. Syd came over," his smile indicated that it was a very good weekend.

"No wonder all your crap migrated from the backseat to the trunk. How is my favorite roommate?"

"Don't start with that. She ain't over that much. Anyway, how'd your weekend go? Any new clients?"

Derek sighed as Sean turned the Passat left onto Azalea Garden Road. "Nothing definite."

Derek had spent the weekend at the professional football

combine, scouting players to sign to his sports management agency. He decided to use it as an opportunity to make some connections with players who had yet to sign with agents and with team presidents and general managers.

Derek and his two best friends from high school, Robert Singer and Rashad Lancer, had started the agency together. They had decided to base it in their hometown area of Hampton Roads. Over the last few years there had been an influx of talent into the pro ranks of all the major sports, from the area. Thus far their endeavor had not been as successful as they had hoped. They had been in business for about a year and a half and had only three clients, one of whom was Robert. He had been drafted into the pro football league by the Miami franchise two years earlier. The other two clients both played basketball overseas in Europe.

Rashad had started out working for a sports management firm in New York, but always dreamed of starting his own. Derek had completed law school at the University of Richmond and was in the process of studying for the Bar exam when his mother suddenly fell ill and died. Rashad convinced him to come back to the Hampton Roads area and help him start the firm. With a small business loan and using a part of Robert's signing bonus they started RDR Sports Management.

"I handed out my card to a few of the players who are probably going to sign as free agents, but the guys that are going to be drafted didn't want anything to do with me."

"Well the draft is still a couple of months away, maybe the calls will start coming in. Besides that the baseball and basketball drafts are coming up this summer and there are several prospects at ODU that I've been talking to for you guys," Sean said as he turned left onto Military Hwy, directly into the late afternoon rush hour traffic.

Sean was a senior at Old Dominion University in Norfolk, and was a top 100 baseball prospect. He had been drafted out of high school three years earlier, but he had promised his mother before she died that he would earn his degree. He had taken summer classes and a couple of semesters of overloads in order to graduate a year early. He had agreed to allow his brother's firm to represent him and had been busy trying to recruit some of his teammates as well as some of the players from the men's and women's basketball teams.

"You guys really need to find a way to get your name out there," Sean said.

"Yea I know."

It took them thirty-five minutes to get from the airport to the townhouse they shared in the Lake Edward neighborhood in Virginia Beach.

Sean parked the Passat behind his brother's Ford Explorer on the street in front of their three-bedroom townhouse. They didn't have a driveway so they had to park at the curb. "I hate traffic," Sean said melodramatically raising his fists above his head and shaking them at the sky as he got out of the car. "There's no way it should take that long to get here from the damn airport."

"Well that's the price of progress," Derek said as he went around to the back of the car and removed his bag from the trunk. The Hampton Roads area had begun to build up its downtown areas in an effort to improve commerce and lessen the areas reliance on the military. The city of Virginia Beach had built what it called Town Center, where high-end restaurants and businesses had flocked. Derek's firm was actually renting space in the main office building, the Armada Hoffler building, for their offices.

Sean was on the phone when Derek brought his bag into the house. "Yea baby, I had a good time too. Yea, especially last night The, uh, extracurriculars where great."

Derek decided to go up stairs and unpack, in order to avoid overhearing anymore of the details of his brother's date. He had the master bedroom since he was the oldest and paid the majority of the bills. The room was furnished with just a dark oak bedroom set that his mother had left him with a dresser, and a nightstand. There were no pictures on the walls. There were a couple of prints leaning against the wall that were a gift from a former girlfriend, but they had been there for about four months and he was not in a huge rush to hang them.

He walked over to the bed and fell face first onto it. He sighed deeply, wondering what he would do if this venture failed. A year and a half and they only had one client in any of the major U.S. sporting leagues. They had signed a couple of second tier basketball players from the local universities, and had negotiated contracts for them with European teams. None of them had signed blockbuster contracts so the commission they were earning was just barely keeping them afloat.

He drifted off to sleep thinking about what he would do if they were unable to get something, anything, to go their way. His sleep was restless as he tossed and turned having dreams of going bankrupt, losing his house, his car, and everything else.

Derek slept for about two hours. He would have slept longer if the phone hadn't rung. It woke him from a dream he could not remember, except for the feeling of complete despair. The fact that the phone continued ringing unanswered after three rings and that the cordless phone from down stairs lay next to his head helped him come to the realization that his brother had left. He groped blindly for the phone finding it a few inches from his right ear.

"Hello," he said more into the pillow than into the phone.

"Hello," the person on the other end's response was more of a question than a greeting. "Is that you, D?"

"Yea, yea. Hey man," it was Robert Singer, his partner at the firm. "What's up?" Derek sat up in bed trying to wake up.

"How was the trip?" Robert asked.

"I'm too groggy to come up with any colorful metaphors, so I'll just say: not good."

"What happened?"

"Man, it's hard to get kids that are about to start making more money than their parents have made in a lifetime, to entrust that money to people they've never heard of. And to people who have never represented anyone they've ever heard of, save for you of course."

Robert was a silent partner in the firm. He had been a star linebacker at The Ohio State University. They had to limit his involvement in the NFL side of the firm, as it could be seen as a conflict of interest for an active NFL player to also be a player agent. So it was agreed that he would only represent and work on recruiting players in other sports.

He had been drafted by the Miami franchise and made his home there for most of the year. He came up during the summers to help with recruiting and to visit his family. "So how 'bout you, any luck with that basketball player from Hampton?" Derek asked.

"I talked and he listened."

"At least you got that far."

"Yea, well that's about as far as I got. He's already been contacted by some of the top firms in the country and they of course have many more recruiting resources than we do."

"Damn. Whose bright idea was it to start a damn sports' management firm?"

"Uh, that would be Rashad."

"Isn't he your best friend?"

"I thought he was yours."

***

The next morning, Derek arrived at the Armada Hoffler building in Towne Center at quarter to eight. The offices were located on the seventh floor of the building. He parked on the first floor of the garage in one of the three reserved spots they had rented. They were considering relinquishing one of the spots since Robert had mentioned staying down in Miami indefinitely.

The office was sparsely furnished, with a desk with the RDR logo on it being the first thing you saw as you entered. The three men shared one office located to the left of the desk and there was a meeting and conference room to the right.

Derek was usually the first one in the office and today was no different. Both Robert and Rashad were hard workers, and that translated into them being gym rats. So they didn't usually get into the office until around nine. Derek spent that time going over the files of perspective clients. He looked over the stats of small college players who were seniors or had declared early for the draft. He liked to focus on those players instead of the big name players because they were sometimes easier to get along with, knowing that they may not be first round material.

Even going after lesser talent had proven to be an unsuccessful strategy. The trio had not found a way to get their names out there, and more importantly they needed to get their clients names out there. Robert suffered a nagging hamstring injury during his rookie season, which prevented him from cracking the starting lineup and therefore getting him no endorsement offers. He managed to stay healthy during his second season, taking over the starting middle linebacker position during the third game of the year. His stats were good but not great and his team struggled to a 7-9 record. They were all hoping that both his performance and the performance of the team improved during the third year and that he could make the pro bowl. That would definitely help garner some endorsement offers, and in turn get some exposure for the firm.

For now they struggled on with the few clients they had, trying the best they could to convince second and third tier athletes that they could represent them. Derek made a few calls to some of the coaches at some of the local colleges trying to get information on players. In particular there was a receiver coming out of Norfolk State that had the chance to be picked up as a rookie free agent. Robert being in the league had helped the company develop some connections with a few scouts.

Derek had been recruited out of high school to play football for Norfolk State. Even though he elected to go to Virginia Tech on an academic scholarship, he had developed a good relationship with the NSU coaching staff. He used that relationship to try to recruit the kid.

"Hey, coach," Derek said into the phone. "This is Derek Ballard."

"Hey, Derek," the coach said. "Bad news."

Apparently another agency had wooed the player while Derek was out in Indianapolis over the weekend. Derek looked out of his office window over at the luxury apartment building that was being built across the street. He wondered to himself if RDR would be around long enough for him to see its completion.

Chapter 3

Derek parked his SUV behind Sean's Passat in front of their townhouse. He had left work early because things were seemingly going from bad to worse. The grass in the small patch of lawn they had needed to be cut, but he didn't concern himself with that, he'd have to get to it over the weekend. Sean was in the living room watching a spring training baseball game and doing his Economics homework.

"What's up?" he said as his big brother entered the room.

"Not much," Derek answered going into the kitchen. He opened the refrigerator door and pulled out the pitcher of Kool-aid.

"Dad called," Sean said as Derek came back into the living room.

"Oh God, what did he want?"

"He and the step-monster want us to come to dinner tonight."

"What did you tell them?"

"Well," Sean said closing his Economics book.

"Oh, no. Tell me you didn't say yes."

"He tricked me," Sean said unconvincingly.

Derek dismissed his brother's excuse with a wave of the hand and a grunt.

"Sorry," Sean said.

"What time do we have to be there?"

"Eight."

Derrick looked at his watch, it was 4:30 and he felt the need to wind down before dealing with his father and new stepmother.

"You want to play a game of Madden? I figure kicking your butt should cheer me up a little," he asked his brother.

"Oh, well if you need cheering up, you might want to pick a different game 'cause you ain't beating me today."

"Just get the sticks."

The two ended up playing two games as Sean called for a rematch after getting beat by fourteen points in the first game. Derek won the second game too, though it came down to a last second field goal. The games did make him feel better, but he was still dreading going out to his father's. They got cleaned up and left for their father's at about 7:30.

Daryl Ballard and his new bride lived in the Ridgely Manor section of Virginia Beach, located off of Weslyan Drive. It was one of the wealthier sections of the Hampton Roads area. He was an investment banker and had made a good deal of money in the stock market. The relationship between the father and his sons was strained. He had left their mother when Derek was eight and Sean was four. He moved to New York to work on Wall Street, but felt that his family would be in the way. He had recently retired and moved back to Virginia after marrying his twenty-seven year old blonde haired blued eyed assistant.

"Hey," she said opening the door to the very modern and very posh waterfront home.

"Hey, Charity," Derek said feigning a smile. "Sorry we're late."

"Oh it's not a problem," Charity said stepping aside to allow the brothers to enter. "Dinner's not even ready yet. Your father is out back on the deck. You want beer?"

"That'd be great," Sean smiled.

"Got any rum?" Derek asked.

"Rum and coke?" she asked.

"Yeah," Derek confirmed.

"Be right out," Charity said walking towards the kitchen. Sean couldn't help but to admire Charity's athletic physique as she walked away. She had been a member of her college's nationally ranked cheerleading squad, and since graduating had maintained her fabulous figure by competing in fitness pageants.

Derek and Sean were making their way through the "Red" room. Charity had asked that each room of the home be painted a different color. Their father had given her full responsibility for decorating the house and she had run away with it. She had filled the house with furniture from the best furniture stores in New York and had it shipped down. She claimed that she couldn't find anything in Virginia to meet the quality she found in New York.

Daryl was in his late forties, but could have passed for thirty-five. He was 6'2" with broad shoulders and an athletic physique. His head was shaved and his face was clean-shaven, but the resemblance between he and his sons, who both had close haircuts and goatees, was still obvious.

"Hey fellas," Daryl was removing the last steak from the grill as his sons came out onto the deck. "How's it going?"

"What's up?" Sean said.

"Hey," Derek said. "It's a little cool for grilling isn't it?"

"Ah, don't be a punk. I'm just finishing up the steaks," Daryl said. "We're going to eat in the sunroom. You want a drink?"

"Charity's getting us some," Sean said, cutting his brother off before he had a chance to respond to being called a punk.

"Good. You guys go back inside and I'll be in with the meat in a minute." Daryl said.

The brothers made their way back into the sunroom. As they sat down at the table, Charity came in carrying a tray with a bowl of salad and the drinks.

"You need any help with that?" Sean said standing up to give her a hand.

"Oh, I got it sweetie," she said with a smile. "I used to be a waitress in college."

She sat the tray down on the stand next to the table. Four place settings were already set on the table along with a bowl of salad, a tray with four large baked potatoes, and a plate of several ears of corn on the cob. Daryl brought the steaks in and joined the group at the table.

"I brought a frosty mug for your beer," Charity said handing Sean his beer and mug.

"Thanks," Sean said smiling.

The four sat down and began dinner. The first few minutes were quiet, except for Sean and Derek complimenting the chefs.

"So," Daryl said as everyone was about halfway through with their thick steaks. "How's the sports agent business?"

"Going alright," Derek lied. His father thought that Derek's choice to start his own business was a bit premature. He had tried to convince him to take the Bar exam and join a law firm after his mother died, but Derek refused.

"Any new clients?" Daryl probed.

"We have a few prospects. I just got back from the combine and some of the guys that play baseball with Sean may get drafted." Derek knew that mentioning his brother would turn his father's attention away from him and onto Sean. His rum and coke hadn't started to affect him yet so he didn't feel like dealing with his father's interrogation.

"So, Sean, you start applying for jobs yet?" Daryl said turning his attention to his younger son.

"No not yet," Sean said with a mouth full of steak.

"Still counting on getting drafted?"

Sean swallowed hard and cut a look at his brother that said *Here we go again.*

"No," Sean finally said, putting his fork down for the first time since the meal started. "Derek said I could work at RDR this summer if I didn't get drafted."

"You think you guys are going to be around that long?" Daryl asked turning back to his oldest son.

Derek literally bit his tongue and took a drink before saying, "I think we'll be okay."

"Well if you need any help, I could always buy in as a silent partner."

Charity's fork hit her plate with a loud clang. "Sorry it slipped."

"No. I don't think that'll be necessary. Thanks anyway," Derek said.

"Well, it's a standing offer."

Charity began coughing as she choked on her coke.

"You alright, baby?"

"Yeah...I'm fine," she said in between coughs.

The rest of the dinner went without incident as the conversation stayed on more mundane topics, like Charity's new Lexus S-class, and the boat Daryl was considering buying.

"Yeah, but I'm probably going to put that off for a while," Daryl said as he and Charity cleared the table. The group moved over into the entertainment room, which Charity referred to as the green room, because of the hunter green color she had had the walls painted. There was a full bar set against one of the walls, a pool table in the middle of the room, and a large projection screen television on the wall opposite the bar.

"So why are you putting off buying your boat?" Sean asked as he sat down on one of the four barstools.

"Yeah, you've never been one to not spoil yourself," Derek's speech was beginning to become a little slurred after the four rum and cokes he had during dinner.

"Well," Daryl said, choosing to ignore the slight jab. "We have to be a bit more sensible, now." He smiled and pulled Charity closer to him.

"We're going to have a baby!" Charity nearly screamed with a wide smile.

Derek blinked and sobered considerably as he watched the couple. He started to speak, but then thought better of it.

"Congratulations, how far along are you?" Sean asked, trying to fill the silence, which was becoming slightly uncomfortable.

"Yeah, congratulations," Derek finally added.

"Thank you," Charity said, still beaming. "I'm about three months, but we decided to keep in under raps for a while. I hope you don't mind. We're going to have a party to celebrate, but Daryl said he wanted his boys to know before anyone else."

"Well, wasn't that great of him?" Derek said, smiling as though he were in physical pain. "Oh, wow. Um, this is great news, and we'd love to stay and celebrate more, but it's getting late. And I have a meeting in the morning and Sean has an econ test, so we should probably get going." He looked sharply at his brother, before Sean could contradict his story about the test.

"Yeah, we should get going," Sean said.

"Oh, no," Charity said with an exaggerated frown. "I was hoping you guys would stay and help us celebrate a bit more."

"The boys are busy men, honey. They can help us celebrate some other time," Daryl said.

"Yeah, you can invite us to the baby shower," Derek said, as he began making his way to the door.

Charity and Daryl walked them to the door where they said their goodbyes.

"Give me the keys," Sean said as soon as the door closed behind them. "You're drunk."

"Here," Derek said tossing the keys to his SUV to his brother. "I am a little tipsy."

They rode in silence for the first fifteen minutes of the trip. Sean had turned on the radio for a few minutes but eventually turned it off, because he couldn't find anything he felt like listening to. Derek simply stared out the window at the passing street lights.

"What the hell was up with you back there?" Sean finally asked, already knowing the answer.

"What are you talking about?" Derek asked still staring out of the window.

"Why were you being such a dick?"

"Cause I feel sorry for Charity and our new sibling," Derek said. "Cause that man doesn't know how to care about anyone but himself. He's gonna leave them high and dry, just like he did us."

"You don't know that," Sean countered. "Maybe he's changed. He's a lot older than he was when we were born and he has already achieved all his goals or whatever. Maybe this is his second chance."

"Second chance?" Derek said, finally turning to face his brother. "Why the hell does he deserve a second chance? He should still be working on the first one."

"We're grown now, D. You have your own business, I'm about to graduate college, and we don't need him anymore."

"Obviously we didn't need him in the first place. Cause we did all that without his deadbeat ass."

"Why are you so bitter? He's been making an effort since he's been back. Yeah, it might be too little too late, but at least he's trying."

"Sean, man. You were too young when he left," Derek said, calming down. "You didn't see how hard it was on mama at first. She really had to struggle to support us, while he was up in New York dating white girls and trying to 'make something of himself'. When what he should have been doing was being a father and a husband."

There was little else to be said, so the two rode in silence the rest of the way home. When they got to their townhouse, Derek went immediately to bed.

The next morning he awoke, his head pounding, mouth feeling as though he had tried to swallow a bag full of cotton balls, and with an uneasy stomach. He walked slowly down the stairs where his brother sat dressed watching Sportscenter.

"You look like crap," Sean said with a smile.

"Thanks."

"I don't know why you drink when you know you can't handle it," Sean said tossing his brother the television remote.

"Where you going?" Derek asked as he bent over to retrieve the remote, which he had bobbled and dropped.

"Meeting my girl for breakfast. See ya."

"Later." Derek took longer than usual getting ready for work. He forced down a piece of toast and a glass of orange juice. By the time he was showered and dressed it was nearly 8:30AM. He didn't arrive at the office building until 9:00.

When Derek walked into the shared office, Rashad was already at his desk looking over the info Derek had brought back with him from the combine.

"What's up?" Derek asked as he plopped down into the plush leather love seat they had placed against the wall of the office.

"You look like crap," Rashad said. Derek didn't respond. Instead he closed his eyes and laid his head back on the back of the chair. "Is everything okay?"

"Went to my father's house last night."

"Oh. He still on you about the business?" Rashad asked.

"Always. It's like he has no faith in me. Not that he would know what I'm capable of, considering he barely even knows me," Derek said finally raising his head to look at his friend. "But that's not the best part. He and the bimbo are going to have a baby."

"No way," Rashad said. Before Derek could respond, the phone on Rashad's desk rang. "RDR Sports Management." Rasahd had a short exchange with the person on the phone before he said, "Yes, I do believe Derek his here, let me see if I can locate him for you." He pushed the button on the phone to put the person on hold and said, "It's one of the kids you talked to at the combine. Sounds like he may be interested."

Suddenly Derek's hangover was an afterthought as he ran over to his own desk

"This is Derek, how can I help you?"

"Hello Mr. Ballard, I don't know if you remember me, but we talked over the weekend and you said some things I found interesting." The young man was an offensive lineman at The Ohio State and was more interested in going to law school than playing pro ball.

"Alan France, right? I told you we are projecting you as a late round draft pick."

"That's what you told me this weekend, sir, but I still have my doubts. Most of the agents I've talked to are saying I'll be a rookie free agent."

"Yeah, and if you don't have the right people fighting for you and getting you ready for your pro day and personal workouts, that's probably where you'll end up. Robert Singer, one of our other clients, and your fellow Buckeye, has an intense off season training regime that will get you into the best shape of your life."

"So you're telling me if I sign with you I'll get to work out with Robert Singer?"

"That's right. Robert has designed workout programs specific for each position and he can cater it to your specific needs. We want you to get into the type of shape that'll help you perform well on the football field not just at the combine." There was a long pause as Derek gave the young man the opportunity to consider what he had said.

"Can you give me a day or two to talk it over with my father?"

"That won't be a problem, take all the time you need."

"I'll give you a call back soon. Thank you for you time, sir."

"No. Thank you. And I look forward to hearing from you."

Chapter 4

Before meeting his girlfriend, Sean decided to stop and get her some flowers from a local flower shop. They had spent the weekend together while Derek was in Indianapolis, and he wanted to provide her with a romantic greeting since it had been a few days since they had seen one another. This morning, they both had some down time before starting their day. They decided to meet at Sammy's on 29th Street in Norfolk. It was kind of a greasy spoon joint but the food was good and it was inexpensive.

Sean parked his car on the street and decided to empty his backpack so he could hide the flowers. As he entered the restaurant, a young white lady in a t-shirt with the name of the restaurant on it approached him.

"How many?"

"Actually, I'm meeting someone," Sean said as he spotted his girlfriend sitting at a table under one of the several ineffective air conditioners. The temperature was quite warm in the diner. He made his way over to her, his backpack with the flowers in it slung over his shoulder. She was looking as beautiful as ever.

"Sydney, baby," Sean said with a smile. They greeted one another with a hug. Sean didn't want to let go, she smelled so good with the Jennifer Lopez perfume she was wearing. "I've missed you."

"I've missed you too," said Sydney.

Sydney Mitchell and Sean Ballard had been seeing one another for almost two years. They had met during her sophomore year at a fraternity ball. Sean had gone with a girl he had been talking to for a few weeks, but it was a relationship that they both knew wasn't going anywhere.

Sydney was with a group of girlfriends. She had caught Sean's eye as soon as she and her girlfriends entered the room. He recognized one of the girls she was with from high school, and knew that that would be his way to meet her.

"I'm going to say 'hi' to somebody," he told his date, "I'll be right back." She was in a conversation with a friend of her own and he wasn't even sure she had heard him.

Sydney and her friends had found a table to sit at and were laughing at someone out on the dance floor. Though he tried not to stare, his eyes were continually drawn to the attractive girl with, at the time, long hair and an hourglass figure.

"Hey, Tianna. How ya been doin' girl?" Sean said as he approached the table. One of Sydney's friends stood up and gave Sean a big hug.

"Hey I haven't seen you since graduation. What's up?" Tianna smiled.

"Oh, you know me, going to school, playing baseball. What about you?"

"Things are cool. School is going all right." Tianna was still smiling and at the same time wondering why his attention seemed to be more focused on Sydney than anything else.

"So you're not going to introduce me to your friends?" Sean asked.

"Oh, I'm sorry. These are my girls Alicia, Denise and Sydney. Girls, this is Sean. We went to high school together."

"Nice to meet you ladies," said Sean to the girls but more so towards Sydney.

Sean and Sydney's eyes locked for a split second longer than either had intended and Sean knew that he was hooked. As for Sydney, she thought he looked damn good. Sean made sure to exchange numbers with Tianna. A week later, he called her to get Sydney's number.

Sean and Sydney sat down at the table after their embrace.

"I have something for you," Sean said.

"Do I have to close my eyes?" Sydney asked.

"Only if you want to."

"Okay." As Sydney closed her eyes, Sean reached into the backpack and pulled out the flowers he bought.

"All right, you can open your eyes."

Sydney smiled as she saw the beautiful bouquet of yellow tulips with a single red rose in the middle. As tough as he may have seemed at times, Sean could be very romantic.

"Thank you, baby. These are gorgeous."

"Well ya know I do what I can." Sean said jokingly.

"You're so silly," Sydney responded.

"But for real, I just wanted to get them for you to thank you for a wonderful weekend."

"That's so sweet," said Sydney. She gently placed the flowers at the far end of the table. She couldn't wait to tell him about her news.

"Guess what?"

"What?"

"I got a job working for a PR specialist in downtown Norfolk."

"That's great. When do you start?" Sean asked.

"On Monday. It's only part-time but she has assured me that the position will become full-time once business picks up. So I'm putting in my two weeks notice today at Macy's."

"That's great sweetie. Is it a big firm?"

"No. It's just Camille right now."

"That sounds exciting, baby. You'll get the chance to get some experience and show off your talent."

Sydney continued to share her excitement about the opportunity and told Sean about the interview and Camille. Once the food arrived the subject came around to Sean's dinner with his father and stepmother.

"Why is your brother so against giving your dad a chance?"

"I don't know."

"Well, maybe the baby'll give you guys a fresh start."

"We'll see,' Sean said, doubtfully. "Hey, how bout we go out for a celebration dinner tonight after my game? To celebrate your new job."

"That would be great."

After they finished their breakfast, Sean walked Sydney to her car and kissed her goodbye, before going off to class.

*****

"Strike! Two," The umpire said emphatically.

Sean stepped out of the batter's box and cursed himself under his breath for not having swung the bat at the previous pitch. *C'mon Sean*, he thought to himself. *Wake up*. The season had started slowly for him. His batting average was nearly 100 points lower than his career average over the first month of this season.

It was the bottom of the seventh inning, two outs and the score was tied 6-6. There was a runner on second base, and if he could get a hit, Sean could drive in the go ahead run. He stepped back into the box and took a quarter speed practice swing. The pitcher started his wind up and the pitch was on its way. Sean identified it immediately as a curveball from the spin and the pitchers arm angle. He pulled back, stepped towards the pitcher and swung. Sean heard the "ping" of the aluminum bat striking the ball. He felt nothing in his hands so he knew the ball had caught the sweet spot of the bat. The ball sailed over the field between second and third base and landed in the outfield gap between the center and leftfielders. Sean was halfway between first and second as the ball rolled towards the outfield wall. He kicked it into another gear as he stepped on second and ran hard toward third base. The outfielder had thrown the ball to the cutoff man who turned quickly and threw the ball to the third baseman. Sean slid head first into third raising a cloud of dust as he reached for the bag.

"Safe," he heard the umpire say. Sean was left stranded on third at the end of the inning, but the run he drove in proved to be the difference in the game as Old Dominion held on to win 7-6. Sean also made a wonderful defensive play in the top of the ninth inning to end a potential rally. His defense often fed off of his success on offense.

After the game, Sean showered and changed in the locker room with his teammates. He gave a quick interview to a reporter for the school newspaper and to the beat reporter for the Virginian Pilot. He hurried out of the building, looking at his cell phone to check the time. It was 6:25 PM and he was supposed to be meeting Sydney at 7:00 at Fellini's on Colley Avenue.

"Hey bud," he heard as he turned to head towards his car. He looked around and saw Daryl smiling and walking towards him.

"Dad? Hey. What are you doing here?"

"Came to watch your game," Daryl said extending his hand to his son.

"Why didn't you let me know you were gonna be here?" Sean said shaking his father's hand.

"Last second. I actually didn't get here until the second inning. You played pretty well today. Game winning hit, nice defense."

"Yea, hopefully this'll get me out of the slump I've been in."

"Well let's hope so. What are you doing now? I'd like to take you out to dinner."

"I'm supposed to be meeting my girlfriend for dinner at Fellini's," Sean said.

"Oh, ok...well."

"Why don't you join us?" Sean asked.

"I'd love to," Daryl said smiling.

"Great, you know how to get there?"

"No, but I have a GPS, so I can find it."

"Alright, well I'll see you there."

They walked in opposite directions towards their cars and headed over to the restaurant separately. Sean was happy that his father had made the effort to come out and see him play. Derek was right when he said that Sean did not remember how hard it was when Daryl left. All he ever really knew was life without Daryl and his desire to have his father in his life. His phone rang.

"Hello," he said.

"Hey, babe," it was Sydney. "I'm running late, I'll be there around 7:30."

"Everything okay?"

"Yea, rough day, I'll tell you bout it when I see you, and you can tell me all about the game."

"Okay, I have a surprise for you," Sean said.

"What?"

"My dad's gonna join us for dinner."

"Really? I guess you'll fill me in on how that happened when I get there too, huh?"

"Yea."

Sean and Daryl arrived at the restaurant at around 6:45pm. Sean stood at the door and waited for his father. Fellini's was a favorite of many Norfolk residents. They serve gourmet pizzas as well as traditional Italian dishes. The two men were seated immediately as there was a light crowd.

They ordered their drinks, appetizers of fried calamari and garlic bread.

"So you enjoyed the game?" Sean asked.

"Yea," Daryl said. "I'm not a huge baseball fan, but I enjoyed watching you play."

Sean smiled. He felt like a kid earning his father's approval.

"Sorry, I gave you such a hard time the other night, about going pro, I just feel like you should keep your options open."

"Of course," Sean said. "I understand all that. Why else you think I'm working my tail off to graduate a year early? I'm not looking at baseball as a lottery ticket. It's just that I've been dreaming about playing pro ball since I was a kid. If mom hadn't gotten sick, I would probably be playing now instead of in school."

"What do you mean?"

"I was a fourth round pick out of high school, but she made me promise to get my degree. If she hadn't been sick I might have just said screw it and went and played anyway."

"You would've disobeyed your mom?" The look on Daryl's face was a mixture of shock and disbelief.

Sean sighed and took a sip of his sweet tea. He started to speak, but then reached for a piece of calamari and chewed. He took another swig of his tea to wash it down.

"Yea," Sean said. "Mom and I had a rough go of it for a while after Derek went away to school. He tried so hard to please her and be perfect for her. I'm not sure if it was because he blamed himself for you leaving or because he was trying to make up for it, but he made it pretty difficult on me.

"He made straight A's, was always helping around the house and just being the perfect son. And there I was, a C student obsessed with becoming a professional baseball player. I played all year round. I would cut grass and clean gutters to pay for traveling teams. Thankfully I started to do so well that one of the AAU coaches gave me a 'scholarship'. When I got that call from the Cubs I about jumped through the roof. But mom 'asked' me to get my degree first and how could I say no with her being sick?"

Daryl looked at his youngest son for a long time before speaking. "What do you mean you had a 'rough go of it' when Derek left for school?"

"Well, like I said he was the perfect son. When she came home the house was clean he would cook dinner sometimes. I was hardly ever home. I had my own stuff going on, so she would get pretty irritated with me sometimes. We had some blow ups and then she got sick, and...well...."

"Hey," Sydney said as she approached the table.

"Hey, babe," Sean said standing up from the table and giving Sydney a hug. Daryl also stood and shook Sydney's hand. "This is my dad, Daryl. Dad this is Sydney."

"Nice to meet you Mr. Ballard," Sydney said ignoring Sean's informal introduction.

"Nice to meet you too, Sydney."

The three sat down at the table and the waiter came over to get Sydney's drink order. They decided to order one of the specialty pizzas as well. The conversation turned to Sydney.

"So why'd you get off late?" Sean asked.

"Some lady was trying to shoplift a blouse and I had to slow her down until security could get there. So when I started talking to her she started throwing gummy bears at me."

Daryl and Sean both laughed.

"It's not funny," Sydney laughed. "There were all warm and

sticky. I think they had been in the bottom of her purse for months."

Daryl and Sean laughed harder.

Sydney sighed and waited for the laughter to subside. "Ya'll done?"

"I'm sorry, babe, but that's funny," Sean said wiping away a tear.

"Hmm hm, whatever," Sydney said. "I'm just glad I got to put in my two weeks notice today. So Mr. Ballard Sean said you just moved back to the area? Has it changed much from what you remember?"

"Yea, quite a bit actually, it's amazing some of the changes, but I want to talk about you two? How did you guys meet?"

"He does that," Sean said.

"What?" Daryl asked.

"Control conversations."

"It's fine, I like talking about us," Sydney said smiling at Sean. "We met at a fraternity ball during my sophomore year, Sean's freshman year."

"Older woman? Good job son," Daryl said smiling.

Sydney giggled.

"Yea, I saw her with a girl I knew from high school and knew I had to meet her, so I went in a worked my magic," Sean said.

"Never the cocky one, that's my baby," Sydney said.

"I'm not cocky," Sean said raising an eyebrow.

"I know you aren't. I was just kidding."

"So that means you're both graduating this year," Daryl said. "You guys should have a graduation party at my place, we have plenty of room."

"That'd be awesome, dad, thanks."

"No problem. So what happens after graduation?"

Sean and Sydney looked at one another. The question had come up, but neither had been sure of the answer yet.

"We aren't really sure yet," Sean stated cautiously. "It kind of depends on when and where I get drafted and what Sydney decides to do with her career."

Daryl could see that the subject was a touchy one and decided to change it. "Where are you from Sydney?"

"North Carolina, right outside of Charlotte. I came up here for school. Just wanted to get away from home, but not so far that I couldn't get back if I needed to."

"Siblings?"

"Nope, just me."

"Oh, you got a spoiled one?" Daryl said to Sean.

"I am not. That is such a horrible stereotype. Not all only children are spoiled."

"No, not *all* of them," Sean said earning a pinch from Sydney. "Ow. I was just kidding."

Once the pizza arrived the conversation stayed on more fun topics. Daryl told stories about his time in New York and they talked about the excitement of Charity's pregnancy.

Chapter 5: First Date

It was Saturday, and Camille was excited. The Lyons account and her new assistant, who really seemed to have her stuff together, were both going to start on Monday. She had finally gotten a full night's sleep in her bed instead of on the sofa. Mr. Lyons had loved her proposals so much that he had already recommended her to some other local business owners. Things were really beginning to look up.

She decided to go to the gym a little later than usual, which meant she might not see the handsome and intriguing Rashad Lancer, whom she had developed a nice friendship with over the last week. Her trips to the gym were getting to be a lot less discouraging, and she and Rashad learned that they had some things in common. They were both movie buffs, liked to dance, and loved seafood. So far all their conversations had been in between sets or during their time on the treadmill. Camille was beginning to wonder if he was going to ask her out or not.

Her assumption was correct, Rashad was nowhere in sight. She had a good workout despite not having her workout buddy and left the gym two hours after arriving. She was almost out the revolving doors and...

"Hey pretty lady."

Camille turned around and saw Rashad. He was walking briskly towards her. Thank goodness she had stuck to her regular routine and showered after her workout. She didn't want to scare him off. He looked good and the jeans he had on fell perfectly at his waist and showed off his bowed legs.

"Hey," She had a huge grin on her face. "I didn't see you inside."

"Yeah, I went to cardio boxing today. I like variety in my workout." Rashad said with a similar grin. "I'm glad we ran into each other. I was going to ask if you wanted to go grab a bite to eat."

"Lunch?"

"Well I was actually hoping for a dinner date," Rashad explained.

Camille blushed. She had not accompanied a man to anything in a while. She didn't have any plans for the evening, so she decided to say yes.

"Yes, I would love to get a bite to eat. Where did you have in mind?"

"I was thinking about Rodger Browns. Have you ever been there?" Rashad asked.

"No, It's in Portsmouth, right?" Camille responded.

"Yeah, that's it. Does that sound good?"

"Sounds perfect," Camille said.

"I was thinking we could meet over there, say at about seven?"

She agreed, "Okay."

They went their separate ways. Camille made her way to her car. Rashad walked in the opposite direction towards his car which she assumed was parked on a nearby street. She looked back to see if he had taken a quick glance but when she turned around, he had already disappeared around the corner.

Rashad had in fact glanced back just before he turned the corner. He had found Camille attractive the first time he saw her. He had planned to wait a little longer to ask her out, but once RDR had signed that kid from Ohio State, he felt like he should take that lucky streak and run with it.

He knew that once Monday came it would be down to business, trying to set up some individual workouts with some teams and getting the kid ready for his school's pro day. Once that started he would have to wait until things slowed back down to ask her out, and with a girl that fine, he knew if he wasted time some other brother would scoop her up. Even though they had only spoken at the gym over a few days, he found Camille to be a fascinating woman. She was intelligent, beautiful, and ambitious.

Rashad lived in Admiral's Landing on the corner of High and Court Streets a few blocks away from Rodger Browns. He decided to take the walk to the restaurant despite the cold wind blowing in off of the Elizabeth River. He dressed casually and wearing a pair of loose fitting jeans and a tailored black button up. As he approached the restaurant he realized he had never asked Camille what type of car she drove, so he didn't know if she had arrived yet.

He looked around the restaurant as he walked up to the hostess. He was just about to describe Camille to the young woman, when he heard her voice behind him.

"Hey," Camille said.

He turned to face her and was struck by the infectiousness of her smile and her beauty. She was wearing a pair of dark blue jeans that showed off her figure without appearing painted on. Spring had not yet reached the Hampton Roads area, so she wore a light blue v-neck sweater and a hand knitted scarf.

"Hey. Two, please," he said turning back to the hostess.

"Smoking or non-smoking?"

Rashad turned to Camille hoping that she was not a smoker.

"Non," she said, confirming that she still had a chance to be the perfect woman.

The hostess led them past the bar and over to the left hand section away from the wall of large screen televisions displaying several sporting events and one which was tuned to the cartoon network, for the kids. Rashad often came here after work to relax or to catch a game with Derek.

"Sports on TV, huh? Now I see why you suggested this place," Camille said as they took their seats in a booth.

The two kept the conversation light through the appetizer. They had developed a good friendship and small talk was no problem. Somewhere between the salad and the arrival of the main course, there was a slight lull in the conversation.

"I'm glad you finally decided to ask me out," said Camille.

"Finally?" Rashad said with an inquisitive smile on his face.

"Yea. I was starting to think you weren't going to after a few conversations. Perhaps I should have asked you first."

"Why didn't you?" Rashad inquired.

"Not sure," Camille said slightly shrugging her shoulders but in a playful and flirtatious way.

"Anyway, I'm glad we're here."

Rashad had a smile that could make the sun shine on a stormy day. He had beautiful teeth. He was around 6 feet tall with smooth cocoa brown skin. He took pride in his physique and it showed. She was very comfortable with his presence.

"I know its taboo for a man to comment on a woman's weight, but I just have to let you know you look incredible. Not to say you didn't look good before."

"Oh, so that's what took you so long. You wanted to wait 'til I toned up my *assets*."

They both smiled. Rashad was glad that Camille had a sense of humor. Most of the women he had been dating were so obsessed with their bodies, that they took any comment as criticism. It was nice to meet a woman who was comfortable with herself.

"You take pretty good care of yourself too," Camille smiled.

"I try," Rashad said.

"So, what's your story?" Camille said as the food arrived.

"My story?"

"Yea, who is Rashad Lancer?"

"Well," Rashad smiled. "I'm from right here in Norfolk, well that's not entirely true. I was born in California, and my family moved here when I was six. I have an older brother, Malcolm, who went back to California for college and decided to stay. I'm a graduate of UVA. After I got my MBA, I worked at a sports marketing firm in New York, learned a lot but I wasn't happy."

"Why not?"

"My best friends and I always wanted our own firm, so I came back home and did it. How's that for a story?"

"Pretty thorough," Camille said taking another bite of her meal.

"What about you? What's the story of Camille Jacobs?"

"Well, I'm originally from Florida but my family moved to Hampton because my dad had orders to Langley. I went to Norfolk State, graduated and moved to Chicago with my god sister and her mother for a bit. While I was there, I landed an entry-level PR job with a firm and managed to save a nest egg while I lived with them. I decided to come back to Norfolk and go out on my own with my talents. My brother Gary lives in D.C and my sister Shayla is still in Hampton."

Rashad nodded his head and smiled

"So are you close to your family?" Rashad inquired.

"Yeah, we're cool. I'm pretty close with my brother and sister. I should call them more often. I've been so bad with that lately."

"I think I might talk to my brother a couple times a month. It gets hard, ya know?"

Camille nodded her head in agreement. "Yes, especially when you're busy and trying to get yourself together or get wrapped up in your career. I have however vowed to make appearances at more family functions. Family is important."

"Most definitely," Rashad agreed.

The conversation was going well. They were flirting hard and had several short topic talks about work, movies, college, etc. They laughed hard at some moments during the evening. Camille was hopeful that the night would go well and that he wouldn't do or say something to turn her off. Thankfully he did not.

The conversation continued through dessert. It was nearly ten o'clock by the time either of them looked at their watches but they continued to talk. They ended up leaving around eleven.

"Where are you parked?" Rashad asked as they stepped out in the cold night air.

"Just up the street a ways," Camille said pointing in the opposite direction of Rashad's apartment. "What about you?"

"I walked. I live in that building right up the street there," Rashad pointed down towards his building.

"Really? So how are you gonna pick a restaurant within

walking distance of your place? You must have been pretty confident about how the date was gonna end, or did you just want to make sure you could make a quick get away?"

Rashad laughed. "No, no. I didn't even think about it like that. I just really like this place."

"Whatever," Camille said as she started walking towards her car.

"Seriously," Rashad said. "Next time you can pick the place."

"Who said there was gonna be a next time?" Camille said smiling. She stopped next to her 2007 burgundy Toyota Camry.

"Well, excuse me for being presumptuous, but I thought we had a pretty nice time, at least I know I did," Rashad said.

Camille looked up at him and smiled. "This was a lot of fun, and I do hope we can do it again soon." She moved towards him and gave him a hug. "You want a ride down to your place?"

"No, I'm good. The cold air will do me some good," Rashad said. "Good night, Ms. Jacobs." He opened the driver's side door so that she could enter the car.

"Good night to you Mr. Lancer," he closed the door of the car.

Rashad stood for a few moments and watched as she drove up High Street and made a left on to London Boulevard, before starting his walk home. He made a mental note to let her know that the Midtown Tunnel would be a quicker route for her to get to Ghent.

Chapter 6

Camille was really into Rashad and definitely wanted to see him again. Maybe she could give him a call after her day was over. She was rather excited about the idea of having male company. There would be plenty of time to think about that later. It was Sydney's first day at work and Camille wanted to make sure everything was set up for her. A desk was set up for her with a few supplies. Camille had given her an older brown office chair that had an irritating squeaking sound every time it rotated to the right. Nothing a little WD-40 couldn't solve for a while.

Sydney was on her way up to the office. She was wearing a black skirt suit she bought from Macy's and carrying her portfolio. She thought she'd never find a parking space. The downtown Norfolk area was congested. She arrived around ten minutes to nine.

"Good morning." Sydney smiled.

"And good morning to you. Don't you look nice? Love the suit." Camille was not surprised. Sydney was so professional at their first meeting, she didn't expect anything less.

"Thank you."

"Your desk is here. There should be enough supplies here for you to get started. I will be sure to order more within the next couple of weeks."

"That's fine," Sydney said looking over the desk.

"I don't have a computer for you yet, but we can share mine until we get a couple more clients."

" Well, I have a laptop, so if you want, I could bring that in," Sydney suggested sitting down at her new desk. She noticed that the chair squeaked quite a bit when she turned in it.

"Oh and about the chair," Camille said preemptively, "I'm planning to get you a new one, but in the mean time I'll get some WD-40 at lunch."

"No problem," Sydney said with a chuckle. "It sounds just like my boyfriend's car door."

Camille laughed, relieved that Sydney had a sense of humor.

I'm glad she isn't an uptight stick in the mud. "Well, you can borrow the WD-40 for your boyfriend's car door then."

Sydney was also relieved that things were getting off to a good start. Camille's cell phone rang. She didn't recognize the number. She didn't like answering unknown phone numbers. She studied the number for two more rings and decided to answer.

"Hello?"

"Hello, Camille?" It was a man's voice. One that she could not place.

"Yes."

"Camille Jacobs?" The man asked.

"Yes, Camille Jacobs. Who is this?" At this point, she was very curious who was at the other end.

"This is Tyrone."

Camille was perplexed. She tilted her head to one side...*Tyrone...Tyrone.* The only Tyrone she knew was a guy she met while in college. She knew him for a short time and they lost touch. She recalled him being quite the party animal.

"Tyrone Johnson?" Camille questioned.

"Yea. I saw your contact information in the alumni link on the university web site. Thought I'd give you a call, see how things were going."

"Things are quite well thank you. I must say I am surprised to hear from you."

"I know you must be. Actually, I was calling because I am opening a club and really need someone to work promotions for me. I was wondering if you would be interested in providing me with your expertise."

Camille was flattered. As she thought back to her sophomore year, she recalled him saying that he dreamed of running his own club one day. He was very sociable, outgoing, and knew a lot of people. She forgot that she placed her contact information on the site until he mentioned it. That was okay though. This would be a good business venture.

"Wow. You're really going to do it; open your own club. That's great."

"Yeah, it's on Virginia Beach Boulevard near Military Circle Mall. I am preparing for my grand opening, which is a few months off, but I'm trying to get my ducks in row." Tyrone sounded very enthusiastic and confident.

"I would love to take this on. Perhaps we can meet somewhere to talk about the particulars, you know, so I could get some more details."

"Great. When and where would you like to meet?" Tyrone asked.

"How about we meet at the deli across from the Downtown Marriot sometime this week?"

"All right. Maybe Wednesday for lunch....noon?" Tyrone proposed.

"Okay. I will meet you then. I look forward to seeing you."

"Thanks Camille, I'll be there." Tyrone disconnected.

Camille was excited. The idea of two new clients in less than a week was great.

"Good news?" Sydney asked.

"Very, we may be able to afford that new computer sooner than we thought," Camille said smiling. "That was an old college friend. He's opening a new club and wants us to do the PR for his grand opening."

"That's great," Sydney said.

"Yea, if we keep this up maybe we'll be able to get you a new chair too." They both laughed. "Well let's get you started."

Chapter 7

Derek had begun to feel a little ashamed about the incident at his father's home. He knew he had been out of line but he couldn't help himself. When his father left, he was eight years old. His mother tried to explain why his dad was leaving. She said it did not mean he didn't love him, but to him it still felt like he was unwanted. Sean didn't have the same reaction because he was only four and too young to realize what was going on.

Derek decided that he needed to get away. He needed to get his mind off the news Daryl and Charity had dropped on him. They had arranged for Alan France, their new client from Ohio State, to go down to Miami to stay and workout with Robert Singer. They hoped that with Robert's help Alan could impress the scouts at pro day and possibly get a few private workouts.

Robert and Alan were waiting for Derek just outside the sliding glass doors of the airport. Robert was a prototypical NFL linebacker with movie star looks. He was six feet four inches tall, two hundred and forty-seven pounds of pure muscle. He waslight-skinned and handsome, but not pretty. He had a neatly trimmed goatee and an intricately designed set of cornrows.

Standing next to him, it was hard to tell Alan was an athlete. He was two inches taller than Robert and out weighed him by nearly sixty pounds. The nearly three hundred pound white man looked uncomfortable in the eighty degree Miami heat. He had a well maintained full beard and shoulder length dark brown hair, which he had pulled back into a ponytail.

"What's up, playa?" Robert said giving his old friend a huge hug. "How the hell are ya doin'?"

"I'm good, man. How you been?" Derek smiled. Robert was a great friend and someone who was always there for him.

"Can't complain. Just tryin' to get our boy here ready for the league."

Derek turned his attention to Alan, extending his hand. "How you doing Alan?

"Good, Mr. Ballard, how have you been?" Alan said shaking Derek's hand.

"What's with the Mr. Ballard stuff Alan, I told you it's just Derek."

"Yeah, he tried that with me for a while too," Robert said. "Until I got him in the gym and broke his ass down. Then he was calling me everything but mister." The three of them laughed and Derek could feel his mood lightening.

"Don't laugh too hard," Robert said taking Derek's bag and throwing it into the back seat of his red Escalade. "Cause you're next."

"What?"

"You brought your workout gear, didn't you? I know you didn't expect me to show you the Miami nightlife, without working for it did you?"

Derek's smile faded a little. Robert had always been a gym rat and his two to three hour workouts were hellish and not something Derek looked forward to. But since Robert was footing the bill for this little vacation, he was calling the shots.

The three men went to an exclusive private gym in downtown Miami straight from the airport. Robert had been a Human Nutrition, Food, and Exercise major and had gotten his certification as a personal trainer.

"What's up, Steve?" Robert said to the athletic blonde haired man behind the desk, as he entered the gym.

"Hey Rob. You got clients today?" Steve asked.

"Naw, just my boys," Robert said. "I told Alex he'll have to take on my clients for a while."

"Okay, that's cool."

Robert, Derek, and Alan went to the locker room to change.

"You work here?" Derek asked.

"I picked up a couple of clients as a favor to Steve. Miami's all about name recognition, and having a famous name as a regular at your business can take your place to a new level."

"But he asked you about clients," Derek said.

"Yeah, well after I got my certification I kind of wanted to get some use out of it and it gives me the opportunity to develop some programs and learn about the business aspect of running a gym."

"You want to own your own gym?" Alan asked. It was the first time he had spoken since the airport.

"Whole chain of 'em. Hopefully I can perform well enough to get a big second contract and use that money to get started."

Derek knew that Robert wanted to start other endeavors with his money, but this was the first he had heard of the gym idea. It made him think. Derek had been expending so much energy trying to get the firm off the ground that he had set aside other dreams. Actually when he thought about it he wasn't even sure what it was he ultimately wanted to do. The firm had been a dream that Rashad had convinced him and Robert was a good idea.

The three men worked out hard for an hour and a half. They began with a fifteen minute run around the raised track which encircled the gym. Afterwards they moved on to weight training. Derek could already see a change in Alan's physique and strength level as compared to when he had first seen him in Indianapolis. He knew that having him work with Robert would be a good plan for him and would help to improve his value to teams. Derek struggled a bit as he had been slacking a bit with working out.

After the workout, the three men made their way to Robert's South Beach condo. It was located a couple of blocks off of the beach but still within walking distance of the shopping and nightlife.

"Man, I love this place," Derek said as he leaned on the railing on the balcony of the fifth floor condo. He stared out as the sun began to set over the ocean. He had already changed for the club and was waiting for Robert, who was getting dressed, and Alan, who was showering in one of the two guest rooms.

"I keep telling you to move down here with me," Robert said walking out onto the balcony and handing Derek a bottle of water. He was dressed in an expensive grey outfit. It was specially tailored and did a great job of showing off his physique without making him look like a hulk. "We could set up a second office. With as much talent as there is here in Florida our client list would definitely start to grow."

Derek sighed, "I can't move down here."

"Yo' brother is old enough to take care of himself and you need a change of scenery playa'," Robert said.

"Why do you say that?"

"You look drained, man. You gettin' any?"

"What?" Derek said looking at his friend incredulously.

"You heard me. Are you getting' any nana?"

"You a nasty son of-"

"Don't change the subject, negro. Are…you…gettin'…any…ass?"

Derek turned back to look as the last of the sun dipped into the ocean. "It's been a while."

"How long is a while?"

"Nosey ass."

"Negro, I was the first person you called when you bust yo cherry. How long has it been?"

"I don't know. Three, four months."

"Damn. No wonder you look so down in the dumps, you backed up. Cause you know like I do, that wackin' ain't cuttin' it after about the third week."

"When the last time you went three weeks without gettin' any?"

"You right," Robert laughed. "But not to worry, we shall be rectifying your problem tonight. There are entirely too many lovely and willing ladies in Miami Beach for you to be running around with a hard on and blue balls, my friend."

"You are a nasty son of a-"

"And you love me for it." Robert said putting his arm around his long time friend and leading him back into the condominium. Robert's condo had three bedrooms, a library, a den and three full bathrooms. The floors were all hardwood except for the kitchen which had black marble floors which matched the countertops. The library had built in bookshelves which were filled. He had separated the books by genre. One shelf was nothing but black authors, Zane, Morrison, Dickey, Baldwin, Wright, among others. Another shelf was filled with books on becoming successful in business. The other shelves were everything from autobiographies of athletes and statesmen to computer software books.

Alan came from the second bedroom dressed in black slacks and a blue short sleeved button up shirt. He also wore a new pair of black Prada shoes.

"Wow. You clean up nice," Derek said. "Nice shoes."

"Thanks," Alan said. "Rob bought them for me. I thought it was insane to spend that much on a pair of shoes, but he insisted."

"Hey, if you gonna go out with me, you got to look the part." Robert said grabbing his keys from the kitchen counter. "Ya'll ready to party like rock stars?"

Chapter 8

Sean came home from class at around two o'clock on an early March Friday afternoon. It was the first day in a couple of weeks he didn't have a game or practice and he was looking forward to spending the evening alone with Sydney. Since she had gotten her new job he had seen less of her than he liked. He was glad that she was getting experience and seemed to be enjoying what she was doing, but he really missed her. Today was her last day at Macy's and she would not be getting home until around four.

Sean decided to make himself some lunch and watch television. He had just sat down with his sandwich and chips when the phone rang.

"Hello," he said as he muted the television.

"Hey, Sean. This is your dad. How you doing?"

"Hey," Sean said. "I'm good. How bout you?"

"Good, good," Daryl said. "What are ya'll up to tonight?"

"Well, Derek's down in Miami visiting one of his clients and business partners," Sean explained.

"That's perfect. I was hoping we'd get to hang out without Derek around."

"Actually I was planning to chill with my girl tonight," Sean said. "She just started a new job and we haven't been able to spend a lot of time together lately."

"That's even better," Daryl said excitedly. "Charity and I can take you guys out tonight. How about we get together at Freemason Abby tonight at about seven?"

"Uh, well."

"C'mon, it'll be fun. I'd love to see Sydney again and for her to meet Charity," Daryl pressed.

"Yeah, um, okay seven at Freemason sounds good, dad."

"Great, we'll see you and Sydney at seven. Bye, son."

"See ya," Sean hung up the phone with a sigh. Sydney had been looking forward to the two of them getting to spend some time alone together and he wasn't sure how'd she react to this news.

Sydney pulled up in front of Sean's place at about five thirty. She parked her 1999 blue Honda Civic behind Sean's Passat. Sean was waiting in the doorway for her. She smiled and waved to him. He gave her a half smile in return.

"Uh oh," she said as she walked up to him. "What's wrong?"

"Well," he said as he hugged her. "I know we were supposed to be having a nice quiet evening alone, but I kind of made plans for us."

"What kind of plans?" Sydney said through squinted eyes.

"My dad called and he and the stepmonster want to take us out to dinner."

"Why do you do that?"

"Do what?" Sean said. The two of them stepped inside the townhouse and closed the door. He followed her into the living room where she sat down on the couch.

"Call her stepmontser? I thought you said she wasn't that bad?"

"She's not. I just got used to calling her that because of Derek," Sean explained. "I actually think she's nice."

"Well don't call her that anymore," Sydney admonished.

"Okay."

"I'm serious, don't let your brother influence the way you feel about your dad and step mom," Sydney said pulling Sean down on the couch beside her. She snuggled her head into his shoulder and neck. "Just because Derek hates her doesn't mean you can't give her a chance."

Sean kissed her on the forehead and smiled. "You're wonderful."

"Thank you. So what time are we meeting them?"

"Seven at Freemason Abby."

"What?" Sydney sat bolt upright. "I need to shower and change clothes."

"Why? You look good," Sean said. Sydney was dressed in business casual attire.

"Yeah, but I don't feel comfortable," Sydney said. "Give me a few minutes. I want to put on some jeans."

*****

Sean and Sydney arrived at the restaurant a few minutes after seven. It was a relatively warm night. Sydney felt more comfortable after changing. Daryl and Charity were standing out front of the restaurant waiting for them. They both smiled as Sean and Sydney approached.

"Hey dad, Charity," Sean said as they stopped in front of his father and step mother. "This is Sydney."

"Hello," Sydney said smiling. "It's nice to see you again Mr. Ballard and it's wonderful to finally meet you, Charity," She extended her hand to Daryl and Charity in turn. They both shook it.

They made their way inside the restaurant, and were seated almost immediately.

"Sydney, I love your hair," Charity said ending the lull in conversation that had occurred after they were seated.

"Thank you," Sydney said smiling.

"I've been wanting to cut my hair, but Daryl likes it long," Charity said. "Even still, I don't think it'd look as cute as yours."

"Well thank you, Charity. I had longer hair when I started college and it just got to be a hassle getting ready in the morning. I would jut keep it up most of the time, so I figured why not just cut it. Low maintenance."

"So son, how's baseball going?" Daryl said trying to bring the conversation around to a more masculine topic.

"Pretty good, actually," Sean said. "That game you came to was the start of a hot streak. This is turning into my best season since I got to school. I'm hitting the ball like I did in high school and my power numbers are higher than ever. Robert, Derek's other partner designed an off season weight training program that's really given me some pop."

"Robert's the one that plays professional football right?" Charity asked.

"Yeah. He's also certified as a personal trainer."

"That's pretty impressive," Daryl said. "I wish your brother would get his act together."

“What do you mean?” Sean asked. “He owns his own business.”

“Failing business. Those boys are in over their heads and they need to cut their loses. I hate saying that because I want him to be successful, I'm just afraid your brother's head really isn't in it. Rashad seems reasonably dedicated, but Derek seems like he's just going through the motions.”

Sean wished he could defend his brother and dispute what his father was saying but he had to admit that he had felt the same way for sometime. When Rashad had come to Derek with the idea that year after their mom died, Derek seemed to be in a place where he had no idea what he wanted to do with his future. It had almost seemed to Sean like Derek had agreed just because he didn't want to leave his boy hanging.

The conversation turned to lighter topics after the food had arrived. Daryl turned the attention back onto his son's girlfriend.

“You know Sean you need to lock this girl up to a long term contract,” Daryl said. “A man should try to hold a woman like you as closely as possible.”

“Don't worry about him Sydney, he's just a big mouth,” Charity said laughing.

“I'm serious, why else you think I knocked my baby up,” Daryl said leaning over and kissing Charity on the neck. Sean shook his head.

“Stop it, now. You're going to have these guys thinking you're serious. So Sydney, are you still in school too?”

“Yes, I graduate in May,” Sydney said. Sean was glad to have avoided the potential topic of marriage.

“I still think the older woman was a good choice son,” Daryl commented, earning an elbow in the arm from Charity.

“Go on, Sydney. Don't mind his interruptions.”

“Well, I recently started working for a woman who runs her own marketing and PR business. She has some really great ideas, and it's great to see a black woman unafraid to get out their on her own” Sydney explained. “No offense, Charity.”

“Oh, none taken sweetie. I understand what you're saying.”

The group continued talking and getting to know one another. Sean was happy that Sydney liked his father and step-mother. Even though his brother was still bitter about their father leaving them, he felt like this was a chance to start over.

Chapter 9

On the last day of his visit to Miami, Derek lay in bed with a hangover like none he had ever felt before. His head was pounding and he wasn't sure but he thought there was the distinct smell of vomit coming from somewhere nearby. He sat up on the edge of the bed as slowly as possible. He felt like if he moved any faster he's tip over and shatter into a thousand pieces. He still wore the outfit he had on the previous night, though someone had removed his shoes for him. *Why do I do things like this*? He thought. He didn't drink often mainly when he was out with his boys, but occasionally when he was upset he'd use alcohol to dull the feelings. Unfortunately, once he was sober whatever he was upset about hadn't changed and now he had a tremendous headache to add to it. There was a light knock at the guestroom door. He groaned permission for entry.

"How you feeling?" Robert said as he peeked into the room.

"Why the hell did you let me get that drunk?"

"You needed it, kid," Robert said handing his friend a glass of water. "Every since we were kids you'd get yourself all twisted up about something and then you'd be mopey and a pain for days. For some reason alcohol is the only thing that expedites the process.

"You get drunk, you cry and talk about your feelings for about and hour and then you're all better."

"I cried," Derek said, nearly choking on his water. "In front of Alan?"

"Yea, he ended up taking care of both of us last night," Robert said. "That boy can put away some beer."

"Oh my goodness," Derek said burying his head in his hands. "This is so unprofessional."

"Don't worry about it. Alan's cool, he told me he was glad that we were treating him like a friend and not just a paycheck."

Derek shook his head, though he did feel some relief to hear that.

"Get cleaned up, I'll take you out to lunch before your flight."

****

It took Derek about an hour to get ready, because he was still moving in slow motion. He wanted to clean the room up, but Robert said he had a maid service.

"And with as much money as I'm paying they better not complain about a little vomit."

Alan stayed at the condo watching television, while the two old friends went out for a quick lunch. They sat at an outside table at one of the many beachfront cafes.

"So how are we doing, man?" Robert asked.

"What do you mean?" Derek asked sipping another glass of water.

"The agency I mean. I looked over the books last time I was there and things weren't looking so hot."

"Things aren't so hot. We're struggling just to break even right now."

"What do we need to do?"

"We need clients. If we don't get either a lot more clients or one top notch client I'm not sure how much longer we can stay afloat."

"You think we should cut our losses and just shut her down?" Robert asked the question that Derek had been asking himself for the better part of a year.

He looked at his friend for a moment and then turned to look out at the ocean. He watched the waves crash against the shore as he answered. "I don't know.

"I mean you have football and your gyms potentially. I don't know what else I want to do. I don't even know if this is what I want to be doing. And what about Rashad, this agency is his dream?"

"Yea, well he has his dream and if he wants to keep it going he can, but I think I'm going to sell you guys my portion of the agency."

"Are you serious?"

"My heart's not in it anymore. Honestly, I'm not sure it's ever been in it. I'll still train guys for you and I'll stay a client, but I want to take my money out of the business end of everything."

"Wow," Derek said.

"Yea, I think I'm going to use the money to start my first gym, and I think you need to figure out what it is you want to do before you end up bankrupt and miserable."

Derek didn't answer. He sipped his water and watched the waves crash. His thoughts were as murky as the ocean water.

"We better get going," Robert said, after a while. "Don't want you to miss your flight."

Chapter 10

Camille was waiting for Tyrone to arrive at the deli downtown. She was excited about this meeting. She had arrived a little early so she perused the menu. The turkey and Swiss on toasted sourdough looked good. She proceeded to order as she felt a presence behind her. She turned around and standing there was Tyrone. He was handsome and looked better than she remembered. He stood about six feet two inches. He was wearing a pair of black slacks, a purple shirt and a nice striped tie. It was about seventy degrees out so he didn't have on a jacket. His hair looked like he just got it cut five minutes ago.

"Hungry, huh?" He said smiling.

"Oh, hello I thought I felt someone standing behind me. And yes, I am hungry. I hope you don't mind. I didn't want to be rude not waiting for you and all."

"No that's quite all right." Tyrone said continuing to smile. "Wow! You haven't changed a bit. You still look good."

"Thanks." Camille responded. Tyrone had always been a flatterer, though she was happy to hear that her time at the gym was paying off.

Tyrone ordered something as well. They paid, took their numbers and went to find a place to sit. The place was busy but not too crowded. They managed to get a booth near the window where you could see right across the street to the hotel. Camille sat her brief case on the floor next to the table. Tyrone was carrying a black portfolio which he placed on the table.

"So Tyrone, I have to say I was surprised to get your call. Who would have thought that I would be embarking on a business venture with an old college friend?"

"Yes, well you know what they say...life is full of surprises."

"So what have you been doing since college?" Camille asked

"I don't know if you remember but during senior year, I was a bartender at a club."

Camille tilted her head to the side trying to recall what the name of the club was. She said excitedly, "Club Groove?"

"That's right," Tyrone said. "I bartended for about two years. The money was good. Eventually I was promoted to assistant manager. After all, I did have a degree and I had a good relationship with the owner of the club. That gave me the opportunity to really learn the ins and outs of the business. So when the owner decided to open a second club he gave me the chance to manage it. I loved it and decided I wanted a club of my own. I saved some money, found a location, got a business loan and started construction. Of course that's the abbreviated version of it but you get the idea."

"Well I am glad that you got in touch. I hope that we can make great things happen for your business," Camille said.

"Number 116 and 117." The blonde haired waitress said as she held two plates of food.

"Yes, I had the turkey and Swiss." Camille said.

Tryone removed his portfolio from the table and placed it under the chair. The waitress placed his roast beef and cheddar sandwich on a sesame seed bun in front of him.

"Thank you," he said.

"Enjoy your meal," the waitress said leaving.

"Camille do you mind if we talk while we eat?"

"Oh of course not," Camille said already chewing on her first bite.

"Okay then, I guess I can just get right to it. My club is for the grown and sexy, you know...ages 25 and older. I want it to be a place where people come, sit back, relax and not be gritted on."

"That sounds nice," Camille said. "Is it just going to be a kind of after work, chill spot? What about the weekends?"

"Well, I like the idea of the after work, R&B, happy hour vibe and on the weekends, maybe have some old school hip hop dance club nights."

"Okay, so you said you've already started construction?" Camille asked.

"Yeah, I've provided a lot of direction on how I want the place to look."

"Nice. You said you wanted an R&B vibe on the weekdays, but

have you thought of maybe changing it up some?"

"How do you mean?" Tyrone asked.

"I don't know, I was thinking of trying to offer something you can't get everywhere. Maybe have a jazz night, or a spoken word night, or maybe just an open mic night, where you give local artists a chance to shine."

Tyrone contemplated Camille's suggestions as he took another bite of his sandwich. "Open mic?"

"You know, aim to fill a niche that isn't being filled in this area," Camille said. She could see that she had piqued his interest and knew this was how she could help make this place a success.

"I hadn't really thought of that," Tyrone admitted. "I just wanted a place where adults go get their drink on after work."

"Yeah, but there are plenty of places like that around here. What you want is something special. I think something like making Wednesday a jazz night, and say making Thursday a spoken word or open mic night would, you know, bring in some people who might not usually do the club scene." Camille started to get excited about the ideas herself. Her mind was already starting to consider some ideas she wanted to bounce off of Sydney. But she was getting ahead of herself, because she hadn't gotten the account yet.

"I knew it," Tyrone said with a smile. "I knew you would be the perfect person for this, because you know your stuff. When can you get started?"

"So you're giving me the account?" Camille asked.

"Of course."

"Well, I do need to see the club. I know it's not done yet but it'll help me get an idea of what we're working with. I also need to give you some paperwork to look over."

"That's fine, when would be a good time for you?"

"Actually, I want Sydney to see it too. She's my assistant, so I'll give you a call this afternoon, after I talk to her."

"Sounds good," Tyrone said.

Once the deal was verbally finalized, the conversation turned back into small talk. They finished their lunches and Camille reiterated how excited she was to be working on the project and reminded Tyrone that she would be giving him a call that afternoon.

When she got back to the office, Camille was still smiling from the positive meeting with Tyrone.

"I'm assuming from your smile that the meeting went well," Sydney said when Camille walked into the office.

"Very well," Camille confirmed. "I think this could be huge for us. He liked some of the suggestions and ideas I had and I think with your graphic design talents we can do some really nice stuff. He wants us to come by to take a look at the club so we can get a better idea about what our strategy is going to be."

"You want me to come along?" Sydney asked excitedly.

"Of course, you are my graphic design artist. And with a club the visuals are going to be an important part of the sell."

"When?"

"I told him I'd give him a call this afternoon to set up a time. When's good for you?"

"Since I'm still part time here I haven' quit my job at the department store, so I have to work tomorrow, but Friday or Saturday would work."

"Good, I'll set it up for Saturday morning. I have a meeting with Mr. Lyons on Friday." Just then Camille's cell rang. "Hello."

"Hey there," Rashad's smooth voice said on the other end.

Camille smiled at the sound of his voice. They had seen each other that morning at the gym, but she still liked to hear his voice. "How are you?"

"Good, yourself."

"Very good, actually. I just had a very good meeting with a potential client," Camille made her way into her office and closed the door behind her.

"That's good news. Can I help you celebrate?"

"How do you propose doing that?"

"Dinner. Tonight."

"Where?" Camille asked, her smile growing wider. This would be their third date. The first two had gone well and Camille was really starting to feel Rashad. He was educated, good looking, and well spoken. She had actually started fantasizing about having sex with him, especially when they were working out at the gym and he had a nice sheen of sweat covering his well defined physique. It had been a while since she had gotten any and she wasn't sure if she wanted to hold out much longer.

"Well, this is such a special occasion, how about you let me cook you dinner?"

"Hmm, not only is he tall dark and handsome, but he can cook as well."

"Hey, I'm a southern boy, we know how to burn."

"I guess I'll have to be the judge of that," Camille said with a laugh. "What time should I show up?"

"Around seven. Let me give you the address."

***

Camille parked in the parking deck behind Rashad's building. She walked up to the glass doors and dialed the three digit code to his apartment on the metallic intercom system.

"Hello," Rashad's voice came through the intercom system.

"It's Camille."

"Come on up." There was a dull buzzing sound that emitted from the door and Camille pulled it opened. Upon entering the building, she was struck at how much like a hotel it looked like on the inside. The carpeted halls were long and wide as though they were built for housekeeping carts. She went up the elevator to the third floor and made a right like he had told her to do.

209...211...213...215. That was his place. Before knocking on the door she gathered herself. She was wearing her bootilicious jeans, the ones that showed off the shapeliness of her thighs and butt, a black scoop-neck off the shoulder blouse that showed off the smooth skin of her shoulders and back, and a blazer. It was a little cool out, so she couldn't wear her strappy sandal shoes and had to wear her shoe boots instead.

Rashad opened the door just as she raised her hand to knock. He smiled. He had on a pair of dark Old Navy blue jeans and a thin, tan, thermal fitted shirt. The shirt showed off his muscles...he looked so good. "I thought you had gotten lost."

"No, I was just walking slow, I guess," Camille lied. They hugged and she gave him a peck on the cheek. He was obviously surprised and pleased with the show of affection, as his smile broadened.

"This is my apartment," Rashad said, stepping aside. "It's not very big, but I like it. Take a look around while I finish up dinner."

Miles Davis's *Kind of Blue* was playing in the background. A candle was lit on the living room coffee table. The place was small but nice. The kitchen was immediately to the left. There were all new appliances and ample counter space. Straight ahead was the living room, which was just big enough for a couch, single plush chair and a coffee table. There was a door that Camille figured opened up onto a balcony directly in front of her. The carpet was cream colored and Rashad had contrasted that nicely with a moroon colored leather chair and sofa. He had a 32" Samsung flat panel television on the wall opposite the balcony. It had two bedrooms. The master was immediately to the right upon entering the apartment and the other was around the corner from the living room. There were also two bathrooms, one in the master bedroom and a communal one, across from the second bedroom.

Rashad had converted the second bedroom into an office. He had an L-shaped desk along the far wall and the walls were covered in sports memorabilia. There were autographed jerseys, pictures of famous sporting events, and framed newspaper articles. One of the newspaper articles caught Camille's eye and she walked over to it to get a closer look. It read:

<u>*Lancer Blows Out Knee*</u>

Norfolk, VA- "I heard something pop, and then it went numb for a second. The next thing I know I was screaming at the top of my lungs. I've never felt anything like that before." That was what Rashad

Lancer, the All-American senior tailback at Booker T. Washington High School said when asked about tearing up his knee. 22 blast sweep. It was his favorite play, and one he had run thousands of times, but this time was different. As Rashad took the pitch, he planted hard with his left foot and was about to cut back to his right when 272 pound Ernie Blake from Maury High School, threw all of that weight into Lancer's left thigh, tearing the ACL, MCL, and PCL, the three ligaments that make up the knee, effectively ending Lancer's high school career and potentially costing him several scholarship offers.

"Dinner's ready," Rashad called from the kitchen.

Camille pulled herself away from the article and came out into the kitchen, "Hmm. Smells delicious," she said.

"Have a seat in the living room. Unfortunately one of the drawbacks of having a small place is no eat in kitchen. Hope you don't mind eating on the coffee table."

"Not at all, especially if the food tastes as good as it smells."

Rashad had prepared some broiled pork chops, creamed garlic potatoes, fresh snap beans, and some buttered rolls. They sat and ate and talked. Camille asked about the article and Rashad explained how all the scholarship offers he had received for football were rescinded after the injury and how he ended up taking an academic scholarship to the University of Virginia.

"I tried walking onto the team after I rehabbed my knee, but it never felt right. I always felt a step slow. So I retired from football and decided to work behind the scenes as an agent."

"Wow, that must have been tough," Camille said.

"Yeah, but you can't change the past, I had to deal with the circumstances in my own way. When one door closes another opportunity surfaces."

"So how's the agent business going?" Camille asked.

"Not so great right now," Rashad explained. "We came back here because recently a lot of athletes from this area have been doing well, so we thought with our connections we could sign a few. Unfortunately the bigger firms are gobbling them up. We've tried everything we can with the limited resources we have."

"You going after city kids?"

"Yea, for the most part. We did sign a farm kid from Ohio State recently. I think he has a chance to do well."

"Why not go after more of those?" Camille proposed.

"Farm kids?"

"Yea. Instead of going after city kids, who if they're any good, are used to being spoiled and fawned all over, go after the kid from the small town who may appreciate the personal attention." Camille finished her statement and took another bite of the dinner Rashad had prepared. "Hmm. These chops are so tender, and these potatoes and beans are exquisite."

"Thank you, for the compliment and the suggestion."

"You're welcome," Camille said with a smile. "Where'd you learn to cook like this?"

"Well, mainly from my mom, but I also dated a chef for a while and she showed me a few tricks of the trade," Rashad said.

They finished their meal and Rashad cleared away the dishes, rinsing them and placing them in the dishwasher.

"I know you're driving, but would you like a drink?"

"I'd love one," Camille said. "What do you have?"

"Vodka, rum, and some brandy."

"You have some cranberry juice?"

"Yep, one cosmo, coming up."

One drink turned into several. The alcohol added an extra flirtatious vibe to the conversation. Camille could feel the heat of her own skin as she laughed and drank. Rashad was feeling comfortable as well.

"You are beautiful," Rashad said as he handed her another drink.

"Thank you and so are you," Camille said as she placed her drink down on the coaster and took Rashad's hand in hers. She gently pulled him down beside her. He placed his own drink down and they kissed. Camille thought, he's a great kisser. His lips were soft and smooth. She could always tell from the first kiss how a relationship would turn out. Judging from this kiss, these two could have some fun together. Rashad leaned back and pulled Camille on top of him. They kissed and caressed one another's bodies for several minutes. The situation was getting heated and Camille could feel Rashad's erection against her thigh as she rubbed her leg against his. She pulled away and looked at him.

"Maybe I should go," she said breathlessly.

He blinked but managed not to show his true level of disappointment.

"Are you sure?" Rashad questioned.

"Yes," Camille said but she wasn't sure. Her head was telling her to go but her body was telling her to stay. Rashad had gotten her really excited but she didn't want to feel as if the alcohol had taken over. She began to gather her things and make her way to the door. Rashad got up and followed her to the door. He reached out to open it for her. She turned to face him and said, "What the hell."

Not wanting to give her a chance to change her mind, Rashad picked her up and carried her into the bedroom. He placed her gently on the bed. They began to kiss again, much more intense than before. He proceeded to rub the soft skin of her stomach as he kissed her on the neck. He then placed his hand under her shirt and began squeezing and caressing her breasts. Camille responded by rubbing his crotch. She could feel him through the sturdy cotton of his jeans. She then placed her hands at the bottom of his shirt and pulled it over his head. He threw his shirt to the floor and helped her to remove hers. He quickly removed her black lacey bra and flung it to the side and attacked her dark half dollar sized areolas with his tongue. She responded with a moan of pleasure. Within seconds they were completely undressed. He reached into the nightstand and pulled out a condom.

"Gotta be safe," Rashad said.

Chapter 11

Derek returned to Norfolk on Tuesday evening. He decided to take Wednesday as a day to recuperate and returned to work on Thursday. He arrived at the RDR offices at about ten in the morning, a full two hours later than usual. Rashad was seated at his desk, with his sleeves rolled up and his tie loosened. He had several player portfolios laid out in front of him and appeared as though he were making a list.

"Looks like you're working hard," Derek said as he stuck his head in the door.

"Yea, and you look like crap," Rashad said with a smile. "Miami wore you out, huh?"

"Yea, I'm not as young as I used to be, I guess."

"With as much alcohol as you probably drank I'm surprised you're still coherent."

"What are you doing?" Derek asked.

"I had this thought over the weekend. We've been going after the mid-major and low level crop of players because we figured that was our best bet. But what if we start targeting a specific type of player?"

"What do you mean?" Derek took a bottled water from the mini refrigerator that sat next to Rashad's desk.

"I mean, guys from small towns where personal attention is valued. Like Alan, he's from some small town in Idaho, and he appreciates the way we don't treat him like he's a commodity."

"I thought the reason we set up business here is because we wanted to target players from Hampton Roads," Derek pointed out.

"Yea, but that's not working out too well right now, so we need a new approach."

Derek thought for a moment about what Rashad was saying. It made sense.

"Show me what you got."

Derek was surprised to see that Rashad had done extensive research on potential clients. He had a list of fifteen men and eleven women from small towns, all of whom played on local college teams. Most of them were not likely to go pro and the few who were would be complimentary type players, no bona fide superstars. Still they were possibilities. They narrowed it down to seven candidates: five men and two women. They started making calls to their contacts at the different colleges, trying to get as much information as they could about the seven people. They found out that three of them already had agents, and one had decided to end his athletic career after college. The other three were available and they made plans about how they would approach them.

It was nearly one o'clock when they had finished. They decided to go down to P.F. Chang's for a celebratory lunch. Chang's was an upscale Chinese bistro located on the corner of the street where their office building was. There was no wait and they were seated immediately. After ordering Derek decided to ask Rashad about his new strategy.

"Well, I've been seeing this girl, well woman actually. It was her suggestion," Rashad explained. "She's in the marketing and PR business so that's her kind of thing."

"Wow. Well tell her your partner thanks her."

"You can thank her yourself. I'm going to invite her to your dad's party."

"Damn, I had forgotten all about that."

Derek's father Daryl and his new wife Charity had sent out invitations to a party celebrating her pregnancy. They had decided to make it a combined housewarming and baby shower, so they wouldn't have to alienate the men. It was going to be on Saturday night and even though it was the last place Derek wanted to be, he knew he had to try to show up especially after his behavior the last time he had seen them.

"You know eventually you're going to either have to forgive him or tell him to go jump in a lake, but acting like a jerk isn't getting you anywhere," Rashad said.

"I know. It's just hard you know. I feel like if I forgive him, I'm somehow betraying my mother's memory."

"How do you mean?"

"I don't know. She just made so many sacrifices for Sean and me while he did what was best for him. While he was up in New York making money we were down here struggling. He sent checks but it wasn't his money that we missed. Mom had to be a mother and father to us, and I feel like if I let him back in then I'm saying she wasn't good enough."

"Accepting your dad back into your life isn't going to make what your mom did any less relevant or special."

"I know, I just have to wrap my head around that. Forget all that mess, tell me about this *woman*."

"Man, she is so fly," Rashad said a huge grin on his face. "Her name is Camille. We met at the gym a few weeks and go." Rashad was speaking so quickly his words were beginning to run together.

"You really seem taken with her."

"I know this sounds crazy especially since it's only been a few weeks, but this could be serious."

"Really?" Derek said surprised. As long as he had known him, Rashad had never been in a relationship that lasted longer than six months and he always claimed to be "just kicking it."

"Yea, man. She's got my head spinning."

"You hit it yet?"

"Last night, and man she had my toes curlin'!" A gray haired white woman at the table next to theirs cleared her throat, and Derek and Rashad both laughed. When they spoke again their voices were quieter. "She is so fine."

"Well, I'm happy for you, man. You sound like you've finally found someone to tame you."

"What about you? I thought you were going down to Miami to relax, so I know Rob found a hottie to hook you up with."

"Man, I got so drunk that by the time he introduced me to the girl he wanted to hook me up with I was about three minutes from passing out. I made out with her a bit the next night, but I wasn't really feeling her like that and I don't think she was that interested either, especially after she found out I was an agent and not a player."

"That sucks, dude," Rashad said.

“It’s probably for the best anyway. One night stands never turn out good for me. Remember Susan?”

“Stalker chick. Oh, dude that was so funny,” Rashad said laughing.

“Yea, you weren’t the one getting fifteen voicemails a day and having some crazy broad showing up and scaring off your dates.”

Rashad laughed harder as Derek recounted his experiences. He was unable to get himself to stop laughing until after the food had come.

Chapter 12

Camille had planned to meet Tryone at the club. Sydney would be on her way as well. It was almost ten a.m. They decided to meet early that Saturday so that everyone could move on with their day. The meeting should take no more than half an hour.

Camille was waiting in her car. She arrived a few minutes early. She got directions from Tryone when she called him to set up the meeting. It was a nice building off of Virginia Beach Boulevard going towards Norfolk. The parking lot was spacious, which was a good thing. It was right off the interstate which made it easy to find. Camille noticed a car pulling up beside hers. It was Sydney. Camille got out the car to meet her.

"Hi Sydney." Camille said.

"Good morning, Camille." Sydney responded.

"Thanks for coming out. I know you've got your own things going on today but I really thought it was important for you to be here, you know, to be a part of the process. Hopefully the both of us will get some good ideas on how to market this place," Camille said.

"Oh, no problem. This is great and I'm very excited to be a part of this," Sydney said with a smile.

"So do you know Tyrone from some time ago?" Syndey asked.

"Yes, we were in college together. He found me on the alumni web page so he thought, why not give someone you know an opportunity," Camille said happily.

"Cool," said Sydney.

"Don't let his good looks distract you." Camille warned.

"All right," Sydney chuckled.

Tyrone pulled up at almost ten after. He got out of his car and approached the ladies. He was dressed in gray sweats and a blue hooded pullover sweatshirt.

"Hello ladies. I apologize for my tardiness. I just came from the gym."

Tyrone said sincerely. He extended his hand to Camille showing his appreciation for her and Syndey's patience.

"Oh, no worries. I know how that is. I visit the gym on a regular myself," Camille knew how busy the gym could be on a Saturday morning.

"Please let me introduce you to my assistant. Sydney, this is Tyrone Johnson. Tyrone, Sydney Mitchell."

Sydney and Tyrone extended their hands in unison. Sydney thought to herself, Camille was right. She saw how his looks could be distracting. He had this Richard T. Jones thing happening.

"Nice to meet you, Tryone."

"Likewise."

They all stood there for a second in a comfortable silence and then Tryone interjected. "Shall we?" Camille and Sydney nodded in agreement. They all made their way to
the front door of the building soon to be club.

Tyrone unlocked the door. "Ladies." He opened the door and motioned for them to go inside. The temperature was chilly. He closed the door behind them. "Stay here and let me turn on the lights." Camille and Sydney remained by the door while Tryone scurried to a locked door immediately to the left of the entrance. He flipped the breaker switch and the two women heard the hum of the fluorescent lights coming to life. It took a few seconds for the lights to come completely on. As they waited, they took in the scene and the layout of the club.

The ladies' eyes widened and their mouths dropped as they cased the place. Neither of them expected it to be so spacious inside. To the left there was a free standing bar. In the middle was the dance floor. Surrounding the dance floor were round tables and cushioned chairs. To the far right there was a stage raised about three to four feet above the level of the dance floor. What was even better was the balcony on the second floor which lined three of the four walls of the club. There were more tables and chairs on that level. The place had a welcoming feel.

"So what do you think?" Tyrone asked. "We haven't finished painting and we also want to put in some light effects for club nights."

“I think it’s great. I like the second floor and I like how open it is.” Camille said.

“I agree. It reminds me of some of the clubs I went to during spring break in Florida,” Sydney added.

“Yeah, that’s the look we were going for. I love the clubs down there and I don’t think we have anything like it up here.”

“Until now,” Camille smiled.

“Let me show you guys around.”

Tyrone gave the women a tour of the club allowing them to get a closer look at the features. Camille could see herself coming here to wind down after a day’s work. Maybe she and Rashad could come here together.

“So Tyrone, when’s the grand opening?” Camille was curious. She didn’t think to ask him at their first meeting.

“Well construction is just about two months away from being complete and we want to give you guys a chance to really get our name out there. I was thinking around June.”

“Another big question is what are you gonna call the place?” Sydney questioned.

“I was thinking Destiny but that’s not definite yet. If either of you have any suggestions, please let me know.”

“Well this is your baby we should leave that up to you.” Camille said.

They went on to discuss possible marketing ideas and general ways of sparking interest in attending the club. They parted ways around quarter ‘til eleven, all very excited about what was discussed and the potential of Destiny.

*****

Camille arrived at her apartment with bags filled with goodies from the grocery store. After putting the groceries away, she realized that she had not spoken with Rashad all day. She began to think about their evening together. Thinking about it made her giddy. Her thoughts drifted to the feel of his skin against hers. She was excited about the possibilities. Her skin tingled as she thought about the passion exhibited by his kiss. Her thoughts were broken by the ringing of the phone.

"Hello?"

"Hey there sexy." It was Rashad.

"Hey yourself."

"What have you been doing with yourself today?"

"Well I had a meeting with a client this morning and then I went to the grocery store because my cupboards were bare. I just got back in not too long ago. What about you?"

"I had a few errands to run this morning but right now I'm just chillin'."

"Oh okay, cool. Well, I know we've playing phone tag for the past few days but I really wanted to tell you that I had a wonderful time the other night. Dinner was great and so were the after dinner activities." Camille was blushing.

"And so did I," Rashad said smiling. "Actually part of the reason we've had such a hard time getting in touch with each other is because of the advice you gave me that night."

"What advice?"

"About going after small town kids, it's really paid off," Rashad explained. "We signed two kids yesterday."

"That's great," Camille said. "I'm glad I could help."

"I'd like to thank you," Rashad said.

Camille could feel her cheeks warm as she blushed. "How would you like to do that?" She asked in a sultry tone.

"You're dirty," Rashad said. "I like it. But actually I was hoping you would accompany me to a party tonight."

"A party? What kind of party?"

"My friend's father and his wife are having a housewarming/babyshower party."

"Your friend's dad is expecting a baby?" Camille questioned.

"Yeah, his wife is about fifteen younger than he is," Rashad explained.

"Oh, okay. What time should I be ready?"

"The party's at eight, so maybe seven thirty?"

"Cool."

"Oh, you don't have a problem with interracial couples do you?" Rashad asked.

"Um, of course not. I have friends in interracial relationships. Why?"

"His wife's a Barbie type," Rashad said.

"That's not very nice."

"Well, you'll see what I mean when you meet her. So I'll pick you up at seven thirty."

"See you then." Camille hung up the phone and lay back on the couch. She liked the idea of having a male companion. She hadn't had one in a while and had forgotten what it was like to have built in plans for Saturday night. She was hoping those plans included a replay of the other night.

*****

Sydney left the meeting with Tyrone and Camille and drove to McArthur Mall. She was supposed to be meeting Sean for lunch and a mini shopping trip. They met upstairs in front of the movie theatre.

"Hey babe," Sean said hugging Sydney and giving her a kiss on the cheek. "How did it go?"

"The meeting went great. The club is going to be so nice, once people step inside I think they'll be really pleased. I can't wait to get started on the marketing. It's going to be fun to be a part of something like this."

The two began walking towards the food court. "I'm so glad I met Camille. She's so professional, but at the same time she's cool and down to earth. I know I'm just her assistant, but she really makes me feel like her colleague. I think I can learn a lot from her."

"That's great babe," Sean said. "Sounds like she could be a good mentor. So where do you want to eat?"

They decided to get something from the Chinese restaurant, since it was reasonably priced and Sydney wanted to save her money for a new outfit. She told Sean about the club over lunch and about the plans for the different nights. After they finished they went down to the first floor to find Sydney a new outfit.

"I don't know why you need a new outfit," Sean said. "It's just my dad."

"I know it's just your dad, but I want to look nice, and besides I don't have a nice cocktail dress. All my party clothes are for the club."

Chapter 13: The Party

It was almost seven o'clock. Daryl and Charity were tying up loose ends making sure everything was in place. The house was beautiful. They recently had the patio closed in and also paid a talented landscaper to revamp the backyard. It was very cozy. Charity was wearing a red colored maternity blouse she just purchased from the Motherhood Maternity and a pair of comfortable black pants. She was starting to need the belly room. She was about four months along now. The gray granite island in the kitchen was filled with munchies like peanuts, chips and a veggie tray with broccoli, cauliflower, tomatoes and celery.

"All right. Everything is good out back. People should be starting to arrive soon." Daryl said as he walked in to the kitchen from the patio sliding door. He was wearing a dark brown shirt and pant set. He made his way over to Charity and planted a gentle kiss on her lips.

"How's my girl doin'?" He asked as he rubbed her stomach.

"Just fine", Charity said with a smile. "This is going to be a great night. Celebrating the purchase of our new home and the pregnancy all in one evening." She hesitated for a second before beginning her next statement.

"Listen, I know Derek doesn't care for me very much, but I am going to try my best to get along with him. It's really important that I have a good relationship with your sons."

"It's not you he doesn't care for, it's me. I've tried my best to make amends but...I don't know." Daryl said with a disappointed look and his head slightly hung.

Charity rubbed his back in a circular motion to comfort him.

The door bell rang.

"I'll get it." Charity scurried grinning from ear to ear to find out who their first guest would be. She opened the door and there stood Sean and Sydney.

"Well hey, guys. Congratulations, you're the first to arrive."

"Great." Sydney said.

"Hey, Charity." Sean responded.

Sydney reached out to hug Charity. Sean walked past the two ladies towards the living room with a gift bag.

"Sydney you look great." Charity said as she admired her blouse.

"Thank you." Sydney had on an outfit she picked up at the mall. Her shirt was a rich purple and V-necked with a roomy 3/4 length sleeves that flowed when she walked. It was form fitting just below the breast line and flared slightly at the bottom to cover her butt. Her dark blue jeans were snug in all the right places and her Nine West black pumps were the perfect finish to the outfit.

"And so do you." Sydney grinned.

"Please Sydney, make your way to the living room and make yourself at home. There are some refreshments in the kitchen if you like."

Charity was about to close the door when she looked out in the front of the house to see a few more cars pulling up. She stood there for a moment in the door way with her arms folded waiting for her guests to gravitate towards her.

Meanwhile, Sean was in the living room searching for a place to put the gift he and Sydney purchased. He decided to place it on the coffee table. He walked into the kitchen to join Sydney. She was making herself something to drink and chatting with Daryl.

"So Sydney, how's the new job going."

"It's good. It's only part-time but the woman I work with is awesome. Right now, we are about to start working on advertising for a new club that's opening this summer. I think it's going to be a great experience." Sydney shared.

"You are very talented Sydney. I'm sure you'll learn a lot. Sounds like this could be the beginning of something good," said Daryl.

"Hey dad," Sean said walking in.

"Hello, son." Daryl and Sean exchanged hugs.

Several voices resonated from the living room. People always seem to show up around the same time.

Charity was in the living room laughing and talking, being friendly and hospitable.

"Well, guess I'd better go in and mingle with my guests. Sean, Sydney, please help yourself to anything you like." Daryl exited the kitchen and went to join Charity in the living room. The house was starting to fill up. People began moving about throughout the house and the patio.

Sydney was on the patio with a Malibu rum and coke in her hand, keeping Sean company.

"I hope your brother doesn't act a fool tonight." Sydney said.

"Yeah, I know. He might start trippin' though. He's had a hard time forgiving dad. I talked to him a few hours ago and he said he was going to try. He kind of blames Daryl for mom having to work so hard."

It was almost eight. Derek had parked his car a few minutes before. He decided to sit for a minute so he could get himself together. Somehow, someway, he had to get past this anger he had lingering inside. He had to allow the past to stop dictating his present. If he was ever going to be happy he was going to have to let go of the past.

It was time to go in. Derek flipped the sun visor down and the light came on. He wanted to check himself in the mirror before he got out of the car. The new clippers he bought really did the job. *Well, here goes.* He got out the car and pressed the key pad to lock the door. Derek walked across the street, over into the yard and followed the curved cement path to the door. He took a deep breath and rang the doorbell. He could hear friendly commotion coming from inside. Charity opened the door.

"Derek?" Charity said his name as if asking him to say hello or like she was surprised to see him there at all.

"Hello Charity," Derek said with a forced smile.

"Come on in. Everyone's in the living room. You should find your father there." Charity had a half smile on her face. It was one of those, yes she knows she needs to be nice but it's really hard expressions.

Derek walked in past Charity and made his way to the living room. He glanced across the open space and saw that every corner of the room was occupied with a body. His father was talking to some guests, looked up from his conversation and noticed that Derek had arrived. Daryl raised his hand and motioned for Derek to come over. Derek nodded and walked over to Daryl.

"This is my son, Derek." Daryl said with enthusiasm as her reached around his son's back to give him a half hug.

"Hi Derek." The four strangers said in unison.

Derek smiled and nodded. "Hello." He responded with his hands stuffed in his pockets.

"Son, there's refreshments in the kitchen. I think your brother and Sydney are out on the patio."

"All right, cool. I think I'll go let them know I'm here"

Derek walked towards the kitchen to make a drink. As he was putting ice in his cup, Sydney made her way to kitchen.

"Hey Derek. How ya feeling?"

"Don't even start Sydney."

"What do ya mean? I'm just asking a question."

"You think I'm gonna start trippin. Well don't worry. I've been here five minutes already and everything has gone all right so far."

"Okay Derek. I'm just saying, you know how you can get."

"Yeah. I'm straight."

"Didn't you invite Rashad?"

"Yeah, I did. I guess he's not here yet."

"Listen, I'm out on the patio with Sean. Come out there and sit so we can all chat."

"Alright." Derek finished making his drink and went out to the patio.

Rashad had been a little late picking up Camille. She made a mental note that he may be one of those chronically late brothers.

"You look great." Rashad said.

"And so do you." Camille responded.

"You'll like Derek. He's a cool guy. He's got some animosity about his father's marriage though."

"Is he upset about the fact that she's white or that she's so much younger than his father or...?"

"Yes and yeah that too. I think it's more about how his dad left him, Sean and his mom. In Derek's eyes, he just moved on without considering the consequences. "

"Well, I have to say I have no idea what that is like. I've always had both of my parents in my life. I don't even know how I would have reacted if my dad just up and left us."

"Yea, that would have been tough," Rashad agreed.

They continued talking about their families and delved a little into their childhoods during the twenty minute trip.

"Well, here we are." Rashad had to parallel park across the street in front of someone else's house. Camille grabbed the gift bag from the back seat with the small box inside. They had stopped by Babies' R Us to get a gift card. Camille didn't like giving gift cards as a general rule. She felt like there was no creativity in it, but it was short notice and she had no idea what these people were like.

They approached the door and Rashad rang the door bell.

Daryl opened the door.

"Rashad!" Daryl exclaimed. "Man it's good to see you."

"Mr. Ballard." The men extended their hands at the same time and exchanged hand shakes.

"Who is this lovely woman you have by your side tonight?"

"This is Camille Jacobs."

"Hello Mr. Ballard it's very nice to meet you." Camille extended her hand to shake his.

"Likewise. Welcome to my home. Please make yourselves comfortable and help yourselves to refreshments in the kitchen and there's more room on the patio."

Camille and Rashad stepped into the house.

"Where should I place this? " Camille asked lifting the gift bag.

"Oh, you can set that right in the living room next to the others on the table or in the corner." Daryl said smiling at Camille.

Camille looked around the house and it was beautiful. High ceilings, spacious floor plan, gorgeous artwork, and arches separating the living room from the family room. *One day*, Camille thought to herself. *One day.*

"I'm hungry." Rashad said.

"Me too."

"Come on. Let's go to the kitchen and get something to eat," Rashad suggested.

"Well I was hoping that I could meet your business partner and mingle for a few minutes first," Camille said.

"Yeah, sure. Where is my head? I believe I saw Derek's car outside. He should be around here somewhere."

Rashad and Camille walked into the kitchen where they saw an abundance of refreshments carefully laid on the island.

"The patio is just over here. Maybe Derek is out there."

They walked out to the patio. There stood Sydney, Sean and Derek sipping on their drinks.

Sean and Syndey's backs were to the door, so they didn't see Rashad and Camille come out onto the patio. Derek was the first to see them.

"Rashad, my man," Derek greeted.

Sean and Sydney turned around.

"Camille!" Sydney exclaimed.

"Sydney!"

"Oh my gosh what are you doing here?" Sydney was surprised, excited, and curious about her boss's presence.

"Well, I'm here with Rashad."

"You're seeing Rashad?"

"Well...", Camille didn't know what to say. She was really shocked to see Sydney.

"So you two know each other?" Rashad asked.

"Yes, Rashad. Camille is my boss. Sean, this is my boss Camille Jacobs, the one I've been telling you about." Sydney said smiling and still in shock.

"Wow. Well how about that." Rashad said.

"Well as you've just heard this is Camille. Camille...Derek."

"Hello."

"Hello. How are you?" Camille asked him as if she could sense something was wrong.

"I could be better," Derek responded.

"Okay," Camille said.

"I'm Sean, Derek's brother."

"Nice to meet you," Camille was taken aback by Derek's disposition. Rashad did say he was in a funky mood. *Oh well. Perhaps he'll come around later.*

"Well, I have to say this is a bizarre meeting," Sydney said.

"It is indeed," Camille agreed.

"Why don't we go into the kitchen for something to eat?" Sydney recommended.

"Good idea." Camille followed Sydney into the kitchen.

"Don't be filling her head with no mess, Sydney," Rashad said.

Camille and Sydney walked into the kitchen. Sydney got a paper plate and started loading veggies on it. Camille followed suit except she decided to add some chicken fingers to hers. The ladies doused a section of their plates with ranch dressing. There was a little breakfast bar set up with a few barstools. They put their plates on the bar along with their drinks. Camille had made herself a vodka and orange juice. Sydney just had a coke. She decided to slow down since she already had three drinks and she was a little concerned about her boss thinking she was some kind of lush.

"Camille, I have to say I am still surprised that you're here."

"Yes, I am surprised to see you too. So Sean, your boyfriend, is Derek's younger brother; Rashad and Derek are business partners, Derek doesn't care for his dad and is trying like hell to make the best of this evening."

"That pretty much covers it. I guess Rashad filled you in on the drive over."

"Yea, a little. I think I have enough information to know as much as I need to know. Camille felt it was none of her business. *After all, everyone had problems.* She thought.

“Nice, man,” Derek said giving Rashad dap.

“You mean Camille?” Rashad asked.

“Yeah, man. How’d you hook up with a lady that fine?”

“Lucky I guess,” Rashad said smiling and looking back in the direction of the kitchen. Derek and Sean gave each other a look of genuine surprise.

“Excuse me,” Derek said. “Did I hear you right? Did Rashad Lancer just say *he* was lucky to have a woman? This from the guy whose goal it was in school to sleep with a girl from each of the black sororities on campus.”

“You did not,” Sean said.

“Hell, when he finished with them he moved on to see how many of the white sororities he could get,” Derek added.

“That was a long time ago man, I’ve grown up,” Rashad said not allowing Derek’s teasing to get to him. “I’m glad you’re out of your stank mood, at least, even if it’s at my expense. Seriously though, Camille’s something special, man.”

“Sydney’s really impressed by her,” Sean added. “She has nothing but good things to say about her. As a matter of fact she’s been talking my ear off about her, since she got that job. So, I’m glad you’ve found someone special. And so is Derek, even though he’s being a jerk about it.”

“Well, the jerk’s glass is empty so he’s going to go refill it. Would anyone else care for anything?”

“No, just carry your silly ass somewhere,” Rashad said punching his friend in the arm as he walked away.

As Derek entered the kitchen, there were several people milling around the refreshments and even more around the alcohol. He decided to wait his turn. He ended up standing very near to the breakfast bar, but did not notice Sydney and Camille until he overheard part of their conversation.

“So is Derek all right?” Camille inquired. “He seems to be a little, I don’t know...on edge.”

“He’ll be okay. He’s a cool guy, I think he’s just going through some stuff now with the business and his rocky relationship with his father just kind of makes things a little more tense," Sydney responded.

"I guess I expected a friendlier introduction."

"Excuse me for interrupting. Miss, I don't believe we've met," Derek interrupted catching the ladies off guard and hoping that Camille would play along.

Camille and Sydney turned their bodies around and saw Derek standing behind them. Camille had caught on to the fact that Derek had overheard their conversation.

"Hello. My name is Camille Jacobs. And you are?"

"I'm Derek Ballard."

They exchanged handshakes. Sydney sat there smiling glancing back and forth at the both of them. Both Sydney and Camille were a little embarrassed, but Camille was quick on her feet.

"I hope you don't think I make it a habit of talking about people behind their backs. Rashad had positive things to say about you and I just expected a more amicable greeting but hey everyone has their days. We're only human" Camille said.

"Oh no that's no excuse. I apologize," Derek said.

"Apology accepted and nice to meet you...again."

Sydney continued to smile and glance back and forth between the two. Derek walked away towards the alcohol to make himself another drink. The ladies chuckled as he exited.

"Well," Sydney said with a sigh, "that was interesting."

"Yeah, it was." Camille said.

"So, if you don't mind me asking, how are things going with you and Rashad?" Sydney asked.

"No, I don't mind you asking at all. Things are all right so far. I don't want to speak for him but I'd like to think that right now we're just going with the flow if you know what I mean." Camille answered.

Sydney nodded in agreement. "Yeah take things slow, see what comes of it. It's still early yet."

The ladies smiled and continued eating. Their plates were almost clean.

Meanwhile, the thirty or so guests began gravitating towards the living room. Charity began to open the gifts.

"Perhaps we should find the guys and go in there and be a part of it," Sydney suggested.

"I'm right behind you," Camille said while chewing her last ranch dipped carrot. The ladies disposed of their plates in the tall stainless steel garbage can sitting next to the island. Rashad and Sean had come in from the patio to find them.

"I see you've had a chance to eat." Rashad said to Camille.

"Would you ladies like to go into the living room?" Sean suggested.

"We were just on our in way in there. Where's Derek by the way?" Sydney questioned.

"Last I saw he was making himself a drink," Sydney said nodding towards the kitchen. "He'll find us, let's not be anti."

The two couples made their way into the living room area where the gift table had been set up. Even though it was supposed to be a joint housewarming and baby shower, Charity had indicated she wanted everyone to bring baby gifts. She had spent so much time decorating the house to her liking that she didn't feel like she needed anything else.

"And this is from," she paused as she tried to make out the names on the tag of a little gift bag. "Camille and Rashad." She turned to look around indicating she was unsure of who they were.

"That's us," Rashad said grabbing Camille's hand and raising it with his. "I'm a friend of Derek's and this is my friend."

"Well it's a pleasure to meet you," Charity said across the crowded room.

Camille felt a little embarrassed at suddenly becoming the center of attention, but smiled anyway.

"A gift card, thank you," Charity said, before moving on to her other gifts.

Camille noticed that when they lowered their hands Rashad did not let go of hers. She looked at him and smiled. She looked back up and saw Derek entering from the kitchen. He had what looked like a fresh drink in his hand.

Just then Alicia Keys's "Unbreakable" began to come from Rashad's pocket. "Excuse me." He quickly removed his cell phone from his pocket and silenced it.

"I guess I should have made the 'silence all cell phones' announcement before we started," Charity said getting a chuckle from her guests.

Rashad made his way out onto the covered patio to take the call.

"Hello."

"What's up playa?" It was Robert Singer, Rashad and Derek's partner and best friend.

"I'm good, I'm good," Rashad said. "How about you? How's the training going with the kid?"

"Alan? He's good. I think he's really going to impress at the individual workouts you guys set up."

"That's good to hear. We can use some more good news," Rashad said. "Did 'D' tell you about our new strategy?"

There was a long pause.

"'D' didn't tell to you?" Robert asked.

"Tell me what?"

There was another pause.

"No wonder you haven't called and cussed me out," Robert said half to himself. "I told 'D' when he was down here last week that I wanted out."

"Want out of what? The agency?"

"Yeah, I told him I was going to sell you guys my share of the business. I've been looking to start my own gym down here and with the money I have saved up and if you guys give me about half of what I put up I'll be good to go."

This time it was Rashad's turn to stay silent.

"You there, man?" Robert asked.

"I can't believe this. Are you serious?"

"I'm sorry, Shad. Man, I didn't mean to spring this on you I thought Derek had told you about it. This just isn't for me. I want to be hands on, and a gym is more the type of business where I can do that."

"This is some bull. This was our dream, dude. We've been talking 'bout this since we were kids. We said if we didn't make it to the league we'd be agents. Now you gonna tell me this ain't for you. Ain't that a blip?"

"Yo, man. Calm down. Look, I guess you need time to let this settle in, give me a call when you do." Robert hung up.

Rashad stared at the blinking time on his phone until it went back to the main screen. He heard Camille, Sydney, Sean, and Derek come back out on to the patio laughing and talking.

"Did you see that stroller? That thing was worth more than my car," Sean was saying.

Rashad spun around and stared at Derek.

"What's wrong Rashad?" Camille asked concerned.

"Why the hell didn't you tell me?" Rashad said to Derek ignoring Camille.

"Tell you what?"

"About Robert?"

Derek cursed himself under his breathe. "Man, I'm sorry. I was going to, but you started talking about the new strategy and I didn't want to burst your bubble."

"Burst my bubble? This does more than bust my damn bubble," Rashad said clenching his fists. "You know how much it's going to cost us to buy out his share of the company? That's going to deplete our entire account 'D'. We don't have that type of money."

"Man, you know Rob'll let us slide for a bit on that."

"That doesn't matter, man you should have told me. This affects all of us. This affects our dream."

"*Our* dream?" Derek said, his own anger beginning to get the best of him. "Since when in the hell has this been our dream? The agency was your dream, man. Rob and I just came in with you because you didn't have the money to do it yourself."

"Man, you are full of--," Rashad took a deep sigh to steady

himself.

"What in the world is going on out here?" Daryl said coming out on to the patio. Derek and Rashad were staring at each other fiercely. The rest of the group was staring at the two of them in stunned silence.

"I said what's going on out here?" Daryl repeated.

"Nothing, pop," Derek said turning to his father. "I was just saying my goodbyes. You guys have a wonderful night." Before anyone could stop him Derek left the patio.

Part 2

Chapter 14

Camille hated sitting in traffic. She wasn't complaining though. It was a beautiful Sunday afternoon and the scenery was relaxing as she moved one inch at a time on the Hampton Roads Bridge towards the tunnel that would take her to Hampton. She smiled as she sang along and moved her head back and forth to the smooth tune *Tell Me* by Groove Theory resonating from her speakers.

"It's about time," Camille said out loud as the traffic began to move a little faster. She was on her way now as she finally sped up to about sixty miles per hour. She continued on Interstate 64 until she reached the Hampton Coliseum exit. About ten minutes later, Camille had arrived at her destination. She parked her car in the driveway, got out in a hurry and rang the doorbell to the three bedroom townhouse. She heard footsteps coming towards the door and children's voices saying, "Who is it?"

"Hey girl," Shayla said as she opened the door.

"Hey sis," Camille returned.

Shayla opened her arms wide to greet her little sister. As they embraced, Shayla's two kids: Darius 8 and Tara 6, rushed to the door. Their little arms were wrapped around Camille's legs, squeezing them tightly and stiffening their bodies as to become a part of her legs when she moved.

Shayla was five years older than Camille. She and her children's father had dated since high school. They had separated about two years earlier, when she met her new boyfriend Kris. Shayla was a professional hair stylist. She dreamed of one day owning her own shop, but with having to take care of the kids it had been difficult to pursue that dream. Now as they were getting older she had started making plans to take some business courses at Thomas Nelson Community College.

"How is my niece? And how is my nephew?" Camille said between bending down to kiss each one on the cheek.

"Hey Auntie Camille." Darius said.

"So how was the traffic?" Shayla questioned.

“The normal bumper to bumper all the way to the tunnel,” Camille answered.

“I’m so glad you called. I was wondering when you were going to make your way over here to this side again. I know it can be a pain coming over here,” Shayla said.

“Well, I need to get over here more often. I was just telling a friend how I wanted to get better at keeping in touch with my family.” Camille said this as she followed Shayla towards the kitchen. Darius and Tara had said their hellos and scurried back to the den to continue playing. It looked as if Shayla was in the process of preparing lunch.

“I know you’re hungry,” Shayla assumed.

“Actually I am. What you got cookin’?”

“I just finished fixing some burgers and fries. I seasoned them up myself and cut the potatoes...you know like mom used to do it.”

“I know that’s right. Mom used to make the best burgers,” Camille agreed.

Shayla began to set some paper plates and napkins on the table. Camille helped and got the ketchup, mustard and other dressings for the burgers.

“So...who is this friend you mentioned a second ago?” Shayla asked.

“Oh, his name is Rashad,” Camille had not engaged in a guy talk conversation with her sister in a while. Not only did she come over to see her sister and the kids but she was hoping to re-establish a bond. Even though she and her sister had a good relationship, they both knew it could be a little stronger. When Camille went to Chicago, the phone calls got fewer and farther between. So she figured since she moved back home, there was no excuse.

“I’m listening,” Shayla said in a tone which indicated that Camille needed to continue.

“Rashad Lancer. He’s smart, kind of funny, about six one, bald, dark skinned, nice body.”

“Mmm. Sounds nice. So is everything going okay? I mean do

things look promising?" Shayla asked.

"It's too early to tell yet. We've only been out a few times and well..." Camille paused.

Shayla completed her thought. "You slept with him?"

"Yeah," Camille responded.

"So now you're thinking because you slept with him you messed up an opportunity for something real to happen?"

"Kind of. I mean he's cool and all but I feel like it's just one of those temporary things. At least that's what my gut tells me. He invited me to this housewarming for his business partner's father." Camille responded.

"You didn't tell me he had his own business." Shayla said.

"Him and two other guys are sports agents," said Camille.

"Wow, in Hampton Roads. That sounds challenging," Shayla said.

"Yea I guess. One of his partners was the son of the man who had the housewarming. And get this, the new assistant I have, Sydney, her boyfriend is the brother of the guy. She was already at the house when Rashad and I arrived." Camille explained.

"I bet that was a surprise," Shayla said.

"Yeah, she's cool though."

"So how is Rashad?" Shayla was curious about his talents in the bedroom.

"A lady never tells." Camille grinned from ear to ear indicating that it was all good.

"Say no more my sister. Say no more," Shayla smiled.

"Darius...Tara... come eat!" Shayla called for the kids to come into the kitchen. She fixed their plates and sat them at the table. She and Camille sat at the breakfast bar so they could continue talking.

"So do I get to meet this Rashad?" Shayla asked.

"Maybe. We'll see." Camille was uncertain. She liked him but deep down she didn't know where it was going. Right now she was just going with the flow.

"I have an idea." Shayla said.

"Oh boy." Camille said raising a brow.

"What?" Shayla asked.

"You and your bright ideas." Camille laughed.

"Whatever. Maybe we can grill out, you know have something small. I could invite Kris over and we could just chill." Shayla suggested.

Kris was Shayla's 'friend'. Even though she wasn't with the father of her children, they both insisted on him being there physically and financially for the kids. He and Shayla had managed to stay friends for the sake of the kids. She had been with Kris for about a year. He had a daughter of his own.

"Oh yeah and maybe we could invite mom and dad over too." Camille said.

"Are you being sarcastic?" Shalya asked.

"Yes I am," Camille laughed.

"When was the last time you talked to mom and dad anyway?"

"I called and left a message on the house phone voice mail before I came here. Mom loads my email with all of those silly forwards all the time."

"Well at least she's computer literate. It's hard to keep up with them anyway. They're always on the go." Shayla said.

"Hey, that's exactly how I want to be when I get older: Living my life to the fullest after my kids are grown and out of the house." Camille said as she bit into her juicy burger.

"You know Camille it would be a good idea to have a little family gathering. I talked to Gary and he said he would be making a trip home soon. He said he was thinking about sometime within in the next month and a half or so."

Camille's big brother didn't come home a lot. Gary got a job in D.C. after graduating from Hampton University with a degree in accounting. He had been there ever since. But when he did come home, they always had so much fun together. After several failed relationships, he ended up marrying his high school sweetheart, Lisa.

They had a son who was about to turn ten.

"Yeah, he emailed me a few days ago that he might." Camille said.

"Girl, do you tuck yourself in with your laptop at night? You need to get off that computer sometimes and pick up the phone and call somebody. It's a miracle that you called me." Shayla argued.

"I know, I know. I promised to do better, didn't I?" Camille agreed.

"We'll see." Shalya said chewing her food.

Camille visited with her sister for about an hour and a half longer. On the drive back home, she decided to call Rashad. She was curious about the argument that he had with Derek the night before. It sounded pretty intense and she hoped that he was all right. His cell phone rang and the voice mail kicked in:

"*You've reached Rashad's voice mail. Leave a message and I'll get back to you.*"

Beep!

"Hey Rashad, it's Camille. I was calling to make sure you were all right. Give me a call".

Camille was a little relieved that he didn't answer. She just wanted to leave a message letting him know that she was there if he needed to talk. The drive was just as pleasant going back as it was on the way over. She pushed the buttons on her radio dash until the changer reached her Best of Sade CD. Camille sang out loud with the front windows slightly cracked and with her shades on her face as the wind gently moved her hair. Today was a good day.

Chapter 15

Sunday was usually Rashad's day to rest and get ready for the week ahead. Today, however he was still so pissed off about his boys' betrayal that he needed to burn off the anger. He got to the gym at about nine that morning. He lifted harder than he had in weeks and two hours later he was physically and mentally spent. He decided to skip showering at the gym and drove straight home. He had prepared a protein smoothie before he went to the gym and finished it off when he got home. He lay down on the couch and ended up sleeping until nearly five o'clock.

When he awoke, he showered and was about to prepare dinner for himself when he saw that his cell phone was blinking red, indicating that he had a message. There were actually two messages. The first was from Robert, who had apparently talked to Derek.

"What's up Shad? Look, don't take your frustration with me out on D. I shouldn't have put that on him anyway. I should have told the both of you together instead of one at a time. I guess I was hoping that if he told you, you'd have time to cool off before you talked to me.

"I've seen the books so I know that you guys can't afford to give me everything I put into the company immediately. We can work out a payment plan or something. Man, I really don't feel like leaving this on your phone. Call me."

I can't believe this, Rashad thought. *He's serious. He really wants out. Just 'cause he's in the league he can just leave us behind.* He knew that was not true and that Robert would never abandon his friends, but frustration was getting the better of him.

The second message was from Camille. "*Hey Rashad, it's Camille. I was calling to make sure you were all right. Give me a call*".

He felt horrible because he had refused to tell her what the argument was about and the car ride home was completely silent. The fact that she called did make him feel better. He needed to make it up to her.

He had already cooked for her, and even though he was happy with the outcome of that night, Rashad did not want her to think he was just trying to get her into bed again. He decided to ask her out to dinner.

"Hello," Camille said.

"Hey, sweetness," Rashad said. "This is Rashad."

"I know. How are you?"

"Better, now that I hear your voice," Rashad said.

"Aww, that's sweet."

"I'm sorry 'bout last night. Guess I didn't handle myself too well," Rashad said.

"You feel like talking about it?" Camille asked.

"How 'bout dinner?" Rashad proposed. There was a pause. "We can go out this time. I haven't done my grocery shopping yet anyway."

"Oh, it's not that," Camille half lied. "I just got home from my sister's and I had kind of gotten comfortable."

"Oh," Rashad said trying to regroup. "Well, how about I come to your side? Nothing fancy, you can just throw on some jeans and a shirt and we can go to the *No Frill Grill* in Ghent."

"Ooh I *love* that place," Camille said. "Okay, I'll meet you there in half and hour."

"See you then."

Rashad hung up the phone with a smile. He was glad that she agreed to go, but still wanted to do something nice for Camille. It was Sunday evening so the florist on London Blvd. was closed. The best he would be able to do would be one of those cheap roses from 7-11. He hoped she would appreciate the thought.

When he arrived Camille was already waiting inside the restaurant. The *No Frill Grill* was one of those hidden pleasures of the Ghent section of Norfolk that people who had lived in the area their entire lives had never been to. It was small with what seemed like tables everywhere. They got a small table in the middle of everything close to the bar.

"Thank you for the rose," Camille said as they sat down.

"You're welcome," Rashad said. "I just felt like I should

apologize for acting like such a jerk last night."

"You were upset. It's understandable."

"I still can't believe what happened," Rashad said. "Robert, my partner that plays pro ball in Miami, decided he wanted out of the agency."

"Really?" Camille said. "And you had no idea?"

"None. It was completely out of the blue. And then to top it off he apparently told Derek when he went to visit him and he didn't tell me."

"Maybe Derek felt like Robert should tell you himself," Camille offered.

"I just think Derek was being a punk. Something like that you should let your boy know about. 'Specially since this has to do with our money and our dream."

"So this wasn't Robert's dream? It was just your's and Derek's?"

"According to *them* it was just my dream and they just got in it to help me out. And now that it's not going so hot I guess they want out."

"Derek wants out too?"

"No, but after the way I talked to him last night he might. His dad's been pressuring him to get out and go back to school, and I'm not sure his heart has ever really been in it."

"It sounds to me like you have two really good friends and instead of being pissed at them for wanting out, you should be thanking them for being there for you for as long as they have."

Rashad smiled. "Not only is she beautiful, but she is also brilliant."

Camille blushed. "I'm being serious."

"So am I. I really hadn't thought of it like that. If this really wasn't their dream and they did this for me then I should be thanking them."

The conversation turned to lighter subjects as the entrée's arrived. Rashad was starting to feel a real connection to Camille but wanted to take it slow. *I don't want to scare her off.*

"So on the phone you said you visited your sister today, how was that?"

"It was good," Camille said. "I hadn't seen her and the kids in a while so it was nice."

"How many kids does she have?"

"Two. Tara is six and Darius is eight."

"I bet you're a great auntie."

"I could be better," Camille said. "Like I was telling you before, I've been slacking on keeping in touch with my family. This was the first time I've seen my sister since I moved back to the area and she just lives right across the water."

"At least you're making an effort to change," Rashad said. "That's the first step. I hardly ever talk to my brother. It's hard with him being all the way out in Cali, but I should make more of an effort."

"What about your parents?" Camille asked as she took another bite of her tuna melt.

"They moved to Arizona when I went away to school. So, I don't get up to see them that often. I talk to them every week though. They're happy."

"That's good. After my dad retired from the Air Force, my parents started traveling the world."

"On a retired salary?"

"He was an officer and he invested his money *very* well."

"What about your mom?"

"She ran a daycare out of the house. She loved kids, so our house was always full of them."

"Do you want kids?" Rashad asked.

"Yes I do. What about you?"

"I'm not sure. Sometimes I do and then other times I don't think I'm ready."

"I don't think anybody's ever ready," Camille said. "Not really anyway. I mean, who could ever be ready to have another person's life completely dependent on them."

"Well, when you put it that way, I *know* I don't want kids," Rashad said laughing. Camille laughed too. They continued talking about family and some about work until they finished their meal.

"You want to come over to my place?" Camille asked as they walked out of the restaurant. "I live just over there." She pointed to a four story apartment building across the adjoining parking lot.

"Sure."

They held hands as they walked across the parking lot. Rashad smiled to himself. He had known Camille for about a month and they had only slept together once, but he truly felt like he could fall for her. He could count on one hand the number of women he had used the "L" word with, but he began to think he may have to add to that number soon.

Camille's apartment was on the third floor. They walked up the narrow staircase and Rashad thought about how hard it must have been to move into this place with no elevator. "This must have been a hellish move."

"Professional movers," Camille said. "There's no way I would subject anyone I call a friend to this torture." They both smiled.

As she opened the door to her apartment, Camille was glad she had finally finished unpacking and that her place felt like home. The space was small, as were most apartments in the highly sought after area of Ghent. She had utilized almost every inch without making the place feel crowded. She used wall shelves to hold her many books. There was a very comfortable looking plush couch against the wall opposite the door. There was a window overlooking the parking lot and the No Frill Grill. It had a nice navy blue window treatment covering it. She had a flat panel television sitting on a stand next to the door. There were also a couple of pieces of artwork on some of the bare spots on the wall.

Camille offered Rashad a drink, which he declined.

"I'm going to go change out of these jeans," Camille said. "The remote's on the table. Make yourself at home." She ducked into the bedroom.

She had digital cable so there were a ton of channels to pick from. Unfortunately there was not much on. Eventually he left it on *Boomerang*, which was on HBO.

Camille came back out of the bedroom wearing a pair of dark blue pajama pants and a white Gap t-shirt. "You don't mind me getting comfortable, do you?"

"Not at all," Rashad said. "I know I pulled you away from relaxing to come to dinner."

"Ohh, *Boomerang*! This is one of my favorite movies. I thought Halle was really cute in this movie. What do you think?"

"Of course. Halle's always cute."

"Hmm. Another one of those guys that's in love with Halle."

"In love with her? Hell I'd drink her bathwater," Rashad said with a grin.

"Ew, you nasty," Camille laughed. "What about me?"

"What about you?"

"Would you drink my bathwater?" Camille looked at Rashad seductively.

I'm in trouble, he thought. "Now who's being nasty?"

Camille smiled, "What's the most romantic thing you've ever done for a woman?"

"I can't give away my secrets," Rashad said. "Who knows? If you play your cards right you might get to find out firsthand."

"Wait a minute, buster. What do you mean if *I* play my cards right? You're the one that's courting me, remember."

"If you say so," Rashad said. They sat in silence watching the movie for a few minutes. Rashad was glad they had already reached a point where they did not feel like they had to fill every minute with conversation.

"Would you ever do something like that?" Camille asked as Eddie Murphy and Halle Berry kissed on screen.

"Kiss Halle? Hell yea," Rashad said.

"You're silly. I mean would you hook up with a girl one of your friends was into?"

Rashad was silent for a moment still looking at the screen. He considered talking around the question but decided to be truthful. "I have."

"Really?" Camille sat up and muted the television. She turned all of her attention to Rashad.

"You want me to tell you about it?"

Camille nodded enthusiastically.

She's so cute, he thought. "Back in school I was kind of a playa."

"Really?" Camille said feigning shock.

"Anyway, my roommate worked with this girl at the bookstore. He liked her, but he was being a punk about asking her out."

"So you swooped in?"

"Not quite. I told him to just ask her to hang out with a group of us that way he could maybe talk to her outside of work and with a little alcohol he could loosen up and let her know how he felt.

"Unfortunately, he was his same shy self and she kind of started digging me. We both drank a little more than we should have and we ended up hooking up."

"That's not your fault," Camille said. "It's not your fault if she liked you better. Was it just a one night stand?"

"I told him it was but we actually saw each other for about a month, but I got tired of sneaking around behind his back and broke it off."

"So you didn't like her that much?"

"Not really it was just a fling. What about you?"

"Have I ever done anything like that? No, I'm a good girl," Camille said with a sly smile.

Camille turned the sound back up on the television. Rashad started to gently rub on Camille's knee. She closed her eyes for a second and then opened them, hoping that he hadn't noticed. But it was too late. Camille slowly turned her face towards his. They were staring at one another eye to eye. Rashad gently leaned in towards her and pressed his lips against hers. She fell into his kiss. They both found themselves lost in the moment. Rashad pulled back not wanting to stop but not wanting to over do it. Camille slowly opened her eyes relaxed by the sensation of the kiss.

"I'd better get going," Rashad said to her with his face still close to hers.
"We both have early days tomorrow."

"Uh, yeah you're right. Perhaps that is a good idea." Camille wasn't sure if she meant that or not.

Rashad stood up and picked up his keys off the coffee table. Camille got up as well and walked him to the door.

"This was nice. Maybe we can have an extended evening very soon", Rashad suggested.

"That would be nice." Camille stood in the doorway with a smile on her face.

"Well, I'll call you tomorrow." Rashad said backing away but still facing her.

"Okay," Camille said giddily.

Rashad smiled all the way to his car. He was really feeling Camille and was starting to think this could be his first serious relationship in a long time.

Chapter 16

Camille arrived to work bright and early. It was a beautiful spring March morning. She had her laptop open checking her email. She received another email from her brother, this time confirming that he would be coming home for the Fourth of July. Another email was from Shayla. It read:

Hey sis, thanks for coming over. I enjoyed talking to you. I miss that so much. Love you.

Camille smiled as she read and closed the screen. She missed her big sister too, and she actually started to contemplate when she would make her next visit.

She had a lot to do today and wanted to begin working on marketing Club Destiny. Maybe she could get one of the deejay's to do a plug about it during the afternoon traffic hour. She had to find out if Tyrone was getting a local deejay to be the feature on the opening night. Perhaps he'd want to distribute some postcard flyers. She couldn't wait to trade ideas with Sydney. She would be arriving in about a half hour.

"Morning Camille," Sydney walked in smiling with a Starbucks cup in her hand and her laptop strapped on her shoulder.

"I must have thought you up. You aren't due in for another half hour."

"I know but I wanted to get in early. I didn't know how long the Starbucks line would be so I wanted to get there to give myself some extra time. I should have called to ask if you wanted something. Do you drink coffee?" Sydney asked.

"Only when I really need to wake up. I'm more of a tea drinker."

Sydney nodded indicating that she heard her. "Camille?"

"Yes?" Camille looked up at her.

"I just wanted to say that I'm glad things weren't weird the other night between us at the housewarming. I want you to know that I will always be professional. It was just odd seeing you there. It completely took me by surprise. I guess what I'm trying to say is that if anything happens or doesn't happen between you and Rasahd that I won't be nosy about it. I just don't want things to get weird. Do you understand where I'm going with this?" Sydney seemed a little nervous as she talked.

"Yes. I completely understand. And yes I was surprised myself. But you know we're not that far apart in age. We can talk about stuff. I want to make sure the both of us are comfortable and I appreciate you bringing this up." Camille was impressed and relieved that Sydney was so tactful. It showed that she had a sincere concern for their relationship.

"I want to be sure I don't overstep any boundaries." Sydney said.

"Of course," Camille responded.

"With that said...how is Rashad?" Sydney questioned.

"He's good. I saw him yesterday." Camille wasn't sure how much information she wanted to reveal.

"Good. I'm glad to hear it." Sydney knew what went down the other night from Sean.

Camille thought before she spoke. If she said anything else about her evening with Rashad, it might be risky. She considered herself to be a pretty good judge of character and was confident that the working relationship would be all right if she opened herself up a little.

"We had dinner," Camille said.

"Oh, really. Where?" Sydney asked.

"No Frill."

"Oh I like that place. The food there is delicious and they give you big portions," Sydney smiled.

"Yeah, it was like a last minute thing."

"The weather was nice yesterday."

"It was. I went to see my sister in Hampton."

"Aww, you have a sister? Are you two close?"

"We're getting there again. She's great to talk to. I have a brother too. They're both older than I am," Camille said.

"Oh that's cool. I'm an only child myself," Sydney said.

" Cool," Camille thought about inviting Sydney to her sister's house one afternoon. Camille didn't have friends here she could really call and go hang out with. Most of them were in Chicago.

"Might you be interested in going with me to my sister's house one afternoon on the weekend? You know, like a girls' afternoon together."

"Oh that would be great. I'd like that a lot. Thanks Camille." Sydney was pleased that Camille was making her feel like a friend. She was also proud of herself for what she said earlier.

They put their heads together and came up with some good ideas to market Club Destiny. The ladies worked into the twelve o'clock noon hour and ordered in for lunch.

Camille's cell phone rang as she took the second bite of her sandwich. It was Rashad.

"Hey, you," Camille said.

"Hey, yourself," Rashad said. "I'm not interrupting anything am I? I figured you'd be at lunch."

"No. Yeah, Sydney and I ordered in," Camille said. She mouthed 'Rashad' to Sydney who looked up at the mention of her name.

"Tell, Syd I said hi," Rashad said.

"I will."

"I just wanted to call to say thank you for last night," Rashad said. "You said some things I really needed to hear."

"You're welcome. Have you spoken to Derek yet?"

"No, he called and left a message saying he was going to work from home today. He has a tendency to let things fester."

"Well, maybe you should make the first move," Camille suggested.

"I may have to. Anyway, enough about that. Do you have plans this weekend?"

"Not as of yet, no."

"How would you feel about going away with me?"

Camille's hand went to her mouth in surprise. She tried not to pause too long.

"I, uh, well, where?"

"Well there's a nice bed and breakfast down in Nags Head that I was thinking we could go down to for the weekend...unless you think it's too soon."

Camille knew she liked Rashad, but *Is this too soon? I've only known this man for a month. I've already slept with him though, and he is good. And not just in the bedroom, he's a great guy who has his stuff together. But...* "I don't know. Can I let you know later?"

"Um," Rashad was a little put off by Camille's hesitation. Maybe he was moving too fast. "Well, we could push it off—"

"No, no. When I said later, I meant by the end of the day," Camille explained. *Damn, I don't want to scare a good man off, because I'm scared.*

"Oh, well, okay. Just give me a call before 4:30 so I can make the reservation," Rashad said.

"Alright, I will. I'll talk to you soon."

"Okay, bye."

Camille hung up the phone and looked at Sydney.

"What's wrong?" Sydney asked.

Camille took a big bite of her sandwich before answering. Using the time she spent chewing to think. *Why shouldn't I tell her about this? We're both grown. She knows Rashad and maybe she can tell me if this is his regular routine. But maybe she'll go back and tell her boyfriend and then he'll tell his brother and he'll go back to...but they're not talking and—*

"Camille," Sydney said, bringing Camille out of her spiraling out of control thought process.

"Huh? Oh, I'm sorry. Girl, I was in my own head."

"No problem. If you don't want to talk about it, it's fine."

"Rashad asked me to a bed and breakfast," Camille blurted out.

Sydney raised her eyebrows and took a big bite of her own sandwich.

Uh-oh, Camille thought. *Here we go. I'm about to hear about all of Rashad's dirty little tricks.*

Sydney took a sip of her drink before speaking.

"That's great," Sydney said with a smile. "I don't ever remember hearing about Rashad taking anyone he was dating away for a whole weekend."

"Really?"

"Yeah, he must really like you," Sydney said her smile broadening.

"You think so?"

"Yeah."

"So you think I should go?"

"Well, that's up to you, but I would."

Camille picked up her phone at 4:15, she was pushing it but liked playing hard to get.

"RDR Sports Marketing, this is Rashad."

"So how long does it take to get to Nags Head?"

Chapter 17

By the time Tuesday morning came around, Derek knew he had let this argument with Rashad go on as long as it should. As he entered their shared office, Rashad was sitting behind his desk looking through a player file.

"What's up man?" Derek said, unsure if Rashad was ready to talk to him yet.

Rashad placed the folder on the desk and looked blankly at his friend for a moment, before flashing a smile.

"Well that's a good sign," Derek said a tentative smile appearing on his own face.

"Man, I'm sorry for trippin' the other night," Rashad said.

"Don't worry it about man, I should have told you about Rob," Derek said placing his bag down on his desk and then sitting. "I would have probably reacted the same way. Have you talked to Rob yet?"

"Last night," Rashad said. "He said he wanted to use the money to buy into a gym with a friend of his down there. He explained everything, and I told him I understood. He agreed to keep training players we sent to him, at no charge."

"What about the money? How soon does he want it?"

"He said he looked at the books so he knows that he's not going to get everything he put in, but he's okay with that."

"Good, good. What about your friend? Uh, Camille right?"

"What about her?"

"Was she put off by our fight?"

"No, she's cool. She actually gave me some really good advice, and helped me get over it a lot quicker than I may have if I hadn't talked to her about it. As a matter of fact, I'm taking her to Nags Head this weekend."

"Really?" Derek said genuinely surprised.

"Yup," Rashad said.

"Wow, sounds like you really like this girl. That's cool man," Derek said.

"Yeah. I wasn't sure if it was too fast but I'm really into her. She's smart, funny, attractive." Rashad was grinning from ear to ear.

The two continued to chat and eventually directed the conversation to business. They worked into the lunch hour. They went to the California Pizza Kitchen located in Towne Center for lunch and returned to the office at around 1:30. When they returned there was a message from Robert on the voicemail.

"Rashad, D, this is Rob. I need you guys to call me ASAP. The Miami GM wants to have a private workout and interview with Alan, so one of you needs to get you're asses down here like yesterday."

Derek and Rashad looked at one another in shock. They called Robert back and put him on speaker phone.

"What's up man?" Rashad said.

"Hey," Robert said. "I've been trying to call you jackasses for nearly two hours."

"We were at lunch," Derek provided.

"Well, I'm glad the two of you kissed and made up. Are you ready to make some money?"

"What's the news?" Rashad asked ignoring Rob's comment.

"I've been talking Alan up, around the team complex you know. Telling some of the coaches and the guys that I'm really impressed by how hard he works and all. So the GM came to me this morning and said he wanted to meet Alan and give him a private workout."

"Seriously?" Derek said. "That's sweet. When?"

"Tomorrow."

"Damn," Derek said. "I can't go. I promised to go to my dad's to help him paint the baby's nursery. Normally I'd skip out on it in a minute, but after what happened the other night I kind of have to make it up to them."

"What about you Shad?"

"I'm on the first thing smoking," Rashad said.

"I made a reservation under RDR Sports Marketing for the

6pm flight on JetBlue, so one of the two of you needs to show up."

"That means I need to fly home, pack, and get to the airport," Rashad said. "Can you finish making my calls for me today?"

"Of course," Derek said.

Rashad left for home immediately after they got off the phone with Robert. Derek stayed in the office making calls to existing and potential clients. It was 4:30 when the phone rang.

"RDR Sports Marketing this is Derek."

"Hi, Derek. This is Camille. Is Rashad there?" Camille was sitting in the parking garage at Town Center. She wanted to surprise Rashad. She hoped that he wouldn't be put off too much by her arrival. Then how could he? She had just agreed to spend the weekend with him.

"No he left a few hours ago. He's actually on his way to the airport if he's not there already."

"The airport?" Camille was curious. *Where was he on his way to? Why didn't he call to tell me?*

"Yeah, Robert called and said he needed us to represent a client at a meeting with a team that may draft him. I couldn't go because I promised to help my dad with something at the house. So Rashad said he'd go. It was sort of an emergency."

"Oh, okay." Camille was a little thrown off by the news but hey it was business.

"I'm sure he would have called if he had time but he left here in a hurry to get packed and what not," Derek explained. "He spoke very highly of you this morning."

"Oh did he now? Well what did he say?" Camille questioned.

"Aww now you want me to blow your head up."

"No, it's not like that. I was just curious." Camille was relieved that Derek was so friendly especially after their first encounter at the party that evening.

"You know I wanted to apologize again for my acting a fool that night. It was rude and I'm sure you had a horrible first impression of me. Anyway, I'm usually pretty cool and, well, I'm sorry."

"No need to apologize again. Every family has its stresses. I'm actually trying to get closer to my sister and brother now. I've been in my own world for a while not really keeping in touch. All of us have growing to do."

"You're right about that. I've had some issues with my dad. It's getting better. It's taken a long time but I think I'm coming around."

"Life is too short and family is important. If he's making an effort, then it's good that you are meeting him halfway. People grow up. They get wiser and learn from their mistakes. He's older now and knows how crucial it is that he has good relationship with you and your brother."

"I thought your work was in PR not counseling." Derek joked.

Camille laughed. "It is. Let's just say I've had some practice. People like to tell me their problems."

"Is that right?"

"I mean I've always been one that my friends have kind of loaded their issues out on. So I listen and try to be as objective and positive as I can. Plus I was a resident advisor in my dorm junior year in college. "

"Ahh. Good ol' college days. Where did you go to school?" Derek asked.

"Norfolk State. And you?" Camille asked.

"Virginia Tech." Derek replied.

"I had some good times in school." Camille said.

"Yeah, me too," Derek added.

Camille was still sitting in her car. They had been talking for several minutes and she didn't realize that is was getting close to five o'clock.

"You know I just realized the time. Not that I'm in a rush but I didn't mean to keep you on the phone. I've actually been sitting here in the parking deck. I should let you go," Camille said.

"In the parking deck here outside the office?" Derek asked.

"Yes, I was going to surprise Rashad," Camille said.

"I had no idea you were here, you've been sitting in your car the whole time we've been talking." Derek was surprised. "Listen. I'm on my way out of the building. We were having a pretty good conversation. Maybe we could continue it over tea."

Tea? He drinks tea? Camille laughed.

"What's so funny?" Derek asked.

"I expected you to say coffee. You know the line men use: 'Wanna grab a cup of coffee.'"

"No I don't drink too much coffee. I prefer tea, it's easier on the stomach."

"I'm a tea drinker too. I only drink coffee if I *really* need that pick me up in the morning." Camille smiled.

"So what d'ya say?" Derek asked.

Camille sat there only for a second before she answered. "Sure, why not. Where?"

"There's a Barnes and Noble right across the street. We can meet there, "Derek suggested.

"All right," Camille responded.

They each hung up the phone. Derek gathered his bag and began to lock up the office. Meanwhile, Camille put her car in drive and exited the garage. It only took her three minutes to get to the store parking lot.

What was I thinking? I mean he's Rashad's friend. I could use this opportunity to find out more about him. I'm grown and I can keep company with whomever I choose. Besides, it's just tea.

Derek was in the parking lot. He sat there a second. *This is cool. After all, if Rashad was serious about this girl, I'd be seeing more of her anyway being that we're boys and all. It was just socializing. It's harmless.*

Each of them got out of their cars and walked towards the store. They could see each other walking across the parking lot.

Camille reached the entrance door first. Derek approached.

"Camille, it's nice to you see you again," Derek said.

"Yeah, you too."

Derek opened the door for Camille. "Ladies first."

Camille entered and Derek followed. The two walked over to the Starbucks counter to order.

The cashier had thick red hair pulled back in a pony tail. She had a big smile on her face.

"Hello Sir, what can I get for you today?"

"Yes, I'll have an Earl Grey Tea please and," Derek looked over at Camille.

"Camille what will you have?" Derek asked.

"Oh, uum, I'll have the same."

"You know I can pay for my own." Camille offered.

"That's all right. It's the least I can do for being so rude that night."

"That'll be $4.57," said the young red head.

Derek gave her a five dollar bill and she gave him back his change. Their order was ready in no time.

"Here you are, sir," the girl said handing Derek their tea. "Have a nice evening."

"Thanks." Derek had the two beverages in his hand gesturing Camille to lead the way to a seat. She found one by the window.

"Do you like cream or sugar in your tea?" Derek asked.

"As a matter of fact I do like to put a little milk in my tea and two sugars," Camille said.

"Okay, I'll be back." Derek took the two teas. He prepared hers just the way she said she liked. *What am I doing?*

He walked back to the table, set the beverages on the table and sat down.

Camille took a sip of her tea. "Mmmm. This is good. Thank you."

"Oh, no problem." Derek took a sip of his as well.

Camille immediately went into conversation. "So, exactly how long have you and Rashad known one another?"

"Since high school," Derek answered.

"So it's safe to say you two know each other well?" Camille asked.

"Yeah," Derek paused. "Oh no."

"What?" Camille smiled.

"Don't go asking me a whole lot of questions," Derek said as he shook his hand back and forth in front of his face indicating that he had no intention of betraying his friend's secrets.

"I wasn't even gonna go there," Camille assured him.

"Okay. I know how women are. They try to use the friend to find out a slew of information about their guy," Derek said.

"You're not gonna give me any dirt, huh?" Camille asked.

"Nope."

"So, why did you invite me here?"

"Why did you accept?" Derek came back.

The two sat for a moment and nervously sipped their tea.

"Was your dad upset about the fight you and Rashad had at the party?" Camille asked.

"A little. I have to go help him paint as a sort of penance. I'm going to try to smooth some things out. Everyone keeps telling me I need to give him a chance, so I think I'm going to really try."

"That's good," Camille said. She began to use her fingernail to flick the cardboard sleeve that was on the cup. *It's just a friendly cup of tea.*

"You feel like walking?" Derek asked.

"Around the store you mean?"

"Yeah," Derek said.

"Sure."

The two got up from the table and walked to the magazine section. Camille stopped and picked up Ms. Magazine. She began flipping through the pages.

"What's that you got there?" Derek asked.

"Oh, Ms. You ever heard of it?" Camille asked.

"No, I can't say that I have."

Camille peeked at what he had in his hand. "I see you have

Sports Illustrated. Go figure," she smiled. "What kind of books do you usually read?"

"Lately autobiographies about coaches and athletes." Derek answered. "And how about you?"

"I've read a lot of black fiction novels. But I also enjoy self help and inspirational books." Camille answered and he nodded taking a sip of his tea.

They continued walking and talking about their favorite authors and books, some of which they had in common. The two had been in the store for nearly an hour. Camille's cell phone rang. She looked at the number. It was Rashad. *Shouldn't he be on the plane?*

"Hello," Camille answered.

"Hey, you. You haven't tried to call have you?" Rashad asked.

"Actually I called the office earlier to see if you wanted to grab a bite. Derek told me that you had to rush to Miami. I thought you would call when you got a chance. Shouldn't you still be on the plane?" Camille asked.

"The itinerary had a layover in Charlotte which is a little weird. I thought the flight would go straight to Atlanta and then to Miami. So what are you up to right now?"

"I'm in the bookstore." Camille was hoping he wouldn't ask any more questions.

"Cool. Looking for anything in particular?" Rashad questioned.

"No just winding down, walking around." *That sounded stupid.*

Derek had disappeared into the next isle. Camille was glad. It was harder to think with him right there in her face.

"Hey, I gotta go. I'll give you a call when I get to Miami."

"I'll be looking forward to it."

"All right then I'll talk to you later," Rashad said.

"Okay, have a good flight." Camille hung up the phone. She went around the corner to find Derek standing at the poetry section. He was holding a book by Nikki Giovanni.

"*Cotton Candy on a Rainy Day,*" Camille said.

"You like poetry too, huh?" Derek asked.

"Yeah. It relaxes me, puts me in another place," Camille said.

Derek nodded in agreement. He looked at his cell phone to check the time. Maybe he should wrap this up. "You know I'd better get going."

Camille agreed. "Yes, I think I'm gonna head out too."

"It was nice talking to you. I don't have a lot of female friends. I'm usually with my brother or my boys. It's nice to get a female perspective on things," Derek said.

"I'm glad I could be of service. I'll send you my bill."

They both laughed as they made their way to front of the store and said their goodbyes as they exited. Camille got in her car. She immediately called her sister. The voice mail picked up. "Shayla, I did something dumb. Well, I think I did something dumb. Need to talk. Call me."

Derek sat in his Explorer for several moments before he started it. *It was just a cup of tea and a conversation. It was just two new friends getting to know each other. It was...it was dumb is what it was.*

Chapter 18

Derek finally convinced himself that the outing with Camille was just a friendly get together and meant nothing. It was silly for him to have even thought it meant anything. She was Rashad's girl.

He put on a pair of old sweats and one of his older Tech t-shirts. He had called his dad on the Sunday after the party to apologize for the blow up with Rashad. In an effort to make up for it he agreed to help his dad paint the nursery. He would go into the office until about noon to make some calls and go over to his dad's at lunch time.

He pulled up in the driveway at about 12:30. Charity's car was gone, which he counted as a small blessing. He didn't know if he had the energy to deal with her cheeriness. He rang the bell and heard his dad call for him to come in from somewhere inside the two story home.

"Hello?" he said as he entered the foyer.

"I'm upstairs," Daryl called.

Derek made his way up the carpeted staircase. He felt as though his feet sank into the plush carpeting. Charity and Daryl loved to pamper themselves. The nursery was the smallest of the three upstairs bedrooms and was located next to the common bathroom.

"Hey, son," Daryl said. "He was stirring a bucket of sea green paint with a stick. The floor was covered with a drop cloth and there were two roller trays along with two rollers on the floor. There were also several paintbrushes of varying sizes at Daryl's feet.

"Where's your brother?" Daryl asked.

"He had a game up in Maryland," Derek said.

"Well, that's okay I guess. Gives us a chance to talk."

There was actually very little talking at first. Daryl explained to Derek what he wanted done and they got started. The painting was going well, but the conversation was stalled. Camille's words about family needled Derek into making small talk.

"So you excited?" Derek asked.

"Huh? Oh, yeah, I guess," Daryl said.

"You guess?"

"Well, I think the emotion I'm feeling more than anything is fear," Daryl explained.

Derek was a little surprised to hear his father say that he was afraid. He stopped painting and turned to look at Daryl.

"'Fear'?"

"Yeah, I guess I'm scared of screwing up...again," Daryl said.

It wasn't the first time Daryl had admitted that he had made a mistake leaving his sons, but it was the first time Derek allowed himself to hear it.

"Why would you?" Derek said starting to paint again. "You're older now. You have plenty of money, and you have your tr-," Derek stopped himself from slipping into old habits.

"You can say it," Daryl said. "My trophy wife. I know that's what you think of Charity, but I really do love her. I think at first it was kind of an ego thing to know I could still get a young hot cheerleader type, but she's more than that. You might hate me for saying this but she reminds me a lot of your mother."

A twinge of hatred squeezed Derek's chest, but he allowed it to pass. "Really? How so?"

"She's determined, fiercely loyal, and beautiful. Those were some of the same things I loved about your mother."

"If you loved her so much that you married someone like her, why didn't you just stay married to the original?"

"Your mother and I had our problems too. We didn't let you guys know, but we were unhappy for a while before I left. Your mother was comfortable here. She felt safe. Your mom loved to feel safe," Daryl paused as if sharing a private moment with himself. "She wasn't a risk taker. That's the biggest difference between your mom and Charity."

There was a long silence that ensued after Daryl's comment. Derek wanted to yell at his father. *A risk taker? She was sure as hell more brave than you've ever been! She raised two boys by herself while you were off sewing your damn oats.*

But instead he simply said, "I think if you had given her a chance she may have surprised you. Mom had to take a lot of risks once you left. She went back to school and got her real estate license and started her own business. Doing that as a single parent was a heck of a risk."

"You're right," Daryl said. "I hate that I had to leave in order for her to realize her full potential. Unfortunately I think we both had to get away from one another to do that."

"Are you saying that your leaving was good for mom?" Derek asked turning again to look at his father.

Daryl stopped and turned to his son. "Let's take a break. I have some beer in the fridge." The two men walked downstairs and sat down at the bar.

Derek could tell his father needed a minute to think about his answer and decided to allow him that. They were both nearly half done with their beers before Daryl answered Derek's question.

"Yes. I do believe my leaving was a good thing for your mother. I know it was hard for her and that was because I was dumb and didn't give her the help with you boys that I should have. I wasn't making very much when I left, but when I started making money I more than made up for it."

Derek laughed.

"What's funny?" Daryl asked.

"You think it's your money we missed?" Derek could feel himself getting angry and decided to bite his tongue.

"Don't hold back. I deserve anything you have to say," Daryl said.

"You're right you do, but I've been yelling at you and cussing you for years now and it hasn't gotten either of us anywhere."

"True."

"Look, I have a lot of hurt feelings left over from you leaving, but I'm going to try to get past them. I think you deserve...no we deserve that. A friend told me that life is too short and family is to important to allow hard feelings to linger."

Daryl smiled. "Thank you."

*****

Derek left his father's house at around quarter to six, after helping to put a second coat of paint in the nursery. He decided to stop at the Target on Military Highway across from Janaf shopping center to pick up a few things for the house. Maybe he'd pick up a new DVD to watch that night too.

He stood in the movie aisle looking at the $7.50 movies leaning absentmindedly on his cart, which was filled with toiletries.

"Hey you," he heard the voice from behind him.

He turned and found himself smiling as he saw Camille coming down the aisle towards him. "Hey," he said. "What's up?"

"Not much, just picking up a few things," Camille said. "You too, I see?" She nodded toward his shopping cart.

"Yeah, I just left my dad's and decided to stop by on the way home. You live near here?"

"Well, I live in Ghent, but I was on this side to see a client," Camille explained. "So, how did the painting with your dad go?"

"Very well, with partial thanks to you."

"Me?"

"Yes. The things you said yesterday really got me thinking and I've decided to make an effort. I think today was the first day I've really talked and *listened* to my father in a long time. And that's all in large part due to what you had to say."

"Well, I'm glad I could help," Camille said smiling.

"Let me thank you properly. Have you eaten?"

"No, I was just going to grab something on the way home or eat a Lean Cuisine."

"Lean Cuisine?" Derek said looking at Camille doubtfully. "You don't need to be on a diet."

"Thank you," Camille blushed a little at the compliment. *Is he flirting with me?*

"I'm sorry," Derek said, misreading Camille's blushing.

"For what?"

"I just totally made you uncomfortable, didn't I?" Derek asked.

"No you didn't," Camille said touching him lightly on the forearm. "Believe me, I take all the compliments I can get." *Am I flirting with him?* "Anyway, you don't have to thank me anymore."

"I feel like I should," Derek said. "Let me take you to dinner." *What am I doing?* There was a long pause, before Camille answered and Derek knew he had made a mistake.

"That'd be great," Camille said. "I'm starving."

"Where would you like to go?"

After a few minutes of debate, they decided to meet over at Ruby Tuesday's which was in the same shopping plaza as Target. It had a salad bar, which meant that Camille had the option of eating healthy if she wanted, and Derek was craving a burger which was their specialty.

Just a thank you dinner with a friend. Derek thought as he drove over to the restaurant. Even though his intentions were totally innocent he still felt a twinge of guilt.

He's just a nice guy, who wants to say thanks, Camille thought as she pulled her car into the parking space at Tuesday's. Derek was waiting at the door of the restaurant for her when she exited the car.

Derek couldn't help but admire Camille as she approached him. She was wearing a pair of navy blue pinstriped slacks with a white top. The slacks where fitted just enough to show off the work she had been putting in at the gym. She carried herself with a grace and class that many of the women he had dealt with lacked.

"After you," he said opening the door.

They were seated immediately and their waitress was with them before that had even gotten situated.

"Can I start you two off with something to drink?" She asked.

"I'll have a sweet tea," Derek said.

"Same please," Camille said.

They stayed silent until the waitress returned with their drinks. Both pretended to be concentrating on trying to decide what to order. They placed their orders, Camille was getting a turkey sandwich salad bar combination, and Derek ordering a bacon cheeseburger. After ordering, Camille immediately got up and went to the salad bar.

When Camille returned to the table, she discretely handed Derek a pack of crackers. "Shh, I don't think they saw me," she said looking over her shoulder.

Derek laughed. "Okay, thanks," he slid the crackers into his lap without looking at them. "No one noticed anything did they."

They both laughed.

"You know you're really a cool chick, Camille," Derek said.

"Oh so I'm a chick now, huh?"

"Sorry. You're a very cool woman. I see why Rashad is so taken with you," Derek said.

Camille hesitated a little at the mention of Rashad's name. "Yeah, I think he's cool too."

"You said you went to NSU," Derek said changing the subject. "Have you been here your whole life?"

"No, I was a military brat and I spent the last few years in Chicago," Camille explained between forkfuls of her salad.

"The windy city, huh?" Derek said. "I visited there once last summer. We were trying to sign a kid from Northwestern. Did you like living there?"

"I did. I really did. The nightlife is wonderful and there are so many things to do all the time. It got hella cold during the winters though. I've never seen so much snow."

"I'll bet," Derek said. "I'm sure you had plenty of guys wanting to help keep you warm, though."

Camille again blushed at his compliment. "Actually I had a boyfriend for a while, but he couldn't handle how dedicated I was to my career so for the last year or so I had to rely on a warm blanket and a cup of hot chocolate."

"There's nothing wrong with being a career minded woman," Derek said.

"Not everyone thinks that way."

"True. I guess some guys haven't entered the twenty-first

century yet," Derek said.

"He wasn't a Neanderthal or anything. We just had different priorities. It was a rough break up," Camille explained. "What about you? No special lady in your life?"

Just then the waitress approached the table with the food. She placed the turkey sandwich down in front of Camille and placed Derek's burger in front of him. She also refreshed their drinks.

"I'm waiting," Camille said just as Derek took the first bite of his burger.

"No," Derek said after swallowing. "There's no one. After my mom died I was pretty torn up for a while, and when I did finally start dating I had a bad experience that scared me off for a while."

Camille placed her sandwich down and gave Derek her undivided attention.

"What?" Derek asked.

"Details, buddy."

"Oh, no. I'd rather not relive that," Derek said.

Camille looked at him through half closed eyes, "That bad, huh?"

"Let's just say, I had to change my number *twice*."

"You must have really put it on her," Camille said smiling.

"Excuse me," Derek said surprised.

"You heard me. You must have really blown that chick's back out," Camille said taking a bite of her sandwich. "That or she was just plain crazy."

Derek shook his head and took a bite of his burger.

"It's okay you don't have to admit it, but I know there's only one reason a woman would blow a guys phone up like that."

They both chuckled. "You're crazy." Derek said as he locked eyes with Camille. They held eye contact a moment longer than either had intended. The rest of the dinner was nice, though they avoided anymore taboo subjects. They talked about family and their pasts, and shared numerous laughs. Camille found herself admiring Derek's smile and surprising easy going nature. *Nice teeth*, she thought which was accompanied by a twinge of deja'vu.

As they finished their meals Camille began to reach for her purse.

"What are you doing?" Derek asked. "I told you I was treating you to dinner as a thank you."

"You don't have to do that," Camille said smiling. "The company was thanks enough."

"Well, thank you, but I still insist," Derek said handing the waitress his card before she even placed the bill on the table.

"Thank you," Camille said.

Despite the fact that both were enjoying the company and wanted to continue talking they both felt uneasy about staying any longer. They reluctantly ended their night together when the waitress returned with Derek's card and receipt.

Derek walked Camille to her car.

"This was fun," Camille said.

"It was," Derek said.

"Yeah," Camille opened her car door and turned to face Derek. "You say you were in Chicago last summer?"

"Yeah," Derek said confused. "Why?"

"No reason, just kind of cool that we were in the same place at the same time, you know? Small world."

They stood looking at each other for a moment, neither speaking nor wanting the moment to end. Finally, Derek extended his hand for a handshake. "It was good seeing you again, Camille. I'm sure we'll be seeing plenty of each other."

Camille looked down at Derek's hand before taking it in hers. "Yeah. Take care, Derek."

*****

When Camille arrived home she immediately went to her bedroom. She was a bit of a packrat and kept almost anything she thought might be of use later. She pulled her little step ladder from under the bed and used it to reach a Nike shoebox in the back of the closet. She stepped down from the ladder and sat down on the bed. She opened the box which was filled with hundreds of business cards. She began flipping through quickly and finally stopped on the one she was looking for. She pulled it out of the box and read it aloud.

"Derek Ballard, RDR Sports Marketing. Son of a b-" the phone rang. "Hello."

"Hey pretty lady," it was Rashad.

Chapter 19

Shayla was finally getting around to calling Camille after a busy couple of days. Darius and Tara definitely kept her going. She was also trying to spend some time with her boyfriend Kris. Shayla flipped her cell phone open and she dialed Camille's number.

Camille was in the process of getting dressed. She heard her cell phone ring and looked at the phone number on the screen. She picked up in a hurry.

"Shayla, sis I'm so glad you called." Camille was dying to share with her sister what happened the other day and just recently last evening.

"Girl is everything all right? I'm sorry it took me so long to call."

"That's okay. Listen, something weird happened between me and Derek. Well, it wasn't really weird just...well I don't think it should have happened. I don't know where to start."

"Okay, I'm not following you. Who's Derek?"

"Let me start over. Rashad invited me to join him for the weekend at Nags Head and I accepted."

"WHAT? Whoa." Shayla exclaimed excited for her sister.

"I was going to stop in to surprise him at work. So I sat in the parking deck at Town Center and called his office. Derek, his friend and business partner, picked up the phone and he told me that Rashad had to go to Miami for a business meeting on short notice. Anyway, Derek and I ended up talking on the phone, meeting at Barnes and Noble for tea and..."

"And?" Shayla questioned.

"Well nothing. I mean we had a good conversation. Neither one of us came on to each other or anything but something was there."

"So now you're feeling guilty and a little awkward because you had an innocent...or maybe not so innocent discussion with your new man's best friend," Shayla replied.

"Yes," Camille said.

"Well how did it get to that point? I mean whose idea was it to chat over tea?"

"Derek's but that's not all."

"I'm listening," Shayla said smiling but on the edge of her seat and curious about what in the world was next.

"I ran into him at Target last night and then we had dinner."

"Camille..." Shayla tried to interject.

"Here's the kicker. I've seen him before. I ran into him at the airport last summer in Chicago. I rushed home and went through my collection of business cards and found his. Can you believe that?"

"Camille?" Shayla asked to get her to slow down.

"Yeah?" Camille sat at the edge of her bed out of breath from filling her sister in.

Now that Shayla had her sister's attention, she didn't know where to begin or how to respond to all of this information but then she said, "Don't let this turn into drama. What are you going to tell Rashad?"

"Well, I wasn't planning on tell him anything."

"You're still going away with him for the weekend?"

Camille hesitated for a second before she answered as if she had second thoughts herself. "Yeah," she said with apprehension in her voice.

"All I'm saying is that you don't want this to turn into a stressful and ridiculous situation. What if Derek goes and tells Rashad about the two of you spending time together? I mean what if he just happens to mention it?"

"No, I don't think he will. I mean, he's not going to put his friendship with Rashad on the rocks because of something so innocent," Camille said.

"But look at how you just reacted to the situation."

Camille was now lying flat on her back on the bed. Her sister was right. What if this did turn into something awkward and unsettling? Well it was already that, but what if it turned it to something more?

"Camille?" Shayla asked to make sure her sister was still

there.

"Yeah, I'm here," Camille responded.

"Listen, maybe you should back out of this romantic weekend thing with Rashad. I'm not trying to be negative here. I would just hate to see you get caught up in something that you could have avoided from the beginning. One thing that is obvious is that Rashad must really be into you. It's a dangerous thing to play with somebody's feelings."

"You know what? I'm going to forget about this Derek thing. I mean this is silly. Rashad is a cool guy. I want to enjoy myself with him this weekend." Camille said.

"Okay sis. Just remember what I said."

"All right," Camille answered. "Shayla?"

"Yeah?" Shayla responded.

"Thanks," Camille paused for a second. "I love you."

"Love you too sis," Shayla answered. "You keep me informed of what's going on and don't hesitate to call me. I don't care what time it is."

"Okay," Camille said.

The two hung up their phones. Camille was relieved that she could use her sister as s sounding board. She walked to the mirror and looked at herself. *You're gonna forget about this and have a good time this weekend. This man likes you, you like him and everything is gonna be all good.*

Camille got herself together and finished getting dressed. She had a busy day ahead.

*****

Rashad sat at the kitchen table in Robert's Miami condo. He ate a bowl of cereal while reading the sports section of the newspaper. It was nearly nine, but he was the only one in the condo awake.

The meeting with the team had gone very well and so he, Robert, and Alan had gone out to celebrate. The other two men had truly let loose and gotten more intoxicated than either had intended. Rashad, who hadn't been out clubbing since he had started dating

Camille, decided to take it easy.

His flight was scheduled for one o'clock so he was hoping that one of the two would be up in an hour or two so they could give him a ride to the airport. He had finalized the plans for his weekend with Camille, but he still needed to get home to pack. Rashad was looking forward to this weekend. He loved spending time with Camille. He wanted this weekend to be special.

One of the things he was really looking forward to was sleeping with her again. They had only been together the one time and it was great. He had decided to not try to force anything and so a second time had not yet occurred.

Robert stumbled out of his bedroom eyes still half closed, still wearing the pants he was wearing the previous night. As he entered the kitchen the faint smell of cigarette smoke and alcohol accompanied him.

"You stink," Rashad said smiling.

"Good morning to you, too," Robert said opening the refrigerator and removing a cartoon of orange juice. "Alan up yet?"

"Nope," Rashad said. "Guess that means you won, huh?"

"Won what?"

"The way you two were putting them down last night, I thought you were having a contest to see who could drink the most and not die."

"The jury's still out on whether or not I'm dead," Robert said as he poured his juice. "That was the drunkest I've been in a while."

"I thought you and D got pretty wasted when he came up."

"Yeah, but I had to stay half way sober, you know how he gets when he's drunk," Robert said. "What about you? You used to be a beast, and I was looking for you to be my wingman last night."

"Man, I might be done with all that," Rashad said.

"Done with what? Women? You ain't turning gay on me are you, not that I'm judging or anything, I'm just saying."

"No, ass. I'm talking about the womanizing. This girl I'm talking to...she might be the one."

Robert nearly choked on his orange juice. “I’m sorry. I thought I heard you suggest you might be settling down.”

“I’m not saying I’m getting married tomorrow or anything, I’m just...well, she’s really special. She’s the type of woman who makes me feel like I can be myself and stop frontin’.”

Robert sat and studied his friend for a long moment. The haze from his hangover was lifting and he could see that Rashad was being genuine. He smiled and said, “That’s good, man. I’m happy for you.”

“Thanks. But like I said, I’m not even sure if she feels the same way. Hopefully after this weekend things will be a lot clearer.”

Chapter 20: The Weekend

Camille was already prepared for the weekend. She over-packed but felt it was better to be safe than sorry. They had intended to leave that morning but because Rashad was out of the office for most of the week, he decided to go in for a few hours to catch up on some work. It was one o'clock in the afternoon and Rashad was on his way to pick up Camille.

It took about thirty minutes for him to reach her place. The early April weather was beautiful. It was definitely a spring afternoon to remember. There wasn't a cloud in the sky and the temperature was about 75 degrees. Rashad approached Camille's door and rang the doorbell. Camille looked through the peephole to make sure it was him. A single woman living by herself couldn't be too careful. She smiled big as she opened the door. She was wearing a pair of kakhi capris with brown sandals and a pink scoop neck shirt. Rashad had on a pair of dark blue jeans, a graphic tee which was fitted and showed off his nice arms, and a pair of the new Jordan's.

"Hi." Camille said.

"Hi." Rashad responded. "You look cute."

"Thank you and so do you."

Rashad stepped in. "It smells good in here."

"Yeah, it's this new candle I bought from the Yankee Candle Company. I'm always lighting candles." Camille walked into her bedroom and spoke loudly so he could hear her. "I'm getting my bags. I'll be out in a just in a second."

"Take your time." Rashad had a seat on the plush brown couch. He saw a picture on the coffee table which appeared to be a family portrait. "I don't remember this picture from last time. Is this a picture of you and your family?" Rashad asked in a voice loud enough for Camille to hear in the bedroom.

Camille was on her way out with her bags. She spoke to Rashad as she searched the living room and breakfast bar area for her keys. "Oh yeah I did a little more unpacking since you were last over. That's my parents, brother, sister and me. I was like fourteen in that picture."

"You said your sister lives here in the area right?" Rashad asked.

"Yeah, in Hampton. Maybe I can take you out there to meet her one day soon. She hardly ever comes on this side," Camille said coming back into the living room.

"I'd like that." Rashad agreed.

"All right. I finally found my keys. Okay I'm ready." Camille had tossed a large bag on her right shoulder and reached for her suitcase until Rashad stopped her.

"Let me get this." Rashad picked up her suitcase and headed for the door.

"Are you sure you need that bag on your shoulder? It feels like everything you need is already in this suitcase," Rashad said jokingly.

"Very funny. You know women have to pack *everything*." Camille smiled.

Camille locked and shut the door. The two walked slowly to the car taking short flirtatious looks at one another.

"I am looking forward to this being a wonderful weekend." Camille said.

"Me too, Camille. Me too."

It was a nice drive. Rashad had turned on the air conditioner almost immediately, and the system worked so well that Camille actually had to ask him to turn it down after a while. Rashad had brought along his Caselogic which held over one hundred and fifty CDs. He allowed Camille to play deejay for the trip.

"You have some really good stuff in here," she said as she flipped through the case. "Tribe, the Roots, Billie Holliday, Miles Davis, Thelonius Monk."

"Yeah, I love music," Rashad said smiling. "I used to use it to get my mind off of things when I was rehabbing my knee and to keep my spirits up."

"That's cool. I think music is the one thing I don't think I could live without."

"Well that's because you are the perfect woman."

Camille blushed at the compliment and smiled. She went back to silently flipping through the case admiring the collection. She thought carefully about her selections. She was pretty sure that Rashad was looking for this to be a romantic getaway but she wasn't sure how in tune with that thought she was. Her mind kept drifting back to how comfortable she had been with Derek and how much she had enjoyed his company. *That's stupid, Camille,* she thought. *You have this fine brother right here ready to wine and dine you and you're thinking about his best friend. WHAT'S WRONG WITH YOU?*

"You okay?" Rashad asked.

"Huh, oh. Yeah I'm fine, just thinking about business," she lied.

"How's that nightclub marketing going?" Rashad asked. "That sounds like a really nice place. Somewhere black folks can chill out without worrying about a bunch of thugs bringing some nonsense."

"Yeah, I think it's going to be nice," Camille agreed. "Tyrone's planning the opening for around the beginning of June, so Sydney and I were thinking about really starting the push towards the middle of this month. Sydney's got some really good ideas for flyers and maybe a billboard on the Boulevard."

"That sounds great, what about radio and TV?"

"We're pricing stuff now," Camille said. "He's not sure of his budget quite yet. He wants to make sure the construction is complete before he worries about advertising costs."

"That's smart. Maybe, I can take you to the grand opening."

"That'd be nice."

"What about your meeting? The one in Miami."

"It went great. They seemed really interested in making Alan a late round selection. And the work that Rob's been putting in with him has really made a difference. He's so much stronger than he was and he's gotten quicker too."

"When is the draft?"

"The last Saturday of this month, but Alan won't get picked up until Sunday unless something crazy happens. Speaking of crazy, you know we've picked up six new clients since we started using your advice?"

"Well I'm glad I could be of service. My consulting fee is ten percent, so I'll be expecting my check," Camille said smiling.

"How 'bout I pay you back with services?" Rashad said with a sly grin.

"Ooh, you dirty." They both laughed.

They arrived at the beachfront bed and breakfast at around four, just in time for check in. The Carolina Rose belonged to a friend of Rashad's from the University of Virginia. Elizabeth Nance had turned her family's century old home into a place where people could come and forget about the rest of the world for a little while. When her grandmother died, Elizabeth inherited the home and decided to turn it into a bed and breakfast, which catered especially to African Americans. She named it after her grandmother as a tribute.

As they entered the foyer, Camille was struck by the history that seemed to ooze from every pore of the building. The walls were adorned with family pictures and portraits, some of which she guessed were probably as old as the house itself, and some which were older. The foyer and stairs were dark hardwood floors and the living room, which was to the left, was covered in plush dark blue carpeting.

A young dark faced man greeted them at the door. "Good afternoon, welcome to the Carolina Rose. My name is Felix. How can I help you this afternoon?"

"Good afternoon, Felix," Rashad said. "I have a reservation for the weekend, Mr. Rashad Lancer."

"Yes, Mr. Lancer we've been expecting you. Ms. Nance wanted to be here personally to greet you, but she had an urgent matter come up. Let me show you and..." Felix had obviously worked in the hospitality industry long enough, not to assume that a man and a woman who were spending a weekend together were married.

"Camille," Camille offered. "Just call me Camille."

Felix led them up to their room. The upstairs hallway also had hardwood flooring and instead of family photos the walls were decorated with art depicting Africans and African Americans. Camille recognized a piece by Jacob Lawrence and a couple by Paul Laurence Dunbar.

"This is the Nina Simone suite," Felix said opening the door to the bedroom. "As you can see there is a king sized bed with the finest 1200 count thread cotton bedding. There's a comforter in the chest here at the foot of the bed, in case you get chilly. The fire place is gas operated. The controls are here on the side panel. The plush carpeting will ensure that you are comfortable if you decide to walk around barefooted." He walked around to the other side of the bed and they followed.

"The bathroom is the most modern aspect of our establishment. There is a Jacuzzi tub, here and a stand up shower over here. A double vanity because, we know some people don't like to share." He turned and walked back around the bed to the door. Every night we slide a breakfast menu under your door. Simply choose what you would like, mark either 'in bed' or 'dining room', and select a time and breakfast will either be brought to you or be waiting for you downstairs. If you don't mark a time it will be served by 9:00am. If you have any questions, comments, or concerns please let me know."

"Thank you Felix, this is all wonderful," Camille said smiling.

"Enjoy your stay," with that he left the room closing the door behind him.

"This is wonderful, Rashad," Camille said sitting down on the edge of the bed.

"Yeah, I visited this place back in college before Liz converted it, and it was a nice house, but now it's incredible. She's done a great job of keeping the historical feel and adding some nice modern touches."

"Yeah. So you got to meet the real Carolina Rose?"

"Liz's Nana? Yeah, she was a neat lady."

"Were you and Liz an item?"

"No, she knew me too well to ever get involved with me," Rashad said with a smile of nostalgia. "I was a bit of a player back in those days. She was just a good friend, kind of like a sister."

"That's the second time you mentioned being a player?"

"Don't act like Sydney didn't dish some dirt on me," Rashad said.

"Sydney only had kind things to say about you, actually. But now that you brought it up, let's hear about your player days."

"How 'bout we talk on the beach?"

"Okay, let me get changed."

"Can I watch?"

"There'll be plenty of time for that later," Camille said with a smile as she wheeled her bag into the bathroom and closed the door.

I sure hope so. Rashad thought.

It was still early in the tourist season and still a little cool, so Camille and Rashad had much of the beach to themselves. Camille had actually changed into jeans and sneakers because the air coming off of the ocean was still cool. Despite the chill in the air, the mid afternoon sun sparkled off of the ocean, and the soft sound of the waves breaking on shore made them both feel relaxed. They walked for a while in silence, listening to the lapping water and cawing seagulls over head.

"So," Camille said, rekindling the earlier interrupted conversation.

"So, what?"

"Tell me about these playa days. You already told me about stealing your friend's crush."

"Hey, you said that wasn't my fault," Rashad said.

"I'm just giving you a hard time," Camille said laughing. "Seriously, though were you like a gigolo or something?"

"A gigolo? Who am I Richard Gere?" Rashad said with a smile. "No, well, I mean it was college. People do stuff in college that they might not do under normal circumstances."

"Like?" Camille pressed.

"You know let's talk about something else," Rashad said.

"Why? What's wrong with this subject?"

"I don't know. Maybe it's just best to leave the past in the past. My past experiences taught me a lot, but I don't think recapping them is all that important. What if we just go forward from where we are?" He stopped and faced her. He put his arms around her waist and pulled her towards him, kissing her gently on the cheek.

Camille wanted to be upset at his avoidance of the conversation, but instead found herself feeling warm and safe in his strong embrace.

"You're trembling, are you cold?" Rashad asked.

"Yeah, it's a little chilly."

"Well, let's get you back to the room and get you warmed up."

When they arrived back to the Rose, Elizabeth Nance was waiting for them.

"Rashad," she said smiling as she opened the door. Rashad hugged her picking her up off the ground.

"Hey Liz, how are you doing girl?"

"I'm good. It is so good to see you."

Camille couldn't help but smile as the two old friends reacquainted themselves. Elizabeth was a strikingly beautiful woman. She had dark almond color skin that appeared to be flawless. Her hair was cut short like a boy, but it only accentuated the classic streamlined features of her face. She had a dancer's body, with long legs and arms which were accentuated by the royal blue sleeveless backless dress she was wearing.

"This is my friend Camille," Rashad said turning towards her.

"It's a pleasure to meet you, Camille," Elizabeth said extending her hand.

"You too, Elizabeth," Camille said shaking hands with the woman. "This place is amazing."

"Well thank you. And please, just call me Liz. Do you guys have plans for this evening?"

"Not yet, no," Camille answered.

"Well, if it's not an imposition my husband and I would love to take you guys to dinner."

"*Husband*? When did you get married?" Rashad said shocked.

"I'll tell you all about it over dinner," Liz said mysteriously.

"Bribery, an old trick but still effective. What do you think, Camille?"

"That'd be wonderful," Camille said. *At least in mixed company I won't have to worry about...*What was she worried about? She liked Rashad and had slept with him once, so why was she so nervous about this whole thing. She could not shake the memories of her brief encounters with Derek.

"Well, it's five now. What do you say we leave at about six thirty?"

"That's sounds great, we'll meet you down here at six thirty then," Rashad said.

Camille and Rashad made their way upstairs back to their room.

"She seems really nice," Camille said.

"Yeah, she's a great girl," Rashad said. "You can have first shower."

"Thanks. She's beautiful, too," Camille added. "You mean to tell me you never tried to get with her?" She asked as she went into the bathroom. She left the door cracked so they could continue talking.

"I never said that, I said she knew me well enough not to get involved," Rashad explained.

"Oh, okay," Camille said as she got undressed for her shower. The stand up shower was large and had beautiful dark tiled walls. There were two shower heads, so it was obviously made for a couple.

She let the warm water wash over her face with her eyes closed. She nearly screamed when she heard Rashad's voice.

"Mind if I join you?" he asked stepping into the shower.

Even though she was a little taken aback by his boldness, Camille was aroused by the sight of Rashad's naked muscular body. Her eyes roamed all over his physique. He stepped close to her as he closed the shower door and the smell of his cologne sent a shiver down her spine.

Should I go there? I mean we've only done it once. He brought me here for this romantic weekend and I know he's expecting a round two. But not right now. I have to look good for this evening. But how could I say no? He looks so good. Hell, whether I wanted to go there or not, he's ready.

Camille kept herself turned away from Rashad, trying to ignore him. She wanted him as much as he wanted her, but the time she had spent with Derrick was beginning to cloud her mind. The feelings she had for Derrick when they were together was more than just a friendship thing. She was finding herself more and more attracted to him and the more she tried to push those feelings away the stronger they became.

This is stupid, she thought. *I have this fine ass man right here who damn near blew my back out the only time we did it and I'm thinking about some guy that I barely even know. And it's his best friend at that.* "Ugh."

"You okay?" Rashad asked. As they turned to face one another for the first time since he entered the shower, Camille's was surprised that she had grunted out loud.

"Yeah, I'm-" her words caught in her throat as she noticed his erection in its full glory. She swallowed hard and forced herself to look into his eyes. "I'm fine and I'm finished."

Rashad watched as Camille exited the shower door.

"I'm sorry," Rashad called after her. "I couldn't help it. I really did just want to shower with you."

"It's fine," Camille said. "I was getting pruney so I figured I'd go ahead and get out."

"You sure I didn't scare you off?"

"It's not that big," Camille said sarcastically.

Rashad laughed. "Well, as long as I didn't offend you."

"Why would you being attracted to me offend me?"

"I don't know. You just ran out of here so fast, I didn't know what to think."

Camille tied her towel around her and opened up the shower door. She motioned with her index finger for Rashad to lean down to her. As he bent down bringing his face closer to hers, she placed a hand on either cheek and kissed him passionately. As she saw his manhood beginning to rise again she pulled away.

"I'm not trying to tease you. I just want you to know that I like you, and we have the entire weekend to get reacquainted and for you to pay me back for my advice with your 'services'."

Rashad licked his lips and smiled. "You're something else."

"Better than average?" Camille smiled back.

"Definitely."

Camille and Rashad made their way downstairs for dinner a few minutes before six thirty. Camille reached out and placed her hand lightly into Rashad's. He looked at her and they both smiled warmly.

Liz stood at the bottom of the stairs with her arms locked with a tall white man. He looked like a Men's Health model: dark hair, blue eyes, and a perfect smile. He was dressed in khakis and a button up dark blue dress shirt. Camille looked up at Rashad and saw a slight look of shock in his face.

He didn't know she married a white guy. I wonder how he'll react. Camille thought.

Rashad and Camille reach the bottom of the stairs. Rashad immediately extended his hand towards the man.

"Hi. I'm Rashad", he said as he shook hands with the man.

"Rashad this is Ian, my husband," Liz said.

"It's a pleasure to finally meet you Rashad," said Ian. "Liz has told me so much about you."

"Likewise, except I haven't heard much about you," Rashad responded.

"Well, I'm sure we'll all get to know each other better over dinner. There is a wonderful seafood place up the road that we'll take you to," Liz said.

"That sounds lovely," Camille said.

The two couples drove separately since Ian and Liz lived in the opposite directions of the restaurant. Rashad was rather quiet during the drive and Camille wondered if he was as cool with the interracial relationship as he initially appeared.

"Hey over there, are you all right? You're mighty quiet." Camille questioned.

Rashad hesitated before he answered. "Yeah, I'm straight. Why do you ask?"

"Well you haven't said much since we got in the car. I was just wondering."

"I was just surprised to see Liz with a white guy."

"Why? "

"I've never known her to express interest in dating outside her race. You saw the B and B with the all of the black history and memorabilia. She's always been very proud of her heritage."

"Well she can still be proud of her heritage. Just because she married a white man doesn't mean she has lost a sense of who she is."

"I know I know. It's just weird I guess. I'm sure he's nice guy," Rashad said as he followed Ian's car into the restaurant parking lot. They found a spot near the door even though the lot was nearly at capacity.

The restaurant, The Dunes, was located overlooking the Atlantic Ocean. Liz had had the foresight to make reservations. The restaurant was amazing. The entire wall facing the ocean was made of glass and the view of the moonlight reflecting off the water was breathtaking. Each table was covered with white linen tablecloths and there was a candle burning on each. Besides the light from the moon and stars that was the only light in the restaurant. Despite being filled to capacity the atmosphere was extremely intimate and romantic.

"This place is amazing," Camille said as the group was seated at a table near the window.

"Yeah, this is where Ian proposed to me," Liz said smiling at her blushing husband.

"Really? Well this is the perfect place for a proposal," Camille said.

The four chatted lightly as they decided on what to have for dinner. Apparently this was Ian and Liz's favorite restaurant and they had tried everything on the menu and were not afraid to share their opinions. After placing their orders and starting on a bottle of wine the conversation turned from food to relationships.

"So how did you two meet?" Liz asked.

"At the gym," Camille responded.

"Oh Lord, Shad are you still doing that?"

"What do you mean still?" Camille asked as Rashad rolled his eyes and sighed.

"Well, let me tell you 'bout this man. He's picked up more-"

"Honey," Ian said cutting his wife off in mid-sentence.

"It's cool," Rashad stated. "She's been doing that to me since second year."

Even though she was curious, Camille decided not to feed into Liz's comments, but did make a mental note to dig a little deeper when she and Rashad were alone.

"So tell us about how you two met," Camille said.

Liz and Ian looked at one another and smiled.

"Well you know all the wonderful modern upgrades to the house you were commenting on earlier? You can thank Ian for those. He was my contractor. He designed and did most of the renovations himself."

"Wow," Rashad said. "You did a great job."

"Thanks," Ian said. "Normally I let my guys handle most of the hands on stuff and I just supervise, but when I saw Liz I just felt like I wanted to make sure she had the very best I could give her."

"Ahh, that's so sweet," Camille said.

"Yea, he's great," Liz said leaning over and kissing her husband. Just then the food arrived. Once again the conversation turned, this time from relationships back to food as they enjoyed the wonderful selection of seafood.

"That was the best crab cake I've ever had," Rashad said as he placed his fork down after finishing his final bite. "Thanks for suggesting it, Ian."

"I'm glad you enjoyed it," Ian responded as he continued to enjoy his grilled tuna. "It's definitely one of my favorites here."

"Excuse me, I have to go to the ladies' room," Liz said.

"Oh, I have to go too," Camille stated.

"Okay. Well you boys play nice," Liz said as she stood up from the table. She was a bit unsteady after her third glass of wine.

Camille placed a hand lightly on her elbow to steady her as they walked towards the ladies room.

"Still can't hold her alcohol I see," Rashad said.

"Yeah, she's a bit of a lightweight," Ian agreed with a smile.

"So, Ian, do you mind if I ask you a question?" Rashad wasn't sure if he should go here but he was just curious.

"No sure ask away," Ian said with ease.

Rashad straightened his back a bit and cleared his throat before he spoke. "So how does it feel to be a married to a black woman?"

A small smile came upon Ian's face. He took a sip of what little was left of his wine. "I had a feeling you would ask me something like that."

"If I'm out of line-"

"No, no, it's okay." Ian replied. "Liz is a smart and beautiful woman. She makes me laugh, she's kind, considerate, generous, confident... she gets me. It's like we're on the same page. She's the air I breathe. I love her. Yes she's a black woman but I just see a beautiful woman who takes my breath away every time I look at her, every time I touch her. As far as our color, I don't worry about what other people think. At the end of the day, we come home to one another and it's all about us, no one else. And yes, there are cultural differences but we enjoy many of the same things. We understand those differences and it doesn't make us uncomfortable."

Rashad nodded his head as if he agreed and understood. "All right man. That was from the heart."

"You're damn right it was." Ian smiled and downed the rest of his drink in one gulp.

Liz and Camille were at the mirror retouching their makeup and primping their hair. Camille slowly reapplied her lip gloss. She didn't know if she should 'open the door' to what Liz was trying to say at the table but she was so curious.

"So Liz, tell me how much of a player Rashad really was?"

Liz looked at Camille in the mirror as she touched up her lip color with her MAC lip gloss.

"Perhaps I shouldn't have said that. Sometimes my mouth gets me in trouble." Liz said shaking her head at her own stupidity.

"No please. I mean I like Rashad. He's very attractive...sweet...funny. I'm just curious."

Liz smiled at Camille before she began to speak. "Well," Liz started, "Rashad was quite the ladies man in college. I mean he is attractive and he's always had game. He just has this way about him, a confidence. He was the one girls wanted to get a dance with at the party or club, you know what I mean."

"Okay so you sayin' he was a ho?" Camille asked.

They both laughed.

"Let's put it this way, he never went without but he wasn't out there like that. There were a couple of girls he was really into. I mean he was selective with who he went there with. But you know that was college."

"Yeah. I was just wondering. I mean everyone has a past."

"Yeah." Liz agreed "He's really into you though. I can tell."

“Oh yeah?” Camille asked.

Liz indicated yes with her brows raised, nodding her head slowly. Camille smiled. The women clutched their purses and exited the restroom. They made their way back to the table. Ian and Rashad were laughing.

“Hey we wanna laugh too.” Liz said.

The two men stood as the women approached the table. Both extended kisses to their date.

“I was just telling Ian about the first time you met Derek,” Rashad said.

Liz immediately began laughing and shaking her head, “I was drunk. I was drunk.”

Camille sat dumbfounded as the other three all laughed about the private joke.

“I’m sorry Camille. I didn’t mean to leave you out.” Rashad finally said. “Second year, Derek came to visit one weekend from Tech. We went to this Heaven and Hell party that Liz told me about at some frat house. By the ti-”

“Heaven and Hell party?” Camille asked.

“Oh girl those things are a trip.,” Liz said. “You start at the bottom floor of the house and you have to get like two or three shots or drinks to be allowed up to the next floor where there are two or three more drinks you have to drink to be allowed up to the attic where the last drink is. The first floor is hell, the second is purgatory, and the third is heaven. You are guaranteed to end up messed up!”

“That sounds crazy,” Camille said.

“Yeah it was,” Rahad said. “So like I was saying. By the time we get to the party Liz is half way through purgatory and all the way drunk. And she is just talking shit to all these frat boys telling them they ain’t nothin’ and that she will drink them all under the table.” he paused as he tried to stop himself from laughing. “So we catch up to her as she is about to get her last drink on the second floor. I’ll never forget it. It was called a Flaming Dr. Pepper.”

“A what?” Camille asked.

"A Flaming Dr. Pepper, I have no idea what's in it, but they give you this shot and they set it on fire, you drop it in a mug of beer and chug it and supposedly the aftertaste tastes like Dr. Pepper." Liz explained.

"So anyway, Liz drops in the shot and starts to chug just as we come up behind her. She slams the mug down on the table and lets out this tremendous belch."

"Tasted just like Dr. Pepper," Liz added.

"She turns around and Derek is making this face like 'Damn' you know, cause that shit was kind of unladylike. But Liz sees the look on his face and goes off. I mean she is laying into him: 'Who f do you think you are?' 'Sorry ass mother f.' 'Don't be f-ing judging me.'"

"I was sooo drunk," Liz said hiding her face in her hands. Ian laughed and put his arm around his wife.

"It gets better," Rashad said as tears began to roll down his eyes. "So Derek is standing there dumbfounded with his mouth hanging open and Liz is still just laying into him when all of a sudden she just pukes all over him. All over his new jersey and Tims." The three of them are in complete laughing fits as Liz hides her face further into her hands and tries to make herself as small as possible.

"I was so drunk!"

Camille and Rashad returned to their room after dinner. She ate too much so all she really wanted to do now was lie down. Rashad was showing her such a good time that she owed it to him to be more receptive to his advances. Besides, she hadn't had a good time like this in a while.

Rashad and Camille approached the door. They looked at one another and smiled simultaneously. He opened the door. "Ladies first."

Camille stepped inside and he followed. She immediately removed her shoes, kicking one off and then the other, leaving one by the door and the other by a chair that was placed in the corner.

"I hope you enjoyed dinner," Rashad said.

"Yes, I really had a good time. Your friend Liz is cool and her husband was very charming." Camille responded.

"I'm glad." Rashad smiled. "This is good," he said as he sat on the edge of the bed taking off his shoes, "we both needed this relaxation. It's always good to get with friends and just chill...you know?"

"Yeah," Camille agreed.

"Are you all right?" Rashad asked.

"Oh yeah, I'm good. Why do you ask?" Camille questioned.

"Just making sure," Rashad said smiling. "I'm gonna get out these clothes, throw on some shorts."

"I'm about to get changed into something comfortable myself. Do you need to go the bathroom? Because I was on my way in there for just a few minutes," Camille said.

"Oh you're good. I'll be fine out here," said Rashad.

"Okay." Camille made her way to the bathroom and closed the door behind her.

She let out a soft sigh as she looked at her reflection in the mirror.

Don't trip. There's a good-looking man on the other side of that door waiting for you. Get it together.

After Camille finished convincing herself, she opened the door. She came out with nothing on but a pink tank top and panties to match. Rashad was across the room staring out the window he opened partially, taking a moment to admire the view.

"The view from this room is beautiful isn't it?" "Rashad said still staring out the window.

"Yes it is but the view over here is just as nice," Camille responded.

He could not control his mouth which parted slightly when he turned around and saw her standing there. Her petite but athletic frame looked appetizing.

"You look so sexy," Rashad said.

Camille smiled as she walked over to the bed. "Thank you."

Rashad made his way to the chair near the window. Camille sat on the edge of the bed. Rashad sat on the edge of the chair with his hands clasped and arms resting on his legs. He leaned in to her and smiled.

"So what's up?" Rashad asked.

"What do you mean? I wanted to get comfortable."

"Yeah but I bet you don't usually sleep in a tank top and panties."

"When the weather's nice," Camille blushed.

"Okay." Rashad said.

Rashad had not yet changed into his shorts but he had a feeling there was no need to change at all.

Rashad slowly made his way over to Camille. She was sexy as hell. He took his left hand and gently stroked her hair. He moved his face closer, placed his lips on hers. The kiss started out gently. Their tongues met and each followed the others lead, back and forth, up and down. Already, Camille's body is tingling and she was getting wet. Rashad's penis was getting harder. His right hand made its way to her ass as he slid it against her just enough to place it between her skin and her panties. He squeezed it tight. Camille had both her arms wrapped around him. She caressed his back but it wasn't long before both of their hands were out of control.

Their kissing and breaths were harder now, more intense. Still kissing, Camille walked forward as Rashad walked backwards towards the bed. Both their bodies fell on the mattress. Rashad removed her tank top in a hurry. He stopped for a few seconds to admire her perfect brown breasts. Camille was on her back. Rashad was on top of her looking deeply into her eyes. He gently licked her left nipple and flicked it with his tongue. He grabbed it in his hand and began to suck on it. Camille let out a soft moan. Their hands were going crazy. She was rubbing his head, back, chest, and ass.

He made his way inside her. Their bodies began to dance in a perfect rhythm. There was a crisp but calm breeze flowing in from the window.

Chapter 21

It was the last Sunday of April. The NFL draft had started the day before. They knew that Alan was not going to be chosen on the first day of the draft, but they were hoping the positive vibes they were receiving from some scouts and teams meant that there was a good chance he would be selected some time on the second day.

Derek, Rashad, Camille, Alan, his father Patrick, Sean, and Sydney had gathered at Derek's father's house for a draft party. Derek was in the kitchen unwrapping a tray of hot wings he had picked up from the grocery store. He didn't notice Camille enter the kitchen until she cleared her throat.

"Oh hey," he said looking up from what he was doing.

"How are you?" Camille asked.

"Good, you?"

"I'm good. Charity told me I could just help myself to something to drink."

"Oh yeah, there's soda in the fridge and water on the door," Derek said.

"Thanks."

Camille fidgeted with the stack of plastic caps for a moment before pulling one off the top.

"So, you haven't said anything to Rashad about our dinner?" Camille asked.

"No!" Derek said. "I mean, no. It was harmless, just two people with a mutual friend hanging out." He realized the absurdity of the comment but it was the best he could do.

Camille smiled. "Well, yeah. I agree."

"Good. I heard you guys had a nice weekend," Derek said, changing the subject.

"It was pretty cool," Camille said pouring herself a cup of tea.

"You got to meet Liz? She's a character isn't she?"

"Yeah, she's interesting," Camille said.

"I had never met any one like her," Derek agreed. "She's actually toned down since college."

"That's what I hear," Camille said. "They told me about the first time you two met."

"Oh, lord," Derek said smiling. "Yeah that was an experience. She just laid into me like I was an ex or something. I'm still scared of her. And she never did pay me back for my Tims. I was too scared to ask."

Camille laughed.

"I'm serious. That girl's hardcore. Hopefully being married will calm her down."

"I doubt it," Camille said smiling. "Her husband seems pretty scared of her too." She laughed and placed her hand on his arm.

They had fallen back into the comfortable conversation that they both enjoyed. Thoughts of anything outside of that room faded.

"Hey babe," Rashad said entering the kitchen. "Finding everything okay?"

Derek and Camille moved away from one another quickly.

"Yeah, sweetie. I was just talking to Derek," Camille said.

"Oh yeah, I'm sure he's a lot friendlier than last time you saw him."

Derek and Camille both glanced at one another.

"Remember? The party?"

"Oh yeah, yeah," Camille said. "That was a pretty intense evening."

"Yeah," Rashad agreed. "I'm sure you'll see a few more blow ups between us if you hang around for a while."

"Really? You guys argue a lot?" Camille asked.

"No, that's why they're so intense when we do," Derek said. "Well let me get this food into the living room." He picked up the tray of wings and left Camille and Rashad alone in the kitchen.

Rashad picked up a cup and got some ice and water out of the door of the fridge.

"He's a nice guy, huh?" Rashad said.

"Who, Derek?" Camille asked. "Yeah, he seems pretty cool."

"Yeah, I just wish he would open himself up and find

someone." Rashad said. "He's been so uptight since his mom died. He needs a good woman."

"Yeah, that would probably be good for him," Camille agreed. She quickly pushed away the next thought that entered her mind.

Rashad's cell phone rang, "Hello." He said and immediately began to smile as he quickly walked back into the living room with his hands held high above his head. Camille followed closely at his heels trying to figure out what was happening.

"Someone would like to speak to you," Rashad said handing the phone to Alan.

The man on the television approached the podium just as Alan said hello and also began to smile.

"With the sixth pick of the fifth round, the Miami Dolphins select offensive guard from *The* Ohio State University, Alan France."

Alan's father had started screaming before they had finished calling his name. Everyone in the room cheered in celebration. Derek and Rashad embraced as they saw that their dreams were finally starting to come true. Alan had to step out on the patio so that he could hear his conversation with the team's general manager and head coach.

"Yes sir, I look forward to getting started. I will see you tomorrow." Alan hung up the phone and immediately fell to his knees. His father put his hand on his son's shoulder and knelt down beside him and they thanked God together for their blessing.

Alan, his father, Rashad, Derek, and Robert all flew down to Miami the next morning to meet with the Miami coaches and general manager to begin negotiating his contract.

*****

Camille was glad that the guys would be gone for about a week. She and Rashad had seen each other nearly everyday since getting back from their weekend at the Carolina Rose. While she enjoyed the time they spent together, she felt like she was not getting as much work done as she would like. Thank God for Sydney. She had designed mailers for Lyon's Electronics which gave him enough of a bump in his foot traffic through the store that he decided to sign a yearlong contract. Mr. Lyon's also sent other business her way though his connections at the Rotary Club. Camille was ecstatic at the state of her business and how it was beginning to flourish. This week would give her the opportunity to really turn up the heat on the nightclub project, and send her company to a whole new level.

She sat in her office going over some of Sydney's ideas for the club and she smiled. *This girl is good.* She thought. She looked at the clock on her computer screen it was 8:57 in the morning, Sydney would be arriving any minute and just then Camille decided she was going to do better than keep the promise she made to Sydney in her interview.

She heard the door of the office open and Sydney's greeting, "Hey girl."

"Hey, when you get settled could you come in here for a moment."

"Sure let me just put my stuff down," Sydney answered. "What's up?" She said as she entered the office a few moments later.

"I was just looking over your proposals for the club promotions," Camille began. She forced herself not to smile as to not give away her intentions.

"That bad, huh? Well they were just my first drafts, I can rework them," Sydney said taking a seat across from Camille.

"Actually," Camille could no longer contain her excitement, "they're great. You are really talented girl."

"Well thanks," Sydney said smiling. "I've learned a lot from you."

"Thanks for the compliment, but you have natural ability that I have nothing to do with. You know when I interviewed you I told you that once business picked up I would start giving you fulltime hours, and I want to follow through on that."

"Thank you so much."

"What I didn't realize is that you were so talented and how much of an asset you would be to me. I know I've put a lot on you lately and since you are graduating next month I want to put you on salary."

Sydney let out a little yelp of joy.

"I probably can't pay you want some of the big time places can, but I really don't want to lose you so, we can negotiate a fair salary."

"Ok then. Sounds great." Sydney smiled inside and out. She was excited about the bright outlook of her future.

Chapter 22

"I love it," Tyrone exclaimed. He, Camille and Sydney were having a meeting at Camille's office to discuss the marketing ideas for Club Destiny. "It's exactly what I was looking for. I mean, 21 to get in but I want the atmosphere and the music to say
'this is a laid back grown folks spot where you can come relax, mingle, dance and enjoy yourself without having to worry about a lot of drama.'"

"I understand that." Sydney agreed. "I mean I consider myself to be mature for my age and I've been to some clubs where young adults just get out of control over something stupid, the girls are half dressed, and the guys are just, well, being 19, 20 year old guys. They're idea of having a good time is completely different from the crowd you want to attract to your club."

Tyrone looked at Camille with a small display of disbelief and then over to Sydney again. Camille smiled at him with an 'I told you so' look. He gave a little smile and nodded his head a couple of times.

"Exactly. And this is no disrespect to people your age."

"Oh no, none taken," said Sydney. "People appreciate different things as they get older."

"This is exactly the type of thing we need to be discussing." Camille said. "It's important for us to know what kind of environment you want for your business. I believe it is vital to establish this from the beginning. We want to be sure our marketing efforts will be effective."

"Well, we've been here close to an hour. What do you say we put our first marketing idea into action," Camille said to Tyrone.

"Yes, let's," Tyrone agreed with a big grin.

*****

Camille and Sydney made arrangements for Tyrone to advertise the club opening on air at one of the local radio stations. Tyrone had just arrived at the station. He pulled the front door open which had a big red and black sign that read HOT 101.5 on it. Camille and Sydney were sitting comfortably on the leather couches in the lobby area. They both stood up when they saw him enter.

He went to check in at the receptionist desk. Sitting there was a young woman in her early twenties. Although she was sitting behind a tall counter, one could tell she had a petite frame. She had pretty brown eyes, long eyelashes, perfectly arched eyebrows, and full, glossy lips. She was wearing a headset and chewing a piece of gum.

"Hello sir, how may I help you?" The young receptionist said smiling.

"Yes, my name is Tyrone Johnson. I'm here to do the radio spot scheduled for 12:30."

"All right, Mr. Johnson." She pointed to the clipboard on the counter. "Please sign in and have a seat and I'll let the station manager know you're here."

"Thank you very much." Tyrone said.

Tyrone walked towards Camille and Sydney. They were still standing, both with big smiles on their faces.

Tyrone reached out to shake their hands, "Ladies."

"Hello." Camille greeted.

"Hello." Sydney echoed.

"Thanks for setting this up. I've never done an on air promotion. To be honest, I'm a little nervous." Tyrone said as he fidgeted a little with his keys.

"You'll do fine. This has been your dream, to own and run your own club. This is your vision. Just be natural, be yourself." Camille said this with such enthusiasm.

"That's right." Sydney chimed in.

Tyrone paced the floor for about 20 seconds and then, "Hey", he said, "why don't you two join me?"

Camille and Sydney looked at one another and then at him.

"What?" Camille asked.

"I mean I did hire you to help me market the club. It would be great if you could do it with me. It'll also be good advertising for you and your business." Tyrone added.

"That's a great idea." Sydney agreed.

"Oh, I don't know. I mean we never discussed the radio spot

being a team effort." Camille said apprehensively.

Tyrone stopped himself. "You know what, I'm sorry, you're right. You've done enough just by arranging this whole thing. Forget I asked. Really."

Camille had a silent chat with herself in her head. *Maybe it wouldn't be a bad idea. He's right. This would be great exposure. I should take advantage.*

Sydney stood still with a maybe he is right look on her face. She felt like she would be out of line by actually verbalizing anything more.

"You're right, Tyrone." Camille said suddenly.

Tyrone looked at her with a straightforward expression. Sydney did as well.

"You make a good point. Perhaps I will. That is if it's all right with the person in charge." Camille responded.

"All right then," said Tyrone.

A tall woman walked out from a door around the corner from the receptionist counter. She stood about 5'10". She had an athletic build and long dark brown hair. She was wearing a dark blue knee length skirt with a fitted, cream colored, wrap style blouse. She moved gracefully towards Tyrone and with a very calm demeanor, introduced herself.

"Hello, I'm Stacey King, Station Manager for HOT 101.5." She extended her hand. You must be Tyrone Johnson."

"Yes," Tyrone extended his hand, "pleased to meet you." They both exchanged a firm handshake.

"Hello I'm Camille Jacobs. We spoke on the phone."

"Yes, nice to meet you."

"This is my colleague, Sydney Mitchell," Camille said.

"Hello pleased to meet you as well."

"I understand that Mr. Johnson will be promoting his club opening on air today."

"Yes, Ms. King that is correct." Tyrone said smiling. "However, there was something that we wanted to run by you." The station manager stood still waiting for him to continue.

"I know the arrangement was only made for me to do the spot by myself. We were wondering if it would be possible if Ms. Jacobs and Ms. Mitchell could accompany me in the studio." Tyrone inquired.

"Ms. King, we realize this is short notice and understand if it---", Camille said.

"Well, I'm sure we could work something out," she responded. "Have either of you ever done this before?"

"No." Tyrone, Camille and Sydney all said in unison.

The station manager looked at all of them and smiled. "I'll just need to let the deejay know. It should be fine."

Tyrone looked at Sydney and Camille and exhaled a sigh of relief.

"All right everyone. Follow me."

They all followed the station manager. She swiped the badge hanging from her hip to unlock the door. She led them down a long hall way until they approached another locked door. "Good, he's not on the air at the moment." She swiped her badge once again, opened the door. In the room sat the deejay.

"Hey Scoop. How's it going?"

"Hey, Stacey. Going good, going good."

"Glad to hear it. Listen these two nice women are going to be joining in for the on-air club promotion. Do you have any concerns at all?"

"No, that's cool. I can just cue the other mics."

"Great." The station manager said smiling. "Well, you are in good hands. Scoop will let you know what to do. Good luck to you."

As the three of them sat around the console ready to make their radio debut, Camille and Sydney grew more excited and Tyrone began to feel more at ease.

"We've got some guests on the show with us today. There's a new spot opening in town and here to talk about it is Mr. Tyrone Johnson. So man how ya doin'?"

"I'm good man thanks for having me here today."

"So tell us about this new club you're brining to our area."

"Well, I call it Club Destiny. It's due to open on June 19th."

"Now is this gonna be 21 or 25 and over?"

"Twenty-five and over."

"All right, all right. And why don't you introduce these two beautiful ladies, if you will."

"Certainly. This is Camille Jacobs, owner of Mainstream Marketing and her assistant Sydney Mitchell. These are the two responsible for helping me get the word out about Club Destiny."

"Hello ladies," said Scoop.

"Hey, Scoop," Camille and Sydney said in unison.

"Hmm, hmm, damn. My beautiful black queens gettin' it done. Business owner, huh? That's very impressive Ms. Jacobs," Scoop said.

"Well, thank you. And you can call me Camille."

"So, let's get into this next jam from my man Jay-Z and then we will come back and get some more info on Club Destiny." Scoop said turning everyone's mic off. "After this song we can go into some more details about the club. Are you going to talk about that Mr. Johnson?"

"No, I am going to let Sydney talk about that," Tyrone explained. Sydney looked shocked. "You did a great job in the meeting describing the atmosphere I'm looking for, I just think you can say it better than I can."

Sydney smiled as Camille gave her an approving nod and smile.

"And where is your company located Camille?" Scoop asked.

"Our office is in downtown Norfolk."

"Alright, alright we are back with Tyrone Johnson owner of Club Destiny opening on Military Hwy on Juneteenth. That's June 19th for all my unedumacated folks out there." Scoop said as the song ended. "We also have the beautiful Camille Jacobs, owner of Mainstream Marketing located in downtown Norfolk and her lovely assistant Sydney Mitchell.

"So, the club is opening on June 19th, is that significant or just coincidence?"

"I did want the club to open during the summer and the day of true emancipation of our ancestors seemed like a fitting date. We as African Americans have come a long way, with President Obama in the White House, and African Americans doing great things like owning businesses and running radio stations. I just think its time we really begin to support one another." Tyrone stated.

"Amen, brotha. That's what I like to hear. So Ms. Sydney tell us why Club Destiny is going to be the new hot spot."

"Well, there's gonna be a little something for everyone. Destiny is going to be a place where you can come and relax after work with cocktails and a nice extensive menu. On Mondays and Tuesdays Destiny will feature local artists, bands, and singers."

"Wow, so you gonna give the local cats a chance to shine, that's cool."

"Yea, Destiny is really about lifting up the African American culture in all possible ways. We are going to have open mic night for amateur singers, conscious rap artist, and poets. There are going to be a couple of jazz nights an old school night and on Saturdays we are going to feature some of the hottest deejays."

"I hope I'm on that invitation list because it definitely sounds like a spot I'd like to be," DJ Scoop added.

"No doubt, no doubt," Tyrone said.

"Well there you have it. I'd like to thank my guests for being here this afternoon. All of you listening out there be sure to mark your calendars for June 19th and come out to the opening of Club Destiny on Virginia Beach Boulevard near Military Circle ya'll."

Scoop cut to a commercial immediately. "I can't wait to come out and show my support man," he said to Tyrone extending his hand for a friendly shake. "It was nice to meet you all. See you on the 19th!"

Tyrone, Camille and Sydney all thanked him for having them on his show. They were all very pleased with how well the segment had gone. They went out the exit door back to the lobby.

"That went great!" Camille exclaimed.

"It certainly did." Sydney agreed.

"I can't thank you ladies enough," Tyrone said.

Everyone smiled at one another with excitement and high hopes for the grand opening.

"I am positive this is going to be a great experience indeed." Tyrone said.

*****

The weekend was about to begin. Camille invited Sydney to come with her to meet Shayla. She thought it would be a good idea for some girl time and to celebrate marketing Club Destiny and the publicity that Mainstream had gotten. Since the radio spot they had gotten several calls from companies inquiring about their services.

It was a very warm, late Friday afternoon. Camille was expecting Syndey to be over no later than seven o'clock. She had to make sure she went by the store to pick up some necessities beforehand. As Camille was getting her things together to leave the office, her cell phone rang. She looked at the number. It was Rashad.

"Hi there," Camille greeted.

"Hey you," Rashad responded.

"How was your day?" Camille asked.

"Good and yours?"

"Busy. Still going. Trying to wrap some things up. Derek and I have been energizer bunnies all week."

"I heard that," Camille agreed.

"I wanted to call and tell you that I was thinking about you and to tell you congratulations on your marketing pitch for the club. I'm sure your client is excited."

"He is," Camille said smiling. "He says he's happy with the ideas we presented."

"Well I'm glad to hear that. I'll take you out when I get back, you know, to celebrate. What are you up to this weekend?"

"That would be great. Oh, remember Sydney and I are having a girls weekend at Shayla's. Remember?"

"Oh, yeah that's right, you did tell me that. It must have

slipped my mind. I've been so busy this week." Rashad said.

"When are you guys gonna be back?" Camille asked.

"Probably on Sunday."

"Well, maybe we can do a nice dinner in the mid-week or we can wait 'til the weekend." Camille suggested.

"Yeah that would be cool. So when are you leaving?"

"Sydney should be over by seven o'clock. We're gonna leave soon after."

"Okay then. Well, contact me when you get there to let me know you made it all right." Rashad said with genuine concern.

"It's only a half hour up the road." Camille chuckled playfully. "You act like I'm going out of town."

"Hey I just want to make sure." Rashad added.

"Okay, okay. I'll contact you when I get there."

"Promise?" Rashad questioned.

"I promise."

"All right then." Rashad paused. "Camille?"

"Yeah?"

"I love you."

Whoa. He said the three words. THE three words that everyone in a new relationship does not respond to lightly, cannot respond to lightly. The dynamic of the relationship crosses over. Was I ready to cross over with Rashad? What would it mean for me and...

Camille responded slowly, "I love you, too." She felt herself take a deep breath before she said it and held her breath after.

"Okay." She could hear Rashad smiling at the other end.

"Okay." Camille released a light sigh as she responded.

"Hear from you later on." Rashad said.

"Okay." Camille said quickly.

Wow! Camille thought. *What was this beginning of? I know what it means. It means this takes our relationship to the next level. Was I ready for this?*

Camille arrived home from the store with a few things she

needed for her stay with Shayla for the weekend. She put a Sade CD on to relax. Time was moving fast. She had spent more time in the store than she planned.

"Oh, this is cute," Camille said out loud picking up a soft yellow colored shirt that she got on sale a while back. She folded it and placed it on the bed.

"All right. Bras, panties, head wrap, toothbrush, face wash." Her list was interrupted as she heard a hard knock at the door. *That has to be Sydney.*

Camille looked out the peephole and Sydney was on the other side. She opened the door with a huge grin.

"Hey girl," Sydney greeted.

"Hey Sydney, you're early.

"Girl, no I'm not you know it's going on 7:30. You said that so I wouldn't feel bad. Anyway, I got caught up with Sean." Sydney said.

"I'm almost done packing, give me a few minutes. Sit down and rest yourself."

Sydney took a seat on the couch. "Sade, huh? Yeah, I like her."

"Me too girl. She helps me to think, you know. I don't know, puts me in a different place." Camille said in a higher than normal tone and still moving around in her bedroom getting packed.

"Mmmm, sounds like we're gonna have a real nice girl chat this weekend." Sydney replied.

"Oh yes, I'll have to agree with that."

*****

Camille and Sydney arrived at Shayla's around 8:30. She lived in an apartment not too far away from the Hampton Coliseum. Sydney and Camille got their bags from the car and settled themselves in.

"Oh my gosh I am so glad you two are here. Sydney I'm so glad we are finally getting a chance to meet. I have heard so many good things about you. Please make yourself at home." Shayla offered to

Sydney.

"I'm so excited to meet you too. Thanks for having me."

Shayla had given both the ladies a huge hug when they first arrived. The kids were with their father for the weekend.

"Girl, I love my children but it feels good to have a break. Ya'll just wait." Shayla had invited the ladies into the kitchen. "I've got wine, fruit punch, grape Kool-Aid, juice," Shayla said as she opened the refrigerator door. "Hell, let's all just have a glass of wine."

Everyone laughed. "I'll get the glasses," Camille said. She removed three wine glasses from the cabinet and placed them on the counter. Camille stood on the other side of the counter and filled the glasses. Sydney and Shayla were seated on the other side of the counter on the two barstools. Shayla filled the glasses with wine.

"Here's to being blessed." Camille said.

"And to good friends." Sydney said.

"And to family." Shayla said.

"Now remember you're supposed to swirl it, smell it, sip it then swish it around in your mouth, then swallow it down." Shayla said.

"Are you sure you're talking about drinking wine?" Camille asked. Sydney laughed. The ladies all drank, as instructed.

"Mmmm. Where did you get this sis?"

"My neighbor gave it to me. She's into wine. She got it for me as a gift from a wine tasting she went to at a vineyard, thought I'd like it."

"That was nice," said Sydney. She took another sip of the wine and then immediately initiated discussion. "So, let's cut to the chase." Camille and Shayla raised their heads with heightened interest. "Camille, you were playing Sade when I got to your place tonight. When people play Sade, they got something on their mind."

"Is that right, sis?" Shayla questioned raising an eyebrow and taking a sip at the same time.

"What do you mean? There's nothing to tell. A woman can't listen to Sade to just chill and relax from a hard day's work?" Camille said trying to change the subject. She knew she wasn't doing a good job. The ladies looked at her in silence waiting for her to continue.

"All right girl. Spill the beans." Shayla said.

Camille took a couple of more big sips of her wine. "I was on the phone with Rashad and before we hung up, he told me he loved me."

"For real?" Sydney said smiling. "That's great."

Camille had a cross between a blank look and small smile on her face.

"Or is it?" Shayla asked.

"Is it what?" Camille asked back.

"Is it great? You don't look too enthused." Shayla said.

"Well, I don't know. I mean it changes things. Of course the person who utters it first always says it in the form of a question. If the other person says it back, they'd better mean it. If one waits too long to respond, it's an indication of doubt-that perhaps you may be thinking about not being with that person long term. If you say it too quickly, that means that you could be jumping the gun. Saying it back changes things." Camille said.

"So what did you say?" Sydney asked.

"I said it back." Camille said.

"Did you mean it?" Shayla asked.

"I think I did. I mean I just wasn't ready. I didn't expect to hear it is all." Camille responded.

"Were you smiling when you said it?" Sydney asked. "Because you know how you can hear someone's reaction over the phone and all."

"Yeah, I was taken by surprise but he couldn't tell because when I said it back he just said okay and I could hear him smiling." Camille said.

"Well do you think he sounded happy when you hung up?" Shayla asked.

"Yeah, I believe so." Camille said. "Oh, I was supposed to contact him when I got here to let him know I made it safe." She removed her phone from her hip to send him a text:

At sis's safe. Tlk 2u 2mrw morn. Send.

"What did you say?" Syndey asked. Camille told her what she texted.

"Oh, ok." Sydney responded.

"Was that ok?" Camille asked.

"Yeah," Shayla and Sydney in unison.

Suddenly there was a vibrating sound. It was Camille's phone. Rashad was responding.

"Damn that was fast! What he say?" Shayla asked.

"He said:

Gr8. Njy ur eve. Cll u n th morn ☺

"Aww that's nice. He's showing his love and concern." Shayla and Sydney smiled together.

"Cute." Camille said. "I'm just nervous about moving forward."

"Why?" Shayla asked.

"I don't know." Camille said.

"Yes you do. And when you're ready to let us know why, we'll be here ready to listen." Shayla said.

Camille didn't want to get into it but she did have feelings for Derek. She loved being with Rashad and didn't want to mess things up between them or him and Derek. And how could she get Derek out of her head when he and Rashad were best friends and business partners? Was it possible to love two people at the same time?

"All right ladies. I just finished my glass of wine. Let's have seconds and discuss how we're going to spend the rest of the evening." Camille said eagerly.

The ladies were merry with laughter, conversation, food, and more wine as they watched *Waiting to Exhale* followed by several episodes of *Sex and the City* into the wee hours of the night.

*****

The next morning the ladies woke up around nine o'clock. Camille noticed a text on her phone from Rashad. "The man means what he says." Camille said softly under her breath.

Morn 2U. hope U slpt well. I'll B Thnkn bout U 2dy. HR frm u l8r.

She decided to contact him later. Her head was pounding. Everyone got washed up and dressed. They decided to head out for breakfast to Denny's. It was a beautiful morning. They rode in Shayla's car.

"Last night was a good time." Shayla said.

"Yes it was. It's nice to get together like that." Camille said. There was a nice spring breeze flowing through the window.

"I agree. I had a blast." Sydney added.

They lucked out and got a parking space right in front of the entrance door of the restaurant. It was still busy though. The ladies waited about 15 minutes before they were seated. They all ordered omelets. Camille drank the water she requested from the server with an Aleve to rid herself of the headache she woke up with earlier.

"Hey I have a question for you two?"

Shayla and Sydney looked at her eagerly, waiting for her to proceed.

"Do you believe it's possible to love two people at the same time?" Camille asked.

"Yes. I mean I believe someone can love two people but there's only one that you'd be really in love with." Sydney said.

"I loved two guys at the same time." Shayla said.

"Really, sis? When?" Camille inquired.

"Well you know I had been with Darius and Tara's dad for a while. I mean he was my all. We were together since senior year of high school. In the beginning of the last year we were together, I met Kris. We were at the club. He was a friend of a friend. He told my friend he thought I was cool. Anyway, we ended up calling each other, chatting. Every once in a while turned into more than several times a week. That went on for months."

"The guy you were with didn't suspect anything?" Sydney

asked.

"By that time in our relationship we had grown apart quite a bit. He was working all the time, and there's nothing wrong with that of course. I mean we had two children but it wasn't enough. It was like something was missing. I loved him very much and I ended up growing very close to Kris at the same time. Long story short, he and I ended up breaking up. I loved them both but I Kris and I...." Shayla stopped smiling.

"What? Go on." Camille said impatiently.

"We have similar interests. He's funny. I don't know, he makes me feel good about myself. It's....refreshing." Shayla said.

"Did you ever figure out what was missing?" Sydney asked.

"We were young when we first got together. We didn't try. We worked so hard at making sure the kids had what they needed and ended up neglecting us. I guess by that time it was too late." Shayla sipped her water.

"Do you think you two will ever get back together?" Camille asked.

"I don't know what the future holds. He loves those kids more than anything. We're good apart. No drama. We each want the other to be happy and right now, Kris makes me happy. There's a chemistry there I can't explain. I see good things happening between us, I really do." Shayla had a calm, comfortable smile on her face.

"Wow, when you talk about him, your face just lights up." Sydney said.

"Yeah. So, why did you ask that question anyway, sis?" Shayla asked already knowing the answer.

"Just conversation. That's all." Camille said this with part of her looking at the two with a smile. A deeper part of her was uncertain.

* * * * *

"Are you sure?" Derek asked.

"Very," Rashad answered emphatically. The two men along with Robert sat on the patio of a South Beach restaurant overlooking the Atlantic Ocean. It was around eight in the evening and they had just finished dinner. The late spring breeze coming in off of the ocean was calm and refreshing.

"He is," Robert agreed. "He told me the same thing last time he was down here."

"But...you've only known her for what three months?" Derek argued. "I mean she's a great girl...but you're using the L-word." Derek started to wonder why he was arguing so hard. He tried to convince himself that it was just concern for his friend.

"I know, dude," Rashad said smiling. "And honestly it scared the hell out of me to say it."

"You already told her?" Robert asked with shock displayed clearly on his face.

Rashad smiled and tilted his head to the side sheepishly. "The other day when I was talking to her, before I got off the phone with her I just said it."

"And?" Derek asked forcing himself not to sound too anxious about the answer.

"She said it back," Rashad said his smile growing broader.

"Wow," Derek said. "That's...great. Really, great."

"Yea it is isn't it?" Rashad said. "I mean, I've never met anyone like her. You know I had no plans to settle down, but I think she might be the one."

"As in marriage?" Derek asked.

"Yea, I think so. I've been really thinking about it and I can definitely see that in the future. I mean, I don't think I've ever thought about marrying anyone, but she has my head spinning. Whenever I'm around her I don't think about anything else. All I want to do is make her happy. That's the only thing I can think about is doing whatever I can to make her happy. I really love this girl."

"Here's your checks fellas," the waitress said. "No rush."

"Thanks," Robert said handing the waitress his credit card.

"You don't have to do that," Derek said.

"I know, but my man needs to start saving up for his

wedding." Robert said with a laugh.

"Shut up," Rashad said laughing.

Derek found it hard to laugh along with his friends, but did force a smile.

"Well, does that mean we have to wait until the bachelor party to go to the strip club?" Robert asked.

"Hey I said I was in love not insane. Everybody knows Miami has the best clubs. Let's go."

Chapter 23: Graduation

Camille, Rashad, Derek, Shayla and her boyfriend Kris stood outside of the Old Dominion Ted Constant Center on Hampton Boulevard waiting for Sean and Sydney. Sydney's parents had made the trip in from Charlotte, North Carolina and had spent the day before graduation with Sydney and Sean. Her mother, who was a doctor, had to return to work that evening, so they left immediately following graduation. The beautiful sunny May afternoon made a terrific backdrop for the happy families taking photo opportunities with their graduates. Daryl and Charity had also attended but headed back to their house to finish setting up for the graduation party, which they had agreed to hold for Sean and Sydney.

"I am so proud of Sean," Derek said. "He really busted his tail to get out of school in three years. I'm glad he had Sydney there supporting him."

"Yea, they seem like a great couple," Camille agreed squeezing Rashad around the waist. "She has nothing but good things to say about him."

"Yea, they're great kids," Rashad added returning Camille's squeeze.

"Kids? They're only a few years younger than us," Camille said. "We all have our whole lives ahead of us."

"And hopefully we'll get to spend them together," Rashad said giving Camille a kiss on the forehead. Shayla smiled at her sister and gave Kris's hand a squeeze.

Derek felt an uneasy feeling of guilt and turned away from the two of them and looked back towards many of the graduates exiting the building. He saw Sean and Sydney walking towards them holding hands still wearing their black cap and gowns. Sydney wore a gold sash around her neck indicating that she had graduated with honors.

"There they are," Shayla said pointing at them.

"Hey guys. Congratulations," Camille said as they approached.

"Thanks," they said in unison.

"Hey girl," Sydney said giving Shayla a hug. "I didn't know you were coming."

"Of course I came," Shayla said smiling. "This is Kris."

"Oh, it's so nice to meet you," Sydney said shaking Kris's hand. "Sean this is Shayla, Camille's sister and her friend Kris."

"Nice to meet you both," Sean said shaking each of their hands.

"You too, congratulations," Kris said. He was about thirty-five years old and just under six feet tall. He was thin, but muscular.

"Thanks," Sean said.

"Okay now that the introductions are done it's picture time!" Camille said, pulling her digital camera from her purse.

They took pictures for about five minutes ensuring that everyone had a photo opportunity with the graduates. They headed over to the parking garage to retrieve their cars and head over to Daryl and Charity's for the party. Sydney and Sean rode with Derek, Camille and Rashad took Rashad's car, and Kris and Shayla followed in Kris's car.

"Rashad and Camille make a cute couple," Sydney said as Derek pulled the Explorer on to I-64 east. "Don't you guys think so?"

Derek felt a twinge of jealousy as he heard Camille's name. Today was the first time he had seen her since returning from Miami with Rashad. He was doing his best to avoid being in the same place at the same time as her.

"Yea," Sean agreed. "Rashad seems to be really digging her."

"What has he been saying about her?" Sydney asked Derek.

"Huh? I don't know," Derek said allowing more irritation to enter his tone than he intended.

"Excuse me," Sydney said sitting back in her seat. "I just thought he might have shared since you are his best friend."

"What's your problem?" Sean asked.

"I'm sorry nothing, I'm just a little tired, I guess. It's been a long couple of weeks since the draft," Derek lied.

"Well, you need to be nice to me," Sydney said pouting. "It's my graduation day."

"Yes ma'am," Derek said smiling.

Sean looked at his brother inquisitively. "You sure that's all that's wrong with you?"

"Yea. Why?"

"Just want to be sure," Sean said. "You always get a funky attitude when we go to dad's."

"I'm past that now. I've matured," continuing to display a friendlier mood.

"Well, let's hope so," Sydney said. "You sucked at the baby shower."

"Thanks, Syd," Derek said looking at her in the rearview mirror. "I thought I was coming around until Rashad went off on me."

"Yea, that was cute the thing you did with Camille," Sydney said. "Reintroducing yourself to redeem how funky you acted towards her in the beginning."

"Yea," Derek said smiling as he remembered his first encounter with Camille.

Sean again gave his brother an inquiring look, but this time elected not to say anything.

Rashad glanced over at Camille's legs. She was wearing a light blue thin strapped sun dress. It came down to about mid thigh, and as she crossed her legs it came up just a little higher.

"Damn," Rashad said turning his attention back to the road.

"What?" Camille asked who had been looking out of the window and entranced in the music that was playing.

"You are so sexy," Rashad said. "You want to skip the party?"

"And do what?"

"What do you think?"

"There'll be plenty of time for that later," Camille said smiling. She and Rashad had been spending a lot of time together since he had returned from Miami. He loved making love to her, and let her know that whenever he could.

"I can't wait," Rashad said.

Camille smiled. "I think this is going to be a really fun evening."

"That's all I'm asking for," Rashad said.

"Is that all you can think about," Camille asked.

"No, but it's hard not too, when you look so good."

Camille rolled her eyes. "Thank you. But I was talking about the party. I'm looking forward to everyone getting to spend some time together."

"Yea, Sean and Derek are the closest thing I have to family here. It'll be good for you to get to know them a little better."

"Yea," Camille said as she turned her attention back out of the window of the car. She felt guilty about not telling Rashad about the two encounters she had had with Derek. She knew nothing had happened, but the chemistry she had with Derek made her feel uncomfortable about telling Rashad.

Charity was six months pregnant but Camille could hardly tell with as much energy she was displaying playing hostess.

"Is there anything I can do to help?" Camille offered as Charity moved about the house bringing in a tray of cheese and crackers to the living room.

"Thanks, but we pretty much got everything set up now," Charity said. "I had Daryl do most of the work before you guys got here." Charity winked at Camille and smiled.

"You look great by the way," Camille said.

"Thanks, I've been doing a lot of yoga and Pilates," Charity said. "I love this baby but she is not going to make me lose my figure."

"I hear that," Shayla said as she entered from the kitchen with a drink. "Wish I had been that active with my kids."

"Charity this is my sister Shayla," Camille said.

"Nice to meet you," Charity said. "You look good, how many kids do you have?"

"Two but it took every bit of the six years since I had my last one to recover my figure. You're doing it the smart way, stay active as long as she'll let you."

"I hear ya," Charity said.

Out on the patio Daryl was grilling burgers, hot dogs, and steaks. Sean, Derek, Kris, and Rashad were sitting at the patio table drinking beers and talking.

"Thanks for letting us have the party here dad," Sean said.

"No problem son," Daryl said as he closely examined one of the steaks. "I'm really proud of you and Sydney."

"Well thank you, Mr. Ballard," Sydney said coming out onto the patio with a glass of wine in her hand.

"Uh oh, who gave her the alcohol?" Derek said jokingly.

"Shut up Derek," Sydney said as she sat down on Sean's lap and gave him a kiss.

"Damn, it's too late, she's already getting touchy feely," Derek said.

Sydney stuck her tongue out at Derek before taking another sip of her wine.

Everyone laughed.

"What's so funny?" Camille asked as she and Shayla joined everyone else out on the patio.

"Derek's being mean to me," Sydney said.

"Hey, it's her graduation day. No being mean," Camille said. She started to playfully punch Derek in the arm, but caught herself. She realized that aside from Shayla no one else knew how close they had grown. As far as anyone else knew, they had only met twice and the first meeting was abbreviated.

Daryl had put extra chairs around the patio table, so the ladies sat down next to their significant others. Charity joined the group with a bottle of Fiji water in her hand. She walked up behind her husband and gave him a kiss on the cheek. She loved having people over.

"So, Rashad," Kris said. "Shayla said you're a sports agent."

"Yea," Rashad said. "D and I run our agency."

"Wow, that's awesome. You guys represent anybody I would have heard of?"

"Robert Singer," Derek said.

"The linebacker from Miami?" Kris asked.

"Yea," Rashad confirmed.

"That's pretty cool," Kris said. "I played some b-ball in high school. Had a chance to play some in college, but when my little girl was born I had to go to work. Y'know?"

"Yea, circumstances can get in the way sometimes," Derek said glancing at Camille quickly.

"Yea, but I wouldn't change a thing," Kris said. "I love my little girl."

"Kris, she's not a little girl anymore," Shayla said. "She's seventeen."

"Don't remind me," Kris said evoking laughter from the group.

"Hard having a teenager?" Charity asked.

"Teenage girls especially," Kris said. "You got off lucky Daryl having two boys."

"Amen brutha," Daryl said as he began removing burgers from the grill.

Sean and Sydney cut a quick look at Derek. He did not appear as though he was going to correct the assumption that Daryl had been around when the boys were growing up.

"I just wish I had been around to see them grow into men," Daryl said. "I missed out on them playing high school ball, the prom all that good stuff. She might be driving you crazy now, but cherish these moments, you can never get them back."

"Definitely," Kris said nodding his head.

"Yea, he was crying like a little baby last month when we sent her off to junior prom," Shayla said. "It was so cute." She pulled Kris's face to hers and gave him a kiss on the cheek.

"Hey, I am not afraid to admit that I cried. That was some emotional stuff." Kris said jokingly, evoking more laughter.

"Foods ready," Daryl said. "You guys can help yourselves."

Everyone ate and continued to talk and laugh. As the evening progressed they eventually made their way inside to the entertainment room. Shayla and Kris challenged Sean and Sydney to a game of pool, so everyone else sat and watched the game.

"We got next," Rashad said as he grabbed Camille's hand and raised it.

"I can't play pool," Camille said.

"Don't worry, babe. I'll show you how."

"Ok, but don't say I didn't warn you," Camille said as she sat down next to Derek at the bar.

"He's hyper-competitive too so don't be surprised if he yells at you a bit," Derek said.

"I am not hyper-competitive," Rashad said. "I just don't like losing."

"Is there a difference?" Derek laughed as he got up and walked to the other side of the bar. "Anyone want a drink?"

"I'll have another glass of wine," Sydney said as she stood up from lining up her shot, and nearly whacked Sean with her pool cue.

"No she won't either," Sean said. "She's had about enough."

"Hey...hey...hey," Sydney said. "I am not drunk. It is my graduation and I am celebrating."

"Yes, baby and we are all proud of you, but I think you should chill out for a while on the wine."

"He's just afraid you're gonna pass out before he gets *his* graduation gift," Rashad said eliciting laughter from Derek, Kris, and Daryl.

"Thanks for that," Sean said.

"Ooh, ya'll are so wrong," Shayla said.

"Sean knows I'm just messing with him," Rashad said. "I've been giving him a hard time since he was ten years old."

"And it never gets old," Sean added dryly.

Derek made himself a rum and coke and tossed Kris another beer. Sydney had gone back to the game and had forgotten she wanted another drink. She had just started drinking and did not hold her alcohol well.

"Hey guys, Charity's a little tired so she's gonna go lay down," Daryl announced as he and Charity stood up from the couch.

"Aww, party's over?" Sydney said poking her bottom lip out.

"No you guys can keep having fun," Charity said. "I'll be out like a light as soon as my head hits the pillow."

"And not even a herd of elephants can wake her up," Daryl added.

Charity gave Daryl a playful slap on the arm, "Anyway, it was nice meeting you all. Good night."

Everyone said their good nights to Charity and Daryl.

"What time is it anyway?" Camille asked.

"It's nine," Rashad said looking at his watch. "You ready to go?"

"No, I was just wondering," Camille said.

"I'm gonna get some more ice," Derek said as he walked towards the kitchen carrying the ice bucket from the bar. "Anyone want anything from the kitchen?"

"I'll have a bottle of water," Camille said.

"Me too," Shayla said.

"And grab one for Syd," Sean added.

"Okay, how many hands ya'll think I got?" Derek asked.

"I'll give you a hand," Camille said hopping down from her barstool.

Derek was already scooping ice out of bucket in the freezer when Camille entered the kitchen.

"Where's the bottled water?" she asked.

"There should be some left in the cooler next to the island," Derek responded. He found himself admiring the smooth skin of her shapely legs as she bent over at the waist to dig in the cooler for the water.

"There's nothing but beer in here," she said standing and turning towards him. He nearly dropped the ice bucket as he turned away trying to hide the fact that he had been watching her.

"Oh, well, I think there's more in the fridge I guess."

She approached the refrigerator just as he finished filling the bucket. The smell of her J. Lo Glow perfume invaded his nostrils causing him to momentarily pause. He stepped out of her way, to allow her access to the refrigerator door.

"They should be on the door," Derek said as he broke himself out of his trance and walked over to the island.

"Yea, I found them," Camille said.

"I can carry a couple of 'em," Derek said.

Camille turned to hand Derek two of the water bottles. Her hands ended up in his and the feel of his skin against hers caused her pulse to quicken. As he slowly took the bottles from her hands, they held one another's gaze for longer than both knew was safe.

"I uh…thanks," Camille said, pulling herself away and reaching back into the refrigerator for two more bottles of water.

"You guys doing alright in here?" Shayla said entering the kitchen.

"Yea, sis," Camille said closing the refrigerator door and holding a bottle of water in each hand. Her nipples were hard and showing through the thin material of her sundress. She hoped her Shayla would simply attribute it to the cold of the refrigerator, but she knew by the look on her big sister's face that her own face had given her away.

"I was just heading back in," Derek said.

"Well you can give those to Sydney and Kris," Shayla said. "I'll drink one of the ones Camille has here."

"Will do," Derek said smiling and exiting the kitchen with the ice bucket in one hand and the two bottle of water in the other.

"What the hell, Camille?" Shayla asked taking one of the bottles of water from her sister's hand.

"What?" Camille said feigning innocence as she opened her own water and took and long drink.

"I know that look in your eye," Shayla said. "Did something

happen between you two?"

"No of course not!" Camille said in a whisper. "Are you crazy?"

"No, but you acting like you are," Shayla said also whispering.

"I know," Camille said shaking her head, unable to look her sister in the eyes.

"Hey, babe," Rashad called from the entertainment room. "We're up."

"Okay, I'll be there in a sec," Camille called back. She sheepishly fell into Shayla's arms.

"It's gonna be okay. But you have to get it together, Camey," Shayla said giving her sister a hug. She only used Camille's childhood nickname when she knew she was struggling with something.

"I know, but I don't know how," Camille said.

"You have to stay away from him, and concentrate on your relationship with Rashad."

"I know, I know," Camille agreed.

Part 3

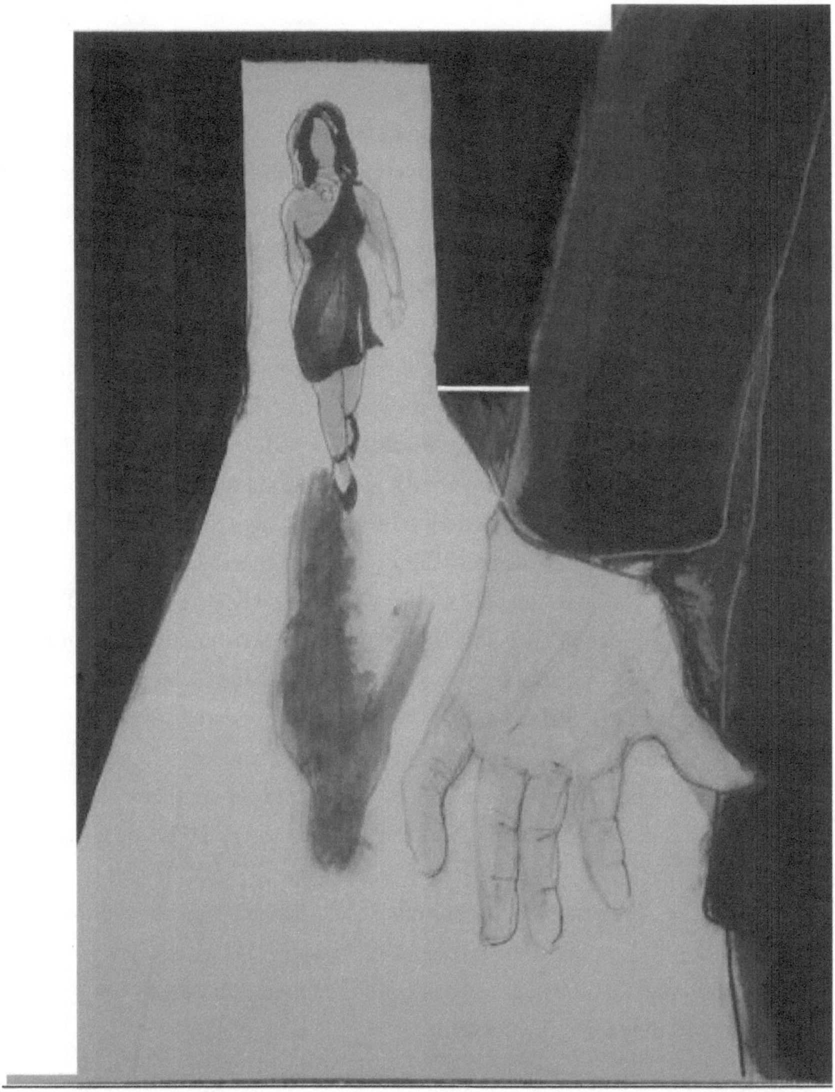

hChapter 24: Juneteenth

"I want to thank you all so much for coming out here tonight. My name is Tyrone Johnson. I am the owner of Club Destiny and I just wanted to say thank you for your support." Tyrone stood on the stage speaking into the microphone. He looked out over the couple hundred mostly black faces and smiled. Even though the club was nearly at capacity there was still a throng of people outside trying to gain entrance.

"Club Destiny is going to be about people being able to come together and have a good time with one another. So in the coming weeks, months, and years we are going to provide you with a place where you can not only have fun but also come out and chill, mingle, and network. My hope is that Club Destiny will help some of you fulfill your own destinies." The crowd applauded and cheered.

"One last thing before I let you guys get back to partying. I would like to thank my fellow NSU alum and friend Camille Jacobs for her hard work in getting all of you guys here. She and Sydney Mitchell, recent graduate of Old Dominion University, were instrumental in getting the word out and I just want to say thank you ladies. And a little plug for them, if you have a business you want to get out there, give them a call. So let me not hold up the party any more, DJ Scoop it's all yours."

The music started bumping as DJ Scoop began playing some hip-hop club grooves and Tyrone made his way off stage. He gave Sydney and Camille hugs as he encountered them standing by the stairs leading up to the stage.

"Thanks for the plug," Camille said.

"The least I could do," Tyrone said. "Thanks so much for this."

"All we did was get the word out," Camille said. "This place is incredible! Even without what we did this place was going to be a success. Heck, it's *destiny*." The three of them smiled at Camille's corny joke. "What you need to do is go mingle."

"Yea, I think I will. Thanks again ladies." Tyrone said walking over to one of the many tables surrounding the dance floor.

Camille locked arms with Sydney and smiled at her. "You know I couldn't have done this without you girl."

"Yea, I know," Sydney said with a smile. "Let's go find our men."

Rashad and Sean sat at a table a little further away from the stage. Over the past few weeks Camille and Rashad had spent every night after work and every weekend together. Rashad had truly been showing her how much he cared about her and it made Camille feel wonderful. She felt like she could ignore the chemistry that she and Derek seemed to have. It was getting easier to ignore since they had managed to avoid one another since the graduation party.

Rashad and Sean stood as the women approached. Rashad hugged Camille tightly lifting her slightly off the ground. "I love you. You are amazing."

"Well, thank you baby. I love you too." She kissed him deeply.

"You too need to get a room," Sean said, earning an elbow in the ribs from Sydney.

"Shut up," Sydney said. "They're cute. I remember when we used to be like that."

"What do you mean used to?" Sean said kissing Sydney.

"Nice try," Sydney said with a look of faux disdain. "Where's your brother? He should be here by now."

"I don't know. He called an hour ago and said he was on his way to pick up his date and he would be here as soon as he could."

"He's bringing a date?" Camille asked surprised.

"Yea, I hooked him up with an accountant I met in the elevator of our building," Rashad explained.

"Really? You didn't tell me that," Camille said. She hoped she was not sounding more interested than she should.

"Yea, she said she had noticed him in the elevator before so you know I worked my magic."

"Whoa," Sean said as he reached for his phone vibrating in his pocket. "Hello.... What?... Ok I'll let her know." Sean hung up the phone. "Derek is outside, but he said they won't let him and his date in because her name's not on the list."

"Oh, well that's because I didn't know he had a plus one," Camille said poking Rashad in the side.

"Oops."

"Well I'll go get them in," Camille said standing up from the table. "I'll be right back."

She made her way around the edge of the dance floor. She was proud to see the mix of well dressed smiling faces as people sweated on the dance floor, flirted at the bar, or just chilled at one of the many full tables. It made Camille smile to know that she was a part of making this possible.

When she reached the door, the bouncer, a large black man dressed in all black, stood between the door and Derek and someone else that Camille could not see due to the girth of the bouncer.

"Hey, Steve," Camille said. "They're with me you can let them in."

"Ok Ms. Jacobs," the bouncer said stepping aside.

As he did so Camille got her first clear look at Derek and his date. Derek looked great. He had a fresh haircut and was wearing a very nice tailored suit with a button up shirt. The top two buttons of the shirt were unbuttoned and she could see a glimpse of his well developed pecks. She felt her cheeks flush a little warm. He allowed his date to move ahead of him. She was a very attractive young lady, with short hair and wearing an even shorter dress. The dress she wore was a dark metal grey, and barely came down past her ass. She had the legs of a runner and apparently did not mind showing them off. Camille felt a slight twinge of...was that jealously?

That's ridiculous, She thought.

"Hey, Camille," Derek said as he entered the club. "Thanks."

"No problem," Camille said giving him a hug. *He smells great too*. "Rashad forgot to mention you were bringing a date."

"Yea, this is Melissa," Derek said introducing his date.

"Nice to meet you," Camille said shaking the young lady's hand.

"You too." Melissa answered.

"We are over here," Camille said leading the way back to the table. As they reached the table Camille allowed Derek and his date to go in front of her so that Derek could do the introductions. She saw the back of Melissa's dress and could feel her heart quicken with what she knew was definitely jealousy. The dress dropped in the back, exposing her entire back and stopping just above the crack of her ass.

This girl is serious. Camille thought.

Derek bought a round of drinks and everyone started to really enjoy themselves. They danced and drank and laughed. Camille noticed that Derek was enjoying himself, but did not seem overly interested in his date. While Melissa was all over him and doing everything she could to let him know she was interested he was spending as much time talking to everyone else as he was with her. Even when they danced, she was grinding on him much more than he seemed to care for, though he did not push her away.

"I have to use the bathroom," Camille said.

"Great, can you show me where they are?" Derek asked.

"Yea, just follow me. What about you Melissa?" Camille asked out of courtesy. Sydney and Sean were on the dance floor, so she felt it her female obligation to ask the only other female at the table to accompany her.

"Oh, I'm fine thank you."

Camille hoped the relief she felt did not show on her face.

The lines to the bathrooms were ridiculous. "Hey," Camille said tugging on Derek's arm. "Tyrone gave me a key to the back office. He has a private bathroom, so we don't have to wait in these lines."

"Ok, lead the way."

Camille walked him up stairs to the second level of the club where Tyrone's office was located. She unlocked the door and entered the immaculate office. The office had dark Berber carpeting. There was a black leather coach against the wall and Tyrone had an ornately carved desk against the far wall with a leather desk chair behind it. There were several pieces of African-American art on the walls.

"Wow," Derek said. "This is a nice office."

"I know right?" Camille said as she made her way to the door behind the desk. I'll be out in a minute.

"No rush," Derek said. He took the time that she was in the rest room to explore the artwork a little closer. He had always enjoyed art but had never purchased any of his own. The one painting was of African-Americans in what looked like a 1920s era club. Another was of a lone trumpeter standing on a darkened stage playing.

"All yours," Camille said walking out of the bathroom.

Derek's breath caught in his throat as he looked at her. He had spent the majority of the night trying not to stare at her, but now as she stood silhouetted in the doorframe he could not help but admire her figure. She was wearing a pair of black Capri pants that flared a little at the bottom. The black heels she wore were not very high, but helped to show off the work she had been doing on her calves in the gym. The white scoop neck sleeveless shirt showed the light layer of sweat that had formed on her cleavage from the dancing. She dabbed at it lightly with a paper towel.

"You okay?" Camille asked.

"Yea, I'm sorry," Derek said. "I was just admiring...this painting."

"Oh, yea. He has some really nice art work."

Derek walked towards the bathroom. There was limited room behind the desk as he had to stop to let Camille move past him. *She smells incredible. Get a hold of yourself, D. Damn! This is your best friend's girl.* He looked at himself in the mirror and splashed some cold water on his face. *Don't be stupid!* He dried his face and opened the door to the bathroom.

"You're gonna get some tonight," Camille said as Derek came out of the bathroom.

"Excuse me," Derek said stopping in his tracks.

"Melissa, wants to give it to you, *bad*," Camille said as she sat on the leather couch, still trying to stem the flow of sweat on her arms and chest. "Believe me. No woman dresses like that on a first date unless they have intentions."

"Whatever," Derek said. "Besides she's cool, but I don't think I'm really feeling her like that."

Camille stood as Derek approached her. "Why not?"

"I don't know. Normally she'd get it in a minute, but...I don't know."

Camille swallowed hard as Derek stood only a few feet away from her. Her eyes were drawn to his lips. *They are thick and kissable*, she thought to herself. She wondered if he was thinking the same. "Well, I guess we should be" she did not get to finish her thought as Derek had quickly closed the gap between them and confirmed that he had been thinking the same thing. The kiss was amazing. She felt herself melting into his arms. She felt his tongue searching her mouth and her tongue answering every unanswered questioned. *Yes!* She felt his manhood press against her and her own juices begin to flow and dampen her panties.

"Let me show you my office," they heard Tyrone's voice from the other side of the door and quickly pulled away from one another. "Oh hey, Camille," Tyrone said as he entered the office with a well dressed young man with him.

"Hey, uh, the lines at the bathrooms were terrible so I kind of used my key," Camille explained.

"Oh, girl don't even trip," Tyrone said. "That's why I gave it to you. I haven't had the pleasure of meeting your friend."

"This is Derek. Rashad's business partner."

"Nice to meet you," Derek said extending his hand. "This place is great."

"Thank you. Nice meeting you as well."

"Well I guess we should be getting back to the party," Camille said.

"Okay, well I'll see you soon," Tyrone said as Derek and

Camille hastily left the office.

"I'm so sorry," Derek said as they re-entered the loud din of the bumping hip-hop and the crowd of people.

"Nothing to be sorry about," Camille responded as she continued to move through the crowd of people.

"But I kissed you," Derek said trying to keep up. Camille appeared to be running away from him and he was not even sure she had heard him.

"Yea, and I didn't stop you."

"I fucked up," Derek said.

Camille stopped and turned to face him. "Look, obviously we both are attracted to one another and we both wanted it. Now it's happened and we have to deal with it, but you know as well as I do that it can't happen again. I am in love with Rashad and I know you are his best friend so neither one of us wants to hurt him. We both fucked up. Yes you may have initiated the kiss, but I sure as hell wasn't about to stop you. God knows what would have happened if Tyrone and his boy toy hadn't come in when they did."

"Tyrone's gay?"

"What?" Camille said confused by the sudden change of topic. "Yes, but whatever. Look, Rashad can never know about this, and we just have to either stay away from each other or maybe you need to go sleep with that hoochie mama downstairs so you can get your mind on someone else. But-"

"You think sleeping with her is going to get you out of my head?" Derek looked appalled. "Don't you understand that I think I'm falling for you."

"Don't say that!" Camille said punching him in the arm. "Don't you dare say that!" Camille did not want to here Derek say it even though it was all she could think about. They looked at one another in silence for a long moment before she turned and walked back towards the stairs. Derek followed silently.

When they reached the table, Derek made an excuse about being tired and having a bit of a headache and wanting to leave. It almost made Camille sick to see how excited Melissa was about helping Derek get rid of his headache. Everyone said their goodbyes and Derek and Melissa headed out.

Melissa lived at River Oaks Apartments on Princess Anne, not too far from the club so it was a quick drive. He had made light conversation with Melissa as they drove, but could not shake his thoughts of Camille and their kiss. A few times he had to ask Melissa to repeat what she had said.

"Wow, your head must be really hurting," Melissa said as they pulled into the parking space next to her Toyota Corolla.

"Why do you say that?" Derek asked.

"You just seem really distracted. If you come up I think I have something for that."

Subtle, Derek thought. *This girl isn't playing.* He took a deep breath and turned off the Explorer. He decided maybe he should take Camille's advice. He *had* to stop thinking about her. If Rashad ever found out about what had happened or if he tried to do something like that again, Rashad would kill him. "Ok, that sounds great."

Melissa smiled broadly, "Great." She was out of the vehicle and walking towards the building before Derek had a chance to think about being a gentleman and helping her out. He walked behind her admiring her ass and legs, she *was* sexy. She was smart and had a pretty good personality. He needed to give her a chance and forget about his unreasonable feelings for Camille.

"My roommate is out of town for the weekend," Melissa said as she pulled her keys from her purse and opened the door. "So you don't have to worry about being quiet." She turned on the light.

As Derek stepped through the door and closed it behind him, Melissa immediately began kissing him and rubbing her hands over his back and ass. She began to undue his belt and tugged at the zipper of his pants. Despite his mental uncertainty, his body responded to her readily. His penis filled with blood as she slipped her hand down his loosened pants and into his boxer briefs.

"I've wanted you since the first day I saw you in the elevator,"

Melissa whispered into his ear.

She knelt down and pulled his pants and underwear down around his ankles in one motion. She began to lick the head of his penis with her tongue and looked up at him as he let out a small moan of pleasure.

"This is better than any headache medicine," she said just before she took his penis into her mouth. They both moaned in unison. Derek's back was pressed against the apartment door. She sucked and stroked his penis with her left hand while using her right to feel on his abs and legs.

Derek reached down and pulled her up and away from him. As she stood he undid the button at the base of the neck of her dress and the front of it fell forward revealing her small but perky breasts. Her nipples were as erect as his penis. Derek leaned in and took the Hershey chocolate colored nipple in his mouth and sucked hard. Melissa moaned loudly and squeezed both of his butt cheeks.

"Do you have a condom?" She asked.

Derek kicked his pants and underwear from around his ankles and reached down to pull his wallet from his pants pocket. Melissa finished undressing, pulling the dress down over her ample butt and thighs. She was wearing black lacey thongs which were also quickly discarded. Derek pulled the condom from his wallet, and quickly opened it and placed it on. He bent Melissa over the back of her couch and entered her from behind, again eliciting a pleasurable moan from her.

"Do you feel how wet I am for you, baby?" She asked sensually.

Derek could feel the wetness despite the condom. She was practically dripping. He began to attack her wetness. He had no intention of making love to her; that he wanted to do to Camille. He shook his head trying to get any thoughts of his best friend's girl out of his head. Melissa moaned loudly as he pressed deeper into her. He reached around and squeezed her small breast playing with the nipple with his thumb and forefinger.

"Wait, wait," Melissa said pushing him back. She turned and jumped into his arms and wrapped her legs around his waist. "Take me to the bedroom."

Damn, this girl definitely knows what she wants.

*****

Sean and Sydney had left about a half hour after Derek and Melissa. Camille and Rashad were sitting at a small round table on barstool style chairs sipping on the rum and cokes they had ordered.

"Wow, it's been an eventful evening. I'm really happy for you and your client. This is a big accomplishment for you both. This seems like it's gonna be a nice spot to come to." Rashad said.

"Yeah, Tyrone is excited. I'm just relieved that my marketing efforts were successful. It doesn't stop here though. We've discussed some other ways to keep the buzz going about the club on a continuous basis." Camille said. As she's saying all of this, her mind is on the kiss she just had with Derek. She'd have to play it cool and relax.

"Hey there!" Tyrone exclaimed smiling from ear to ear.

"Hey there yourself. This is such a great turnout tonight. It's just awesome. People seem to be having a really good time and things seem to be running smoothly." Camille said.

"My sentiments exactly, man. This is nice. The area needs a place like this." Rashad added.

"Thanks man, I really appreciate that." Tyrone said looking at Rashad with an interesting gaze. Rashad thought it a little weird but decided to ignore it.

"Well I just wanted to come over and say thank you for everything and I look forward to continuing to do business with you." Tyrone said.

"Of course. And I look forward to working with you." Camille said smiling and sipping more of her drink.

"Tyrone, I've been looking for you everywhere." A gentleman approached the table wearing a fitted beige colored shirt with black jeans. It was the guy who walked in with Tyrone in the office.

"Oh, right. Okay" Tyrone said nervously. The guy had

approached Tyrone from behind but never stepped beside him. Tyrone appeared as if he wanted to make his friend's unexpected arrival a quick one.

"Well Camille and...I'm sorry, I didn't get your name." Tyrone stated.

"Rashad." Stated with a slight but friendly head nod.

"Okay Rashad. Yeah, you two enjoy the rest of your evening. Camille I'll call you." Tyrone quickly walked off with his friend as Camille responded.

"All right then." Camille grinned as she drank the last of her beverage.

"So much for formal introductions." Rashad commented.

"I'm sorry, I felt like I didn't have the chance to." Camille said apologetically.

"Naw I'm talking about his friend." Rashad said chuckling. "How long does he think he's going to hide that?"

Camille shook her head. "You need to stop. Anyway, are you ready to get out of here? My feet hurt." Camille said.

"After you my sweet." Rashad said.

They both got up from the chairs and did a little dance to the classic old school jam I Ain't No Joke by Eric B and Rakim as they made their way towards the exit.

Camille and Rashad drove separately. They decided that she would follow him to his place for the evening. It was going on 12:30 AM. Camille was on a mission to prove that her feelings for Rashad were real. They had settled in comfortably and both were cuddled on the couch in the darkness. Musiq Soulchild was coming from the speakers.

"You didn't think the night was over did you?" Camille said to Rashad.

He smiled at her and she kissed him hard. He pulled back slightly and looked into her eyes. He lightly touched her chin with his hand. She looked back at him.

"I love you, Camille." Rashad said.

"I love you, Rashad." Camille responded before kissing him again. They made passionate love and fell asleep together on Rashad's slightly plush king size bed.

Chapter 25

The next morning, Camille got up early and left Rashad's place. She lied and said she had some work to get done. She called Shayla from her cell on the way home. "Shayla, it's me. I need to talk do you have some time?" Camille was desperate for conversation about the matter. She needed to get a woman's point of view about this whole thing.

"Yeah girl, what's going on? You sound weird." Shayla reached for the remote to turn the volume down on the television. "Okay I'm listening."

"Remember when I asked you about being in love with two people at the same time?" Camille asked.

"Yeah," Shayla answered.

"Well, I think I am," Camille sighed.

"Does this have anything to do with Rashad's friend?" Shayla questioned.

"Yes." Camille said.

"You're seeing Rashad, right?"

"Yes."

"Did something happen?" Shayla said very concerned and curious.

"Well, you know we had the opening night for Club Destiny last night." Camille said.

"Yeah," said Shayla.

"Derek and I kissed." Camille said quickly.

"Whoa. Okay this is Rashad's business partner and best friend, right?" Shayla asked.

"Yes." Camille said.

"Where?" Shayla asked.

"At the club in Tyrone's office." Camille answered.

"Did anyone see you?" Shayla inquired.

"No," Camille said. "Shayla I don't know what I am going to do."

"So you think you may love both of these men?" Shayla

asked.

"Yes, I think I may. Rashad is great. He's smart, funny, caring and treats me good. But I have this chemistry with Derek that I cannot shake."

"Mmmm." Shayla said.

"Aren't you going to say something else?" Camille asked nervously.

"Give me a second." Shayla had to take wrap her head around what she just heard. "All right. You've been with Rashad for several months now. You have a few options."

"I'm all ears," Camille was ready to hear what her sister had to say.

"You can stay with Rashad and forget about these feelings you have for Derek. Tell Derek it cannot happen."

"Okay what is the other option?" Camille said .

"Go for the feelings you have Derek, if you two agree that you owe it to yourselves to see what's up."

"Okay you said a few. One more makes a few." Camille said intently.

"Well, the last option is to break up with Rashad and leave them both behind." Shayla said. "Listen sis, I'm not telling you this lightly. If you feed into these feelings you have for Derek in any kind of way, it could be destructive to your relationship with Rashad, most of all to his and Derek's friendship. You don't want that hanging over your head." Shayla said with care.

Camille remained silent for a few seconds.

"Hello?" Shayla asked.

"Yeah." Camille answered in a low voice.

"Oh, Camille." Shayla said with a concerned tone.

"When he kissed me, I was spellbound. This part of me wanted it but I totally didn't expect it happen."

"I don't know if this sounds appropriate to say in this situation but sometimes things just have to run their course. Now I'm not saying that you should stay with someone you don't really want to be with or settle. I just mean that things have a way of working out like they're supposed to...for the good. I mean, right now, I would just make it clear to Derek that it's important for you to remain friends." Shayla suggested.

"You're right. Look, I gotta go, I'm about to go through the tunnel. Thanks so much for this. I'll talk to you later." Camille said.

"I love you, girl." Shayla said.

"Love you too."

*****

Derek arrived home around 9:30 the next morning. It had been a long night. Melissa was amazing in bed and had what seemed like and endless amount of energy. He was actually able to stop thinking about the kiss with Camille for the majority of the night, but now as he pulled his SUV up behind Sean and Sydney's cars, his mind began to drift back to the encounter with Camille. He hated himself for kissing her. He and Rashad had been friends since middle school and now he was risking all of those years of friendship for a woman. An amazing and beautiful woman but still, this was insane.

Derek turned the car off, but sat with his head resting against the headrest and his eyes closed.

What am I going to do? He thought to himself. Normally whenever he had relationship issues he would talk to Rashad or Robert about it, but he could not talk to either of them about this. *Robert's a great friend but when it comes to keeping secrets he can't hold water.*

He thought about talking to Sean, but he knew that he could not keep anything from Sydney and once she knew all hell could break loose.

"Fuuuuuck," he whispered as he buried his face in his hands. He pulled his cell phone from his pocket, searched for a number and dialed it. "Hey....Yea it's me. I'm sorry to call so early.... I need to talk. Can we meet for breakfast?... What about Silver Diner?...Yea on Virginia Beach Boulevard....Okay I'll see you in bout an hour."

Derek hurried inside to take a shower and change clothes. Thankfully Sean and Sydney were still sleeping and he could move through the house without being harassed. He stood under the water for a long time trying to will it to wash away his mistake and feelings from the previous night. As he got out of the shower, he heard Sean and Sydney begin to stir in the other room. They were talking, but Derek could not make out what they were saying. He decided to pick up the pace as he got himself together so that he could get out of the house before either of them decided to start asking questions about his evening with Melissa.

He was dressed and heading down the stairs as he heard Sean coming out of his bedroom headed to the bathroom, "Hey, D."

"Sup?" Derek said without stopping

"Where you headed?" Sean had to speak louder as he noticed that Derek had continued down the stairs.

"Breakfast," Derek said. "Be back in a while."

"Oh no thanks," Sean said sarcastically. "We aren't hungry at all. See you later."

Derek ignored Sean's comment and left the house without another word. He arrived at the Silver Diner, a 50s/60s style diner chain that he enjoyed coming to, mainly for breakfast. As he entered to the sound of the Temptations blaring from the television set in the waiting area, he saw his father Daryl sitting on one of the cushioned benches. Daryl stood when he saw his son and smiled.

"Hey, bud. How's it going?" he asked.

"Not good," Derek responded. "Thanks for coming."

"Of course."

Derek waited until they were seated and had ordered before he told his father why he had asked him to meet him.

"I'm sorry I called you so early," Derek said after the waitress had taken their orders and their menus. "I know Charity needs her rest with the pregnancy and all."

"Don't worry about it. That woman's amazing. She had me up this morning at seven so we could go to the gym. She doesn't let me sleep in, not even on a Saturday."

"Well that's good she's still getting around so well," Derek said. He looked out of the window of the diner to the cars passing by on the Boulevard.

"What's going on, D? I know you guys got that kid drafted, but is the business still struggling?"

Derek felt his old feelings of frustration rise up as his father again assumed his business was failing, but quickly pushed them aside. He knew Daryl was just showing concern and not assuming that he was a failure.

"No," Derek said quietly. "Nothing like that." Derek paused unsure of how to say what he needed someone to hear. "Do you remember Rashad's girlfriend Camille?"

"Of course, gorgeous girl and really sweet," Daryl said. "Is she okay? Nothing happened to her did it?"

"No...well...no." Derek again paused unsure of how to proceed. He saw the waitress approaching with their food and decided to just blurt it out. "I kissed her."

"What?" Daryl asked shocked. He was unable to continue as the waitress interrupted with the food.

"Anything else I can get you gentlemen?" she asked.

"No thank you," Daryl said not taking his eyes off of his son. The waitress walked away. "When did this happen?"

"Last night," Derek said. "We were at the opening of the club she's been doing the PR for when I just did it."

"Does Rashad know? Did he see you?"

"No, hell no," Derek said. "I'd probably be in somebody's hospital if he had. No one knows. You're the only person I've told."

Daryl was actually flattered that his son had decided to confide in him, but at the same time knew that this was a heavy secret to carry.

"Well, what are you gonna do now?" He finally picked up his fork and began to eat.

"I don't know," Derek said. His couldn't taste his food. He took a sip of his water and said, "That's kind of why I asked you to meet me. I needed to tell someone, but I also need some advice."

Daryl paused and looked at his son for a long moment.

"Before you say anything, I know I messed up, because you never go after one of your boy's girls. But it just happened."

"Something like that doesn't just happen, Derek. I mean what made you do it?"

"Well we had tea and dinner together on a couple of occasions. It was completely innocent, but there was a spark. She's amazing and in just those couple of times together I think I started to fall for her."

"Is it just infatuation?" Daryl asked hopefully. "Maybe if you get with someone else you can get her out of your head."

"That's what she said," Derek said. "And well I tried."

"Last night?" Daryl asked confused.

"Yea, the girl I took to the club last night."

"You slept with her?"

"Yea, I hadn't planned on it, but after what happened with Camille, and this chick just threw herself at me."

"And?" Daryl asked.

"And now I'm here with you telling you about how I can't stop thinking about Camille. It's crazy. I was up all night having some of the best sex of my life, but as soon as it was over all those thoughts of Camille came rushing back."

"Wow," Daryl said. "You're in big trouble."

Derek looked at his father dumbfounded.

"I'm sorry," Daryl said. "That was insensitive. I just feel like your options are limited. You can pursue this and lose a lifelong friend and business partner and possibly your business in the process, for a woman who may or may not feel the same way and for a relationship that may not last. Or you could wait it out and see what happens with them. If they break up, you could wait a while and then see if Rashad would care if you pursued her. Not likely but who knows. My suggestion would be to do all you can to forget about her. Now if a night of sex like that can't get her out of your head, then like I said, you're in trouble."

"Rashad is in love with her," Derek said. "I've never seen him like this about any woman. He's talking about making a serious commitment to her."

"Damn, son. You really stepped in it."

"I know," Derek said angrily. "You really need to work on the fatherly advice thing, before Charity pops out that baby, because right now you're really sucking at it."

"Don't be angry with me," Daryl said apologetically. "It's just that this is a tough situation. You're only real option is to stay as far away from her as possible, and that's not really an option because then Rashad is going to want to bring her to things you guys do. So you are gonna have to throw yourself into something else, your work, a hobby, or maybe this relationship with the girl from last night."

"Maybe that'll work," Derek sighed. "I sure hell don't have any better ideas. I guess I'll have to just try to focusing on developing something with Melissa." Derek closed his eyes and covered his mouth with his hand. *This is not going to work.* "Thanks for you help."

"I'm not sure I would call it help, but you're welcome."

Chapter 26

After telling his father about kissing Camille, Derek felt a little better. Being able to tell someone about the situation was a relief of sorts. The guilt still overwhelmed him and whenever he looked at Rashad he felt as though he was either going to throw up or blurt out the truth.

For the next week he focused on work obsessively. Whenever Rashad tried to make small talk about their personal lives, Derek would quickly change the subject to something related to work. Rashad attempted to set up a double date, which Derek made up an excuse for not being able to attend.

Derek had spoken to Melissa everyday since the opening of Club Destiny, more at her impetus than his own. He did not want to seem like a complete jerk so he called her on the Sunday following the club opening. She had called him every night since.

At twenty-four, Melissa was a few years younger than Derek. Though the age difference was not huge, Derek did sometimes feel as though he was talking to a college girl. She was intelligent and professional when she had to be, but still seemed to be living the party lifestyle.

"Yea, I go out every weekend wit' my girls," Melissa said during one of their late night conversation.

"Hmm," Derek responded half listening as he flipped through the hundreds of digital cable channels.

"Teetee and I have been roommates since we were freshmen," Melissa continued, taking Derek's acknowledgement as confirmation that he was listening. "She just graduated this May though, partly because we do party so much. Destiny is a cool place to hang. Too bad you gotta be twenty-five to get in. I guess as long as I'm wit' you and uh...what's her name I'm VIP, huh?"

"Camille," Derek said a twinge of some emotion he could not place squeezed his chest.

"What? Oh yeah, Camille. She seemed like cool, peeps," Melissa said. "Kind of up tight though. I mean she was dressed nice, but she has a nice body and should have been showin' it off, y'know what I mean?"

"Yea," Derek lied. Melissa had a fantastic body, but Derek thought she would be more attractive if she left a little more to the imagination the way Camille did. He finally stopped flipping the channel on a European soccer match. He had no idea who the teams were or if the match had any significance and frankly did not care.

"What are you doing on Friday?" Melissa asked.

"Huh?" Derek said realizing she had finally paused needing him to actually respond.

"I said what are you doing on Friday?" Melissa repeated this time in a more sensuous voice. They had only seen each other a couple of times during the week when they had lunch at work. Derek had not been avoiding seeing her after work, but had not been pursuing it either. She had seemed content with the phone conversations, but now seemed to be implying she wanted a possible replay of the previous Friday night.

"I don't have any plans as of yet," Derek said.

"Well...do you want to do something with me?'

"Sure," Derek said. "How 'bout a movie? The new Jamie Foxx movie looks like it may be pretty good."

"Ok," Melissa said.

Derek thought he heard disappointment in her voice. "Unless you want to do something else."

"No, no a movie would be cool," Melissa said. "I haven't been to the movies in forever."

"I mean, if you want to go out with your girls then we can always catch a matinee or something," Derek said.

"No. I'll go home and get changed after work and you can pick me up around seven," Melissa said. "Teetee is back from visiting her parents but I don't think she's much in the mood for going out. They were pretty hard on her about needing to find a 'real' job and said they weren't gonna send her anymore money. And I'm not carrying her broke ass." Melissa raised her voice as she said the last sentence and laughed obviously so her roommate could hear.

"Okay, well I will see you Friday night," Derek said attempting to end the conversation.

"Oh, okay. Well, okay, see you Friday," Melissa said seemingly not as eager to end the conversation.

"Good night."

"Night, night."

Derek decided that despite the humid night he would not wear shorts. The theatre was usually pretty cool and he did not feel like freezing through the movie. He wore a dark pair of loose fit straight leg jeans with a black classic fit polo, which showed off the work he had been doing in the gym. He knocked on Melissa's apartment door and waited for her to answer. A light skinned young lady wearing a pair of Norfolk State University sweats, a white t-shirt, and a black head wrap opened the door instead.

"Hey," she said before turning to yell to the empty hallway. "Your date's here! C'mon in."

"How you doin'? I'm Derek." Derek shook her hand.

"I'm Teetee, nice to meet you."

"You too."

"Have a seat, Meme should be ready in a minute," Teetee said as she sat down on the couch that a week before Derek had bent Melissa over as he entered her from behind. Suddenly, he wondered how much action that couch had seen. Before he had a chance to sit, Melissa came out of the bedroom.

"I'm ready," she said. She was wearing a pair of black stiletto heels with straps that crisscrossed her legs up to mid-calf, black short shorts, and a white scoop neck sleeveless blouse.

"You look nice," Derek said.

"Thank you," Melissa said kissing him on the cheek.

"Alright Teetee," Melissa said as she opened the door.

"Nice meeting you," Derek said as he made his way out of the apartment.

“Hmm hm,” was Teetee’s response.

“You’re roommate okay?” Derek asked as they made their way down the stairs to the parking lot.

“She just mad ‘cause I wouldn’t loan her any money to go out,” Melissa responded. “I told her I ain’t carrying her ass no mo’. She lazy. She got her degree and still workin’ at the mall, ain’t tried to find a job.”

“What’s her degree in?”

“English.”

Derek and Melissa decided to catch the earliest showing they could at Military Circle Mall’s movie theatre. Melissa had not eaten anything after work so Derek bought a bucket of popcorn and a couple of fountain drinks. After the movie, they decided to get some real food and went over to Uno’s Chicago Style Pizzeria in Janaf Shopping Center.

“I can’t believe I’ve never been here,” Melissa said as they were seated by the waitress.

“Yea, me either,” Derek agreed. “It’s been here a while.”

“I know, but when it comes to food, I’m not that adventurous,” Melissa sat on her hands and Derek noticed that chill bumps began to rise on her arms. He had not brought a jacket to offer her so he decided to move and sit beside her in the booth.

“What you doin?’ she asked.

He put his arm around her and began rubbing his hands quickly up and down on her arms. “You look cold.”

“Thank you so much,” Melissa said. “I’ve been freezing since the movie theatre. I’m surprised you didn’t hear my teeth chattering.”

Derek smiled. *Yea, maybe you wouldn’t have been so cold if you would cover yourself up a bit,* he thought.

Melissa smiled back at Derek and leaned in and kissed him. The kiss had none of the sparks that had flown between him and Camille, but it was nice. Unfortunately he knew nice was not going to be enough to get Camille out of his head.

Chapter 27: The Fourth

"Girl, when are you getting here?" Shayla asked Camille. "I thought you said you'd be here early in the morning so you could help me with setting up."

"It's only ten o'clock, sis." Camille was in the process of getting herself dressed. She still had on her robe and head wrap. "I should be leaving here in about a half hour. Rashad should be here in a few minutes. I texted Sydney your address so she can key it in her GPS. She said she didn't quite remember how to get there from the last time."

"Oh ok. Gary, Lisa, and Joshua got here late last night. They can't wait to see you." Shayla said excited.

"Me either. Well, I'd better get off this phone if I'm gonna make it there by eleven. See you in a bit." Camille hurried.

"Ok." Shayla said before hanging up the phone.

Camille heard the doorbell ring. She scurried to the door to let Rashad in. "Hey!" Camille said a little exhausted.

"Why do you sound so...rushed?" Rashad asked. "You look great by the way," he said reaching out to touch her on the butt.

"Because I told Shayla I'd get there early this morning to help her out. And thanks for the compliment." Camille stated. "All right, I'll be about fifteen minutes and then we can get on the road."

"Lisa, I have cereal, fruit and some toast if you want some breakfast," Shayla said to her sister-in-law. Lisa was about five feet three inches tall with a classic bob style hair cut that fell just below her jaw line. She had a medium brown complexion and beautiful skin. She decided to get herself dressed early.

"Thanks Shayla. I'm gonna take you up on that. Gary and Joshua should be getting dressed now." Lisa responded.

Shayla and Lisa heard Gary and Joshua's footsteps coming down the hall. "Good morning, beautiful ladies," Gary cheerfully greeted his wife and sister. He had a dark complexion and stood about six feet. His physique was solid; big boned but not too burly. He made his way to the kitchen where Lisa was preparing a bowl of cereal and toast. He walked behind her and planted a kiss on her cheek.

"You want some breakfast?" Lisa asked.

"Yes, please. Thank you sweetie." Gary answered.

"I thought Joshua came down the hall with you," Lisa said with curiosity.

"Mom, I'm over here," Joshua replied from the living room. He was watching Darius and Tara playing Wii.

"All right, everyone over here to the table for breakfast," Shayla ordered.

Darius and Tara turned off the game and walked over to the table with their cousin as they were told. The table only seated four so Shayla had the children sit there. The table was pretty much set so the kids were able to begin their meal immediately. "Ya'll be sure to say your grace first, you hear?"

"Yes, ma'am," they said altogether.

Shayla, Lisa and her brother were at the breakfast bar style counter. Shayla was up early so she had already grabbed a bite to eat. She was drinking of glass of orange juice to quench her thirst.

"So, when's my baby sister gonna be here?" Gary inquired.

"She should be here by eleven," Shayla answered.

"Cool, I can't wait to see that girl. It's been too long. We've got to do better. Mom and dad are all over the place, traveling and what not. We *all* need to be together this Christmas," Gary said.

"I'm down for that. You know I'm easy when it comes to that stuff. Just tell me where and I'll do my best to be there. Summertime and Christmas is easier of course because of the kids being out of school," Shayla said. "So Lisa, how is work going?"

"It's good. You know its work." Lisa said. She was a policy analyst for the Department of Education.

"That's all I'll say about work. I know how much you hate talking about it when you're on vacation," Shayla remembered.

"Thank you," Lisa said smiling while chewing on a piece of her toast.

"So you play on that Wii much sis?" Gary asked.

"Sometimes, I get in there with the kids and bowl or play some tennis," Shayla answered.

"That's what I'm talking about, baby...bowling. What do you say we play a game after breakfast?" Gary challenged.

"Oh boy, here we go," Lisa said. "He can be so competitive."

"What? Just a friendly game is all. And hey, I've gotten better," Gary responded.

"All right big brother, one game and that's it," Shayla agreed.

"Good. Give me five to ten minutes. We'll even have a cheering section; Lisa and the kids." Gary said with excitement.

"Big brother, you are too much," Shayla said.

Camille and Rashad had just arrived at Shayla's. They had some things in the back seat that Rashad had picked up from the store for the cookout.

"Rashad, are you okay? You look a little nervous," Camille inquired.

"Sort of," he said.

"Why in the world? You shouldn't be really. I mean my brother is a jokester and a little competitive but he's a teddy bear. And well, you know Shayla. There's no reason to be uncomfortable," Camille said trying to reassure him. "It's not like my parents are going to be here."

Rashad took a deep breath and exhaled. "Okay, you're right. I'm trippin'."

They began collecting the bags from the back seat and made their way to the door. The storm door was locked and the main door was open. Camille saw her sister-in-law walking towards them.

"Hey Camille!" Lisa exclaimed. "Oh my gosh girl, let me help you with those bags." Lisa took them from Camille's hands and looked over at Rashad. "Hello there."

"Hello, I'm Rashad."

"Nice to meet you Rashad, I'm Lisa, Camille's sister-in-law. I see you have some bags too. You can follow me to the kitchen."

Rashad walked behind Lisa towards the kitchen. Camille had made her way over to the living room and saw her brother and sister playing an intense game of bowling. "Well, well, well, if it isn't my big brother Gary in competition once again," Camille said smiling.

Gary turned around and shouted. "Sis!" He immediately diverted his attention from the game to his little sister. They both reached out and extended a long, tight hug to one another. Shayla turned her attention from the game as well.

"Hey sis. I'm glad you got here safely. Where's Rashad?" Shayla asked.

"Who's Rashad?" Gary inquired.

"He's probably in the kitchen helping Lisa unload the stuff he bought from the store this morning. Gary come, let me introduce you to my friend." Camille led Gary towards the kitchen. Rashad was emptying the bags with Lisa.

"Rashad, I'd like to introduce you to my family. This is my brother Gary. This is Rashad Lancer."

Rashad had walked out of the kitchen to greet them. He extended his right hand to Gary. "Nice to meet you, man," Rashad said.

"Likewise," Gary replied. The men shook hands.

"And you remember Shayla of course from the graduation," Camille stated.

"Yes, of course. Nice to see you again. Thanks for having me," Rashad said.

"Oh of course," Shayla said.

"Dad, can me and Darius finish you and aunt Shayla's game?" Joshua asked.

"Oh yea, sure son," Gary said removing the strap to the controller from his wrist. Shayla did the same and handed it to Darius.

The boys took the controllers and scurried to the TV set. Tara was sitting on the couch waiting for them to return.

"So I take it you've met my wife Lisa?" Gary asked.

"Yea, we met at the door when we came in," Rashad

answered.

"Cool. Well I'm sure we're all gonna have a good time today," Gary said.

"Oh no doubt," Rashad agreed.

"Camille, I thought you said Sydney and Sean were comin'?" Shayla asked.

"Yea, they'll be here but not 'til a little later on, around 1 or so," Camille responded.

"Yeah, in your face!" Darius shouted as he made a strike.

Lisa, Gary, Shayla, and Rashad all walked in the living room.

"Whoa, I see we got a good game going over here." Gary said.

Everyone either found a seat on the couch or stood around as they watched the two young boys in a friendly competition on the Wii.

The adults and the children got caught up in the game playing. It was nearly 1:30 in the afternoon. Everyone was having a great time and the day was just getting started. Camille had her phone on her hip but had not checked it in the past hour. She looked at it to see if Sydney had tried to contact her. There was one missed text that read:

OMW B thr n 30.

Oh cool. Camille thought. *She sent that around 1 o'clock. She should be here any minute.* She was coming down the hall punching keys on her phone about to send Sydney a response and then...

"Sis, look who I found?" Shayla asked. Camille looked up from her phone and saw her two guests.

"Sydney! Girl I was just reading your text. Hey Sean," Camille extended hugs to them both.

"I want to introduce you to my brother and his wife and their son," Camille said.

"Oh, we just met them," Sydney said.

"Yeah we took care of that," Shayla said.

"Well all righty then," Camille said playfully.

"Rashad...Sean, what can I get you two gentlemen to drink,"

Gary asked with a raised voice from the kitchen and looking in the fridge. "We got Corona's, Bud Light, Miller Light..."

"I'll take a Bud Light," Rashad answered.

"I'll take a Miller," Sean replied.

Gary removed the two beers and grabbed one for himself. Lisa walked into the kitchen as he was closing the refrigerator door. "Oh you ain't gonna ask if any of these ladies in here if we want something to drink?"

"Oh, excuse me miss," Gary said playfully. "My apologies ladies. Gentlemen," he said handing the ice cold beverages to each. Lisa pushed him playfully before getting herself a drink.

Camille and Shayla were standing in the vicinity as they watched the men twist open their beer caps.

"Ladies, what are we having?" Lisa asked. She pulled a grape Hug out for herself.

"I'll have a Corona," Sydney said.

"I think I will too," Camille said.

"I didn't think you liked beer, sis," Shayla said.

"I don't really, but it's a holiday."

"Okay, well give me a bottled water please," Shayla says to her sister-in-law.

"Water?" Gary laughed. "Girl, since when?"

"Whatever," Shayla said. "I'll drink something a little later. Instead of worrying about what I'm drinking, go fire up that grill for me. It's time to get our grub on."

Gary took a swig of his beer and started towards the backyard. "Is everything out there?"

"Yea, I sat it out there this morning. I'll bring the meat out in a few," Shayla answered.

"So Sean, I asked Derek if he wanted to join us but he said he had plans. I just left it alone. I assumed he might be with Melissa." Rashad stated.

"Yea, I think he said he was gonna hang out with her today at one of her friend's cookouts." Sean answered.

"Oh cool." Rashad said taking a gulp.

Camille took a swig of her beer. *I am so glad he's not here.* She thought.

"So Shayla is Kris coming over?" Camille questioned.

"Yea, he should be here," Shayla paused looking at the time on the stove, "any minute now."

Everyone was standing around the kitchen area drinking and chatting freely.

"Sydney, how does it feel to be college grad?" Lisa asked.

"Great," Sydney answered with a sigh of relief. "I love marketing and it was a lot of work. I enjoyed college, but I'm glad it's over."

"Do you think you'll go back to school to pursue a graduate degree?" Lisa inquired.

"I've thought about it. My mom wants me pursue an MBA. I think I'm gonna work for a little while though so I can get some experience. "

Lisa nodded. "Sounds good. Just try to get it done before you have children."

"I hear that," Sydney agreed. "I was in class with a lady who was married with two kids. She used to say how difficult it was to do it all."

"Sean, what did you study?" Lisa asked.

"Economics," Sean answered.

"Two business majors. That's wonderful," Lisa answered.

Rashad approached Camille as everyone else continued in the conversation and leaned in next to her and spoke softly. "Hey I'm gonna go out back and chat with your brother for few."

"Okay," Camille said. Rashad planted a kiss on her forehead.

"Hey Sean, you wanna join me? I'm going out to talk to Gary."

"I'm right behind you," Sean said.

The ladies including Tara were now all in the living room. The boys were outside with Gary, Sean and Rashad. *The Incredibles* was playing on the TV. Tara's eyes were glued.

"This is so nice. Sitting around with friends and family," Shayla said.

"Yes, it is," Lisa agreed. "We should really try to see each other more often. It's not like we're far away. Northern VA is only two and half hours from here."

"True," Shayla said. "Oh I need to take the meat out to Gary. He should have the grill ready." She rose up from the Indian style position she was in on the floor and headed for the kitchen.

Sydney could be quite the conversationalist at times, especially when she started to drink. She was one of those people who would ask a question to get a good discussion going and then sit back and listen to what everyone else had to say. She thought up a question that everyone could answer. "What would be one thing you could change?"

"You mean in your life?" Lisa asked.

"Yea," Sydney answered.

Does it have to be just one thing? Camille thought.

"Mmm. I guess it would be to have spent more time with my father before he died. I was so busy working when I should have been making more trips home. I sure do miss him." Lisa said with a melancholy tone.

"Camille what about you?" Sydney questioned.

She pondered for a bit over the question. She couldn't say what she really wanted. *But no, I wanted it. Sometimes things just happen we don't mean for it to, it just does. Get out of your head.* "I think I would have ended my relationship with Patrick earlier on than I did."

"Who's Patrick?" Sydney asked.

"This guy she was seeing while she was in Chicago. He went loony on her, started trippin'." Shayla answered for her coming back in from outside.

"Really? What happened?" Sydney inquired.

"Things were going well for me at the job. I was going to

networking events and often had late meetings. I was starting to get more exposure professionally. He got a little envious. Started throwing it in my face by saying stuff like, 'oh well, you don't have time for me no more, you always gone, you wanna go find yourself one of those high class brotha's now, I ain't good enough for you no more' ...I had to go. But that's over and done."

"What did he do for a living?" Lisa asked.

"He was a security guard in one of the city buildings," Camille answered. "It's your turn, sis? What would you change in your life?"

"I would have gone straight to college after high school," Shayla answered quickly.

"What would you have taken up?" Lisa said with curiosity.

"Hell, I don't know, I just would've gone."

"Well it's not too late," Lisa encouraged.

"I just think I missed out on the college life experience. You know, parties, staying up late at night in the dorms eating pizza and watching movies, spring break, going out, you know what I mean."

"Yeah," Camille, Sydney, and Lisa all said nodding their heads and then laughing.

"Well, I guess it's my turn. Uumm. I guess I would have gone all the way with Xavier Lewis junior year of high school." Sydney said almost in a whisper and giggling like a little school girl.

"Alright now," Shayla said with her eyes wide open.

"Sydney," Camille said in a 'girl I didn't know you were gonna say something like that' tone.

"Yea ya'll he was fine," Sydney commented.

"Sooo, what stopped you?" Lisa asked.

"I was nervous and a little scared. I don't know, I guess this bigger part of me wanted to wait." Sydney answered.

"Until you were married?" Camille asked.

"No, not that long," Sydney said. "I mean Sean was my first and it was great. I'm glad I waited."

"Well that's beautiful Sydney. Your first experience should be memorable." Camille said.

Their conversation was interrupted by a knock on the screen door. Shayla excused herself and went to see who it was.

"Hey, baby!" Shayla exclaimed. She undid the latch, opened the door, and threw her arms out wide.

"Hey, sweetie," Kris said giving her a kiss on the lips. "I've got a cooler in the truck with some drinks if anyone wants some for later."

"Cool. I'm glad you're here. We can get one of the guys to help you bring it in," Shayla walked him into the living room, lightly pulling him by the hand.

"Kris you remember Sydney from the graduation and of course, Camille."

"Hey, Camille. Hello Sydney, nice to see you again," Kris said politely.

"Likewise," Sydney answered.

"I'm Lisa, the sister-in-law," she stood up to shake his hand.

"Nice to meet you."

"You as well. Glad you could make it down." Kris picked up quickly that the ladies were in full blown girl talk mode so he thought he should exit the area. "The guys out back?"

"Oh yea, Rashad, Sean and Gary are out there grillin' and drinkin'. "

Kris stopped by the kitchen to grab a cold beer out of the refrigerator and then made his exit towards the patio. "Fellas," he said stepping out of the slide door.

The guys said 'what's up' in unison. Rashad had taken over tending to the grill. Sean and Gary were seated on a couple of lawn chairs. Gary got up to greet Kris.

"I'm Gary, Shayla's brother. It's nice to finally meet you."

The two men exchanged handshakes. "I've been telling her we need to hit the road and come for a visit up your way," Kris said.

"Yea, I was just telling her we need to do better from here on out," Gary stated.

"Rashad...Sean. Nice to see you two again. I'm glad you made it," Kris said.

"Of course, no doubt. Especially after you and Shayla came to me and Sydney's graduation."

"Speaking of that, I read in the Daily Press that you got drafted by San Francisco," Kris said. "That was you right?"

"Yea, that was me," Sean said modestly.

"Really?" Gary said. "You mean to tell me I'm sitting here with a professional baseball player and no one told me?"

"Well, I'm not a professional yet," Sean said. "My brother and Rashad haven't gotten my contract done yet."

"Screw that. You got drafted, even if you never make it to the big leagues not many people can say that."

"It's actually the second time he was drafted," Rashad said turning from the grill. "He got drafted out of high school, but wanted to get his education first."

"Nothing wrong with that at all," Gary said. "Man, congratulations. I wish you all the luck in the world."

"Yea, congratulations," Kris echoed. "Don't forget about us little folks once you make it to the big leagues."

"Thanks," Sean said smiling. His phone beeped indicating he had a text message. He read it and replied to the message as the others continued the conversation about baseball players and who they thought were the best. They continued talking about a myriad of topics for the next half hour.

"Hey, ya'll I'll be right back," Sean said looking at his phone as he excused himself and walked back inside the house and towards the front door.

As he walked through the kitchen into the living room, he noticed that the ladies were not in the vicinity. He heard laughter coming from a room at the end of the hall. It appeared to be Shayla's bedroom because he saw a couple of them holding up hangers, admiring some outfits in Shayla's wardrobe. He headed closer to the door and saw a car pulling up near the house. "Oh that must be them," he said under his breath. He unlocked the door and went outside.

"Hey bro," Sean said.

"Hey," Derek said getting out of the driver's side of Melissa's car. "Are you sure Shayla won't mind that I'm here man?"

"Naw, it's i-ight, really. She's not like that, she's cool," Sean said. "Hello Melissa."

"Hey yourself," she answered. She was wearing a pink halter sundress that came a little below her knees with pink flip flops that were about a shade darker. "Thanks for inviting us over. I hope we're not crashing the party."

"Like I told Derek, it's cool. Ya'll come on in." Sean walked Derek and Melissa into the house as the ladies were walking down the hall. Shayla was first in line.

"Oh, I see we have more guests," Shayla said. "Derek, what a pleasant surprise."

Derek! What the hell? Camille thought as she followed suit with everyone else by walking in a little closer to the people circle that had formed.

"I hope it's not a problem that I showed up like this. The cookout we were gonna go to got pushed back 'til later on this evening. I texted Sean about it and he just forwarded me your address. Besides it would have been silly not to spend some time with my brother on the holiday," Derek explained as he tried not to look at Camille. She stood there in shock trying not to bring attention to herself.

"Really forget about it. You're more than welcome. " Shayla decided to introduce herself to Melissa. "Hi there, I'm Shayla, Camille's sister. Welcome."

"Melissa, pleased to meet you. Thank you for having us." The ladies shook hands.

Camille and Derek locked eyes for a few seconds too long. Shayla broke in. "Well, you two make yourselves at home. Why don't we all go out back. They should be done grillin' something already. You two are more than welcome to grab a drink from the fridge if you like."

"Thanks," Derek said.

“Come out here first man.” Sean put his arm around Derek’s shoulder leading him out back.

Rashad exclaimed. “Derek! Man what are you doing here? I thought you might be at somebody else’s crib chillin’ with…,” as he saw her face, “Melissa,” he said surprised. “I didn’t know you were here, it’s great to see you again.”

“You too Rashad,” Melissa said.

Rashad was still at the grill. There was no lull amongst them as everyone joined in on a couple of different conversations that were taking place.

Everyone except for Shayla and Camille were outside. They were both in the kitchen standing at the breakfast bar. Shayla was in serious ‘sistagirl’ mode. “Camille, get it together.”

“What?” Camille asked.

“You heard me,” Shayla said gathering condiments for the food.

“I can’t believe he’s here. Uughhh. I can’t act like that kiss between him and I didn’t happen. I’m not comfortable.”

Shayla just looked her sister in the eyes for a long moment. “Listen, I don’t know what to say about this right now. All I know is you need to get your head right so we can go out here and have a good time. Just don’t draw any attention to yourself that will make Melissa or Rashad suspicious. Okay?” Shayla ordered.

“Okay. You’re right.” Camille agreed.

It was now quarter after five. Everyone was still out back relaxed from the food, conversation and alcohol. Camille was out front taking a breather checking her email on her blackberry. She was in the middle of the driveway looking down at the screen when she heard someone exit the front door.

“Hey Camille, you alright?” Derek slowly walked towards her careful not to get too close.

She continued to look straight ahead punching keys on her phone. Without looking up she responded. “Yeah, I’m good thanks.”

She was nervous about looking him in the eyes. She tried to avoid getting adjacent to him during the entire cookout.

"Always working hard, even on the holiday, huh?" Derek said.

"What? No I'm just...it doesn't matter. What are you doing out here? Where's Melissa?"

"Oh, Pinky, she's inside," Derek responded.

"She looks cute," Camille said. "Be nice." She found it odd to be defending Melissa to Derek.

"Yea, she's cute," Derek agreed. His eyes betrayed that he wanted to add something but chose not to.

"What?" Camille prodded.

"What what?"

"You wanted to say something else. You're the one that brought her here on your arm, so don't go acting like you don't like the way she looks."

"What are you talking about?" Derek asked. "What I was going to say was that you look pretty good today too."

Camille blushed, "Thanks. You're not looking so bad yourself. Looks like you've been spending some time in the gym."

"Oh you noticed did you?"

They had found themselves slipping back into the comfortable conversation that felt so natural to them both. The chemistry between them was more than physical. Despite their attempts to avoid it, when they were alone it was like the rest of the world fell away.

"Yea, I noticed. Hard not to with the way you've been flexing all day showing off for your boo."

"Whatever," Derek said laughing. "I have not been flexing."

Camille laughed.

She's so beautiful when she smiles. Derek thought.

"Hey," Rashad called as he stepped out onto the porch. "Stop flirting with my woman."

Camille and Derek both turned to look as Rashad walked out

to them smiling. Derek could see by the way Rashad looked at Camille that he truly loved her.

"I saw her first," Rashad said as he walked up and hugged Camille picking her up off the ground.

Camille looked at Derek over Rashad's shoulder. He could not read the expression in her eyes.

"I was just trying to get her to come back to the party and stop working so hard," Derek said, trying not to tell his friend a complete lie.

"Good luck with that. She's been a workaholic, especially since the club opening," Rashad said.

"Just want to be as successful as you guys," Camille said.

"And she got jokes," Rashad said.

"Baaabyyy," Melissa said as she joined the group.

"Hey," Derek said as Melissa walked up and snuggled up under his arm.

"You ready to go?" Melissa asked. "Teetee just texted me and said they are bout to get it jumpin'."

"Oh. Uh. Okay, yea we can go," Derek said. The four of them made their way back inside so that Derek and Melissa could say their goodbyes.

As they drove away from Shayla's, Derek could not help but wonder if someone had given Camille the same advice his father had given him. Was she working so hard because she too knew that this thing between them could and would get the best of them if they were not careful?

Chapter 28

"The aroma is heavenly. You really mean business." Camille was over Rashad's place. He was cooking dinner.

"Oh no ma'am. I don't play around when it comes to cooking." Rashad said from the kitchen.

"You haven't told me what is on the menu." Camille stated.

"Baked chicken, steamed vegetables and baked sweet potatoes." Rashad said.

"Sounds yummy. I can't wait to eat it." Camille said.

"Neither can I," Rashad came back.

"You so nasty!" Camille chuckled.

She hoped that she could remain as calm, cool and collected as the night as she stood gazing out towards the water from the apartment patio. Sometimes she was good at not thinking about Derek but other times, her thoughts seemed to run away as if she would be in a stupor. *Everything is going to be okay. No worries. Rashad is the man you're with. He's wonderful. Don't mess this up.*

"All right now. I hope you're ready for some good eatin'." Rashad began making several trips from the kitchen to the dinner table with all the necessities. Camille took notice of his enthusiasm and tireless effort to make this a wonderful and relaxing evening.

"Do you need help with any of that?" Camille offered as she tried to make her way across the room from the patio but he stopped her dead in her tracks.

"Nope. Don't you dare. You just stay right where you are." Rashad said quickly.

Camille stopped at once. She made her way back to the patio. "Yes sir, you just let me know when I am free to come over. I'll be right here on the patio." Camille said.

About five minutes later, Camille turned her body away from the river view towards the inside of the apartment. The room light was dimmed and red candles were lit on the dinner table. Her eyes lit up. She placed her right hand in the middle of her chest in disbelief. As she walked over to the table with her jaw slightly dropped, Rashad stood with his both hands stretched to his sides, smiling like he had just won a dinky carnival prize.

"I'm glad you turned around because I was just about to call you madam. Dinner is served." Rashad bowed.

"Wow, once again you have impressed me," Camille said. She made her way across the room.

"Please be seated." Rashad pulled out a chair for her.

"Thank you very much." Camille said.

Rashad took a seat across from her. Dinner looked delicious.

"You really know how to treat a lady." Camille said.

"I do my best. Especially for you." Rashad grinned.

They were about 10 minutes into dinner. They conversed about work, family and miscellaneous topics. The evening was going perfect. She was completely attentive to Rashad.

" You know I was thinking if tomorrow might you'd be interested in going to Club Destiny for happy hour. It's open mic night." Rashad proposed.

"That sounds great." Camille said.

"I was thinking about asking Derek and Melissa to tag along." Rashad said.

Damn.

"Well wouldn't it be nice if it was just the two of us?" Camille suggested.

"Yeah it would but I thought it would be nice to chill with my boy. I haven't had a chance to chill with him outside of work in a while and I thought it would be cool and I want you to be there." Rashad said.

"All right then sure why not. It'll be fun. This Melissa, she's the one from the club that night right?" Camille asked.

"Yeah that's her." Rashad said. "I think he's been seeing her ever since. And honestly, I'd like for you and Derek to get to know one another a little better. Besides he is my best friend. I've known him over half my life and I plan to have you in mine for a long time." Rashad said.

Camille all of a sudden felt herself become a little uneasy. But she would not succumb to this foolishness. She needed to get a hold of herself. She gave him a smile as she placed her steamed vegetable filled fork to her mouth.

After dinner, the two took a nice stroll and admired the stillness of the night air.

*****

The week before the opening of Club Destiny Sean had been drafted by the San Francisco franchise in the third round of the professional baseball draft. That gave the agency three players in two of the four major North American sports leagues. Derek finally felt as though RDR was going to be a success. They had until mid-August to get him signed, so that gave them only about a month to finalize Alan's contract so that he would be signed in time for training camp and Sean's deal so that he could play some rookie ball out on the west coast.

"How close are we to being done with Alan's contract?' Rashad asked from across the office.

"They're reviewing the final draft of it and should be faxing it back over by the end of the day tomorrow, and once Alan's signature is on it we're all set." Derek said.

"Cool," Rashad said. "So how are things going with you and Melissa?"

"What no segue? You just gonna jump right in with both feet, huh?"

"Well, I'm just saying it's been, a while since the opening of the club and you haven't said a word about what happened that night?"

"What?" Derek said finally looking up from his work. "What happened that night?"

"Exactly," Rashad said. "I hook you up with a fine ass girl and you don't even have the decency to share the details of what happened. She practically put it on a platter for you, so I know you hit that."

"Oh, yea. I mean, yea I slept with her."

"And?"

"And what?"

"D stop playing with me man."

"It was good," Derek said. He decided it was best to start to go along with the course of the conversation and not keep playing dumb. "She damn near turned my ass out. That girl had some tricks I had never seen before."

"Daaaamn," Rashad said laughing. "I knew that girl was a closet freak, as soon as I saw her in that dress. Running around here in those business suits, and coming out to the club looking like that. So you still seeing her or was it a hit and quit it thing?"

"We've been out a few more times," Derek admitted. "Hell, I had to find something to do since you've gone MIA."

"Yea, I know," Rashad said. "I've been spending every free moment I can with Camille. That girl's got me all twisted. You know what I mean?"

"Yea," Derek said and then quickly added, "I've been there, man."

"And besides that I've asked you to hang with us and you always claim you got something to do. Like I bet you got something going on tonight don't you?"

"Not really, I was thinking about asking Melissa to a movie, but I'm not sure."

"Well, why don't you guys come out to Destiny with us for open mic night?"

Derek ran several excuses through his head as to why he could not make it but they were all lame. He had painted himself into a corner and there was no way out.

"I'll call her and see if she's up to it," Derek said.

"No need, I spoke to her in the elevator this morning and she said she'd love to."

Derek looked at his friend in amazement.

"What? Just covering my bases."

"Where's the trust?" Derek said sarcastically shaking his head. "After all these years of friendship, and still no trust."

"Shut the hell up," Rashad said laughing.

Derek kept looking at the clock as the day passed along. He felt like he was counting down to his execution. He made phone calls to potential and existing clients and to some of his basketball contacts to see if some of their clients were going to get looks in the summer league.

Melissa called at around three thirty to confirm their plans for the evening. They agreed to drive separately and meet at the club right after work to take advantage of the happy hour specials. Derek rushed her off of the phone. He wanted to think as little about the possibilities of the evening as he could. He knew it was ridiculous, but he felt like a criminal returning to the scene of the crime.

As five o'clock approached he tried to settle himself.

Rashad was just getting off the phone with a client when he asked, "You ready?"

"Yea, let me put this paperwork away," Derek said.

"Okay, I'll wait for you," Rashad said, "so we can go out to the garage together."

Camille arrived to the club before anyone else. She sat in her car wondering how she would get through the evening. In the two weeks that had passed since their kiss, she had managed to push most thoughts of Derek out her head. She pulled the sun visor down for the mirror.

All right, you can do this. It's gonna be good. She began retouching her lips with the tingly Bare Minerals gloss she recently purchased. She pressed her lips together to distribute the shine evenly before taking a deep breath to steady herself. She decided to make her way into the club and find a table. If she chose a table, she would be in control of some aspect of the evening.

Camille was happy to see that it was a very nice turnout for a Wednesday night. She noticed a good spot to sit down but chose to order a drink first from the bar.

"What can I get you, miss?" The woman behind the bar asked.

"I'll have a cosmopolitan." Camille responded.

"Very well."

Two minutes later the woman placed Camille's drink on the bar. She paid and made her way over to the table. She chose a table off to the side of the stage, away from the speakers. There was a DJ playing some light R&B sounds as some of the staff set up the stage with a microphone. She sat with her drink and waited for the evening to begin.

Derek, Rashad, and Melissa all drove separately from Towne Center. It was a quick drive, but Derek still felt like a man making the slow trek towards the electric chair.

You're being ridiculous, he thought. *Just chill out and be cool.* He pulled into a parking spot next to Melissa's car. She stood behind her car waiting for him to get out.

"Hey baby," she said giving Derek a big hug and kiss on the lips. "I feel like I haven't seen you in forever."

"Yea," Derek said returning the hug. She really was a sweet girl, and an incredible lover, but aside from the physical he felt very little connection to her.

"You guys comin'?" Rashad yelled from near the entrance.

"Yea, we comin'?" Melissa said grabbing Derek's hand.

When the two of them entered the club they noticed Rashad making his way to a table near the stage. There were other people moving around the club and obscuring his line of sight, so Derek assumed that Camille was already seated.

"Guess we follow him, huh?" Melissa said leading the way.

Rashad was giving Camille a hug and a kiss on the cheek as Derek and Melissa arrived to the table.

"Aw, you guys are so sweet," Melissa said as she took her seat.

Derek sat down beside her, pretending to look around the

club at the other patrons. The waitress approached the table as the four of them took their seats.

"What can I get you guys?"

"Rum and coke," Derek said quickly.

"Umm, I think I want a white Russian," Melissa said.

"Jack and coke, please," Rashad said.

The waitress left to retrieve the drinks from the bar.

"So Melissa, I've been meaning to ask you a question. Why are you driving around in a Corolla? I mean no disrespect but you're an accountant you should be making good money." Rashad said.

Camille nudged him with her elbow deep in his side.

"Oh, my Cora Corolla," Melissa responded. Everyone else kind of glanced at one another with a 'oh really' look on their faces trying not to laugh. "You're not the first person to ask me that. I'm tight with my money. It's part of the curse of being an accountant. Besides I've had her since college, she still drives great, and I don't have to worry about car payments every month."

"Well I guess she told you." Camille said laughing.

Melissa smiled at getting Camille's approval. "So how long have you guys been together?" Melissa asked.

"We met in February so I guess about five months," Rashad explained.

"Cool," Melissa said. "You guys make a cute couple, almost as cute as me and my baby." She leaned over and kissed Derek on the cheek.

Camille felt a little nausea, but it quickly passed. She noticed that Derek's reactions to Melissa were a little stiff and unemotional. *He's just going through the motions*, she thought. She decided to feed the fire a bit.

"You guys do make a cute couple," she said with a sly smile, this time earning her own jab in the ribcage from Rashad, who apparently saw the same thing she did.

"Thanks," Melissa said. "I'm so glad Rashad hooked us up. I was waiting for Derek to ask me out, but he acted like he barely even noticed me."

"He was just playing hard to get," Camille said.

"Yea, I know," Melissa said looking at Derek fondly.

Just then their conversation was interrupted by the MC stepping to the microphone. "Good evening ladies and gentlemen," he said in a low smooth voice. It was the same young man that was with Tyrone on opening night.

"I guess he made Tyrone pretty happy," Rashad whispered to Camille. She laughed and punched him in the leg. Derek noticed the exchange and felt a twinge of jealousy. He placed his hand on Melissa's thigh and smiled at her.

"Welcome to Club Destiny's Spoken Word Night," the young man continued. "My name is Phillip and I will be your host this evening. What you will be seeing tonight will be some of the finest poets and wordsmiths in the seven cities. So sit back relax and allow these men and women to take you to new heights, new depths, and unexplored regions of your soul."

He paused and the audience applauded.

"Our first poet for the evening is Ladybug. Everyone give it up. " Philip stepped away from the microphone and a young, brown skinned woman took the stage. She was wearing a black, short sleeve scoop neck shirt with light khaki beach Capri style pants. Her thick hair was back off her face and neck with a black headband in a puffy ponytail that which was actually leveled across the back of her head. Her hooped earrings matched the silver arm bracelet she had on her left arm. The crowd lightly applauded.

"Good evening everyone. This is a little something I wrote while I was in college and it's titled *Fell Through.*"

I don't know if you miss me,
But as you enter my path
I want your arms around me,
And a kiss "Hello"... on my forehead.
Where did that warm feeling in my veins go
And that sudden loss of focus
Come from?
It went cold.
Love.

Five more minutes would...be...so nice.
I gave you me and we fell through.
You fell through on me.
I'll never know you again."

The crowd applauded once again as the woman left the stage. Camille was impressed by the talent level of the performers. Some spoke about pain and heartache, while others spoke with fire and vitriol. Still others spoke about tenderness and love. Camille had written some poetry of her own when she was in college, but she felt like she would never be able to share it with the emotion that these people were. There was an intermission after about an hour.

"That was awesome," Camille said wiping tears away.

"You're crying?" Rashad asked.

"Yes, I'm crying," Camille said. "That was beautiful and so sad."

Derek sat across the table with his hands tented across his nose and his eyes closed.

"You alright, baby?" Melissa asked.

"Yea," Derek said wiping away a tear. "That poem just made me think about my mom."

"Aww," Melissa said hugging him around the neck. "Where is your mom?"

"She died a couple of years ago," Derek explained. Even though he and Melissa had been out on a few dates he had never felt as comfortable with her as he had with Camille and therefore had never really shared more than superficial information with her.

"I'm so sorry," Melissa said stroking the side of Derek's face.

Camille observed the exchange from across the table without saying a word. *He didn't tell her about his mom*, she thought. *He told me about that in one of our first conversations.*

"I have to go to the men's room sweetie," Rashad whispered to Camille.

"Okay," she said still lost in her thoughts.

"Oooh, me too," Melissa said. "I'll be right back baby." She gave Derek a quick hug around the neck and a kiss on the cheek. "Don't miss me too much."

Rashad and Melissa made their way back towards the front of the club to the restrooms, leaving Derek and Camille alone for the first time since their kiss.

"So why didn't you tell her about your mom?" Camille inquired.

"I don't know. It just didn't come up, I guess." Derek said.

"Mmm." Camille said.

"What?" Derek came back.

"Why are playing with this girl?" Camille said.

"Whoa. Where did that come from?" Derek asked.

"This girl really seems to like you. And it doesn't take a genius. I've been sitting at this table watching the expressions on your face every time she made a gesture towards you or commented on something." Camille said.

Derek sat there a little surprised but at the same time could not deny.

"Well, I'm doing exactly what you told me to do which is get you out of my head so don't be so judgmental all right." Derek snapped.

Camille stared at him with a blank look on her face but could not bring herself to say a word in response.

"I'm sorry. I didn't mean to be so abrupt. It's just that I haven't been able to get what happened out of my head. I don't know what to do with myself. Have you had any of this going on at all?" Derek said.

Again Camille sat gazing at him in a state of shock.

"Camille?" Derek said. "Are you okay? Did you hear me?" Derek asked. "Come on, please say something."

"I..." Camille began. "I...think... about you too." She said it slowly not because she didn't mean it but because of what her responding like this would mean.

Derek raised his head a little higher. Now they were both staring into each others eyes, thunderstruck. They were snapped out of their trance by the sound of Rashad's voice.

"Hey pretty lady." Rashad said all smiles not noticing a thing. He gave Camille a kiss on her forehead before he sat back down. Melissa arrived just seconds after Rashad.

"Did you miss me?" Melissa said playfully as she kicked one foot back while kissing Derek on the cheek.

"Well it *was* a quick trip." Derek said nonchalantly.

"I'm glad we did this." Rashad said.

"Me too," Melissa said cheerfully. "I've had so much fun. We should do this again sometime."

"Yea, that would be great," Camille said with a little less enthusiasm. "I'll buy the next round." She waved over the waitress who took everyone's drink order as Phillip introduced the next performer.

They continued to enjoy the poetry and the drinks as the evening progressed. The second set of performers stayed on until about nine o'clock. After the last poet, the deejay began to play some up tempo R&B and hip-hop which got the crowd dancing.

"Well, I think it's about time for me to head out," Derek said.

"You don't wanna dance?" Melissa asked with a disappointed look.

"Not really," Derek said.

"Pleeeaaasse," Melissa said with an exaggerated frown.

Derek smiled at her childish, but kind of cute behavior and said, "One dance."

"I'll take it," Melissa said grabbing his hand and pulling him out on the dance floor.

"You wanna dance?" Rashad asked.

"Sure," Camille responded.

They made their way to the dance floor to join Melissa and Derek. The two couples ended up dancing to a few songs before making their way back to the table.

"You guys are pretty good," Melissa said to Rashad and Camille.

"Why thank you," Rashad said. "You can thank me for all of

Derek's dance moves too. I taught him everything he knows."

"Even how to slow dance?" Camille joked.

"Well, maybe not everything," Rashad said. They all laughed as they gathered their things from the table.

They exited the club into the warm mid-summer night. It was a pleasant evening as the usual humidity that dominates Hampton Roads' summers had granted the area a temporary reprieve. The four of them stood outside of the club for a few moments enjoying the night air and the light breeze that cooled their sweat from dancing.

"You comin' to my place?" Rashad asked.

"Yea, I just have to stop by my apartment to pick up a couple things," Camille said.

"Okay, well I'll have a bath ready for you," Rashad said kissing her lightly on the forehead.

"Thanks," Camille said. "My muscles are a little sore from my workout this morning."

"You want me to wait for you?" Rashad asked.

"No I actually think I'm going to go back in for a minute to speak to Tyrone," Camille said. "I would feel bad coming out to the club and not at least saying 'hello'."

"Well, I can wait," Rashad said.

"Its fine, you go on ahead," Camille insisted giving him a kiss on the lips.

"Okay, if you say so. Alright D, thanks for coming out man," he said giving his friend a hug.

"No problem, kid. Thanks for the invite," Derek said.

"And it was a pleasure as always Miss Melissa." He gave her a peck on the cheek and a hug before making his way to his car.

Camille gave Melissa and Derek hugs and said her goodbyes before going back into the club to find Tyrone.

"Soooo, what are you gonna do?" Melissa asked.

"I don't know," Derek said. "I'm kind of tired."

Melissa gave him the same exaggerated sad little girl look she had given him about the dance.

"Well you know Sean left last week to go play ball, but Sydney's staying at the house cause her lease ran out," Derek said. "She has to get up early for work and I don't want to keep her up."

"Now, why do you think we'd keep them up?" Melissa asked coyly. "I know how to be quiet."

"Well, you sure fooled me," Derek laughed. "Why don't you go home and I'll call you and let you know if she's already in bed."

"Okay. So you promise you'll call?" Melissa asked as he walked her to her car.

"Yes, ma'am," he said opening the door for her. She kissed him on the lips before getting in the car.

"Okay, well I'll talk to you in a little while," she said as she started the car.

"Alright," Derek closed the car door and she drove away.

Derek walked over to his SUV and was just opening the door when he heard, "Hey!"

He looked up to see Camille walking towards him from the club. "Hey yourself."

"You sent Melissa home without you?" Camille asked as she reached the front of the SUV.

"Yea, I'm going to give her a call when I get home," Derek explained. He felt his pulse quicken as looked at her. He jingled his keys nervously. "Sounds like Rashad has another romantic evening planned for you guys."

"Yea, he's great," Camille said. "He's a sweetheart."

"He's a lucky guy."

"What is this?"

"What is what?"

"*This*. This thing we're doing?" Camille said getting animated. "Why are you still here? Why did I stop you from leaving? Why are we doing this to ourselves?" Her hands started to tremble as her emotions began to get the better of her.

Derek closed the door of the SUV and walked over to her. "I don't know," he said taking her hands in his. "I just know that every time I look at you all I can think about is holding you in my arms."

"Stop," Camille said.

"I want to kiss you."

"Stop."

"I want to caress your skin."

"Stop."

"I-"

"Just stop it. Stop it!"

Derek released her hands. Tears began to form in both their eyes.

"I'm sorry," Derek said. He turned to walk back to get into his SUV but felt Camille reach out and take him by the wrist. As he turned to look at her he was both shocked and pleased to feel the warmth of her lips on his own. She ran her tongue lightly across his lips and he responded with his own.

Camille pulled away and looked into his eyes. He started to speak but she placed the first and middle fingers of her right hand over his mouth. She was breathing hard as though she had just finished a brisk run. She closed her eyes for a moment before turning and walking to her car quickly.

Derek stood in the parking lot watching as she got into her car and drove away. He stood there for another minute or so as he watched her taillights disappear down the Boulevard. He got into his own vehicle and drove home.

Chapter 29

Derek lay in bed staring at the ceiling. It was about 2:30AM and he had not yet been able to fall asleep. He could still feel the warmth of Camille's lips on his. He sighed deeply both from the memory and because he knew that he was moving into territory that would be impossible to get out.

How am I going to face Rashad? If he ever finds out about this he will kill me, and he would have every right to. You don't do this to a friend. Why can't I get her out of my head? He reached over and retrieved his phone from the nightstand. He had put it on silence in case Melissa called. He had three texts messages from her: Wht hppnd?; RUOK?; worried U said u wuld call Plz let me knw u ok

As Derek finished reading the final text the phone screen indicated that Melissa was calling. He decided to answer instead of running the risk of her coming over.

"Hello," he said sleepily.

"Are you ok?" Melissa said worried.

"Yea, I'm good," Derek said. "I'm sorry I didn't call you. I started not feeling so well when I got home." He did not like lying but did not want to hurt her feelings. Despite everything she really was a sweet girl.

"Aw, you want me to come take care of you?" Melissa said sweetly.

Derek sighed, he did not want to do this over the phone but he felt like if he did not do it now he would take forever to get up the courage again.

"Melissa," he started, "You're a really sweet girl and we've had a lot of fun, but I just don't think I'm ready to be in a relationship right now."

"What do you mean?" Melissa asked. Derek could hear her voice crack as she held back tears.

"I mean, that I like you and all, but I think you want more of a commitment than I'm ready to give you. So I think its best if we end this now before it's too late."

"Too late?" her tears had given way to anger. "You just used me you asshole. You never cared about me I was just a quick screw and now you've gotten your rocks off and you want to kick me to the curb, well *fuck* you." The phone went silent.

Derek looked at the phone and saw the flashing call time indicating she had hung up. He sighed, put the phone back on the nightstand and rolled over to try to get some sleep. He tossed and turned all night unable to get any restful sleep and felt as though he could not turn off his brain. He finally began to doze at some point just before dawn.

When Derek awoke, the sun was shining brightly through his window. He quickly reached for his phone and saw that it was nearly 8:30 in the morning. He quickly dialed Rashad's cell phone.

"Where the hell are you?" Rashad asked without saying hello.

"Man, I'm not feeling so great," he was using the same lie, but this time he would hold to it.

"Boy, you need to stop letting that young girl keep you up all night. You not as young as you used to be. This ain't college no mo'."

"Whatever, dude," Derek said. "Seriously though, I don't think I'm gonna make it in today. I should be back in tomorrow. I'll try to get some work done from here, though."

"Okay, man. Take care of yourself. Or better yet let Melissa take care of you."

"Very funny. I'll talk to you later."

"Bye," Rashad said still laughing at his own joke.

Derek rolled over and went back to sleep. He finally got up around quarter to eleven. He made himself some breakfast while watching SportsCenter. They were running a story on a professional basketball player that Robert was acquaintances with. He was firing his agent. Derek sent a quick text to Rashad: We nd 2 cll Rob his boy looking 4 new rep.

Alrdy on it, was the response he got back.

Derek smiled. Rashad loved this job and had probably gotten a message on his phone as soon as the story broke. Derek wished his own passion for the job equaled his partner's. He decided to make a few phone calls and send some e-mails in order to not make the day a total loss and to keep his word to Rashad about getting some work done.

It's the least I can do, considering, he thought.

Just before noon, Derek's cell rang. He looked at the screen and saw Rashad's name.

"Hello," Derek said.

"Hey, how you feeling?" Rashad asked.

"Eh," Derek answered.

"Well, we got a problem," Rashad said. "They're ready to finalize Alan's contract and he wants one of us down there with him to make sure everything is in order."

Damn. Derek thought. This would have given him the perfect opportunity to get away from this situation for a few days. "Well can they wait until tomorrow? I could go down when I'm feeling better. I know you went down last time and Camille and you need to spend some quality time."

"No, they want to knock it out today if possible so he can attend the next OTA which starts this weekend. Thanks for the offer though. I'm gonna catch a flight in a couple hours, so I'll give you a call when everything's worked out."

"Okay," Derek said. "Don't forget to ask Rob about his boy."

"You know I'm all over it, dude."

"Alright, then be safe."

"Later."

*****

"Are you all right?" Sydney asked Camille. It was almost noon and Camille had been in and out of daydreams the entire morning. *That damn kiss. Why did I do it?*

"Sure. Of course." Camille answered. She really needed to concentrate on her work. Since the radio spot and the opening of the club, she was starting to see an increase in business.

"You know I've been meaning to ask if you might consider

getting an intern here with us. With the business we're getting now, this would be great experience and exposure for a marketing or public relations major." Sydney proposed.

"Hmm. That sounds like a good idea. It's something we can seriously consider. It would have to be unpaid though," Camille said as she looked intently at her laptop screen.

A cell phone began to vibrate. "Is that you?" Camille asked.

"Naw, my phone isn't on vibrate." Sydney responded. Camille fumbled through her purse to find it was indeed her phone that was going off. She looked at the screen. *It's Rashad.*

"Hello." Camille answered.

"Hey sweetie, how's it going?" Rashad asked.

"Not bad. I have a lot of hits on my website since the club opening. What's up with you? Everything okay?" Camille asked.

"I have to go to down to Miami. There are some issues with Alan's contract and we're trying to get it done ASAP." Rashad said.

"Well didn't you go last time? Why can't Derek go?" Camille inquired.

"Derek called in. He's not feeling well so I told him I'd go. I'll be leaving out later this afternoon. I knew I wouldn't get a chance to see you so I wanted to call to tell you what was up." Rashad said.

Camille felt bad for thinking it but she needed a day or two, maybe even three to think, without Rashad being a presence.

"How long are you gonna be gone?" she asked.

"I'm not sure. Hopefully no longer than a couple of days," he answered.

"All right then well, I guess you gotta go," she said with a melancholy tone.

"I know, I know. Well, listen, I'll contact you before I fly out. I'll be thinking about you the whole time I'm down there you know that right?" Rashad said.

"Ummhmm whatever. This is Miami we're talking about," she said giggling.

"Come on now, *you're* my girl." Rashad said trying to

convince her that he wasn't going to be spending wee hours of the night in strip clubs. "Love you."

"Love you too." Camille responded and pressed END on her cell.

"Everything good, Camille?" Sydney questioned.

"Yea, it's all good." Camille said. But it wasn't all good. Camille was in love with two men: her boyfriend and his best friend.

Chapter 30

On Thursday night, after Rashad left for Miami, Camille went straight home from work for a glass of wine and some TV and went to bed. On Friday she did the same thing except she had about three glasses of wine with a few other alcoholic beverages. It was Saturday morning. She was feeling slightly depressed about this whole Derek situation. She just wasn't up to talking to anybody however she did make sure she answered Rashad's calls. She awakened around 8:30 lying on her back. The tie on her head wrap was repositioned from the front where she knotted it last night to the back of her head. The thick, white Victoria Secret robe she had on was bunched up to her hips and she was wearing one fuzzy sock.

"Ohhhhh." Camille groaned. She put her hands over her eyes then quickly reached for a pillow to cover her face. She had left the blinds open and the sun was beaming in. "Uuuhhhh," she groaned again. "I gotta get up." She rolled out of bed to close the blinds and then plopped herself back on to the bed face down. *Bzzzzzz.* Camille laid still. *Bzzzzzz.* "Stop buzzing." Camille said out loud. *Bzzzzz.* Her phone continued to vibrate. "All right, all right!" Camille forced herself to raise up. "Where are you?" Camille shouted. She pulled herself to the edge of the bed, leaned half her body towards the floor and pulled the covers up. The phone was under the bed. It had already stopped buzzing by the time she got to it. One missed call...Rashad. By now, she raised herself up to a seated position in the middle of her bed with her back to the headboard. She decided to call him back immediately.

"Rashad?" Camille said.

"Camille you sound terrible, sweetie are you all right?" Rashad asked.

"Eeehhh, yeah. I just had a long evening," she said.

"Oh, you went out last night huh?" Rashad asked.

"No, I stayed home. I was just up late watching movies and made myself a few drinks is all." Camille said. "So how's the trip going?"

"Good. I should be taking a flight out tomorrow morning

around 8 o'clock." Rashad said.

"Sweet." Camille said.

"By the way there's something I wanted to talk to you about too but it can wait 'til I get there," he said.

"No, I wanna know now. Please tell me." Camille pleaded in a raspy whiny voice.

"Well, I don't know how you may feel about this but I was wondering if you would..." Rashad hesitated.

"If I would what?" Camille was curious now.

"If you would consider us moving in together."

Camille was shocked. "Uh, I don't know."

"I knew I shouldn't have brought this up over the phone." Rashad said a little upset with himself.

"No, no, it's okay really. I mean I insisted." Camille said to ease his mind.

"The thing is Camille, well, I'm really diggin' you. I think about you when I wake up, when I go to bed and I haven't felt like this about anyone. I was hoping that you felt the same way I did and that perhaps we could talk about moving our relationship to the next level." Rashad said.

Camille felt a mixture of emotions the predominant one being flattery. This man was so good to her. "Wow, Rashad I didn't know you had been thinking about this. Let's talk more when you get home," she responded.

"Okay then." Rashad said with a sigh of relief. Even though she didn't give him a straight forward answer, she still didn't say no. As far as he was concerned, there was a chance she may seriously consider it and if not, at least he put it out there how serious he was about his commitment to her. They each said their 'I love yous' and disconnected.

Damn, damn, damn. Camille thought. *I can't keep doing this.*

*****

The few days without Rashad around were actually quite

good for Derek. Rashad had called on Thursday evening to let him know that Alan's contract had been signed and that he would be able to join the team during the off season training session during the upcoming weekend. Since Alan was a late round pick his contract was not very big and there was no guarantee that he would make the team, but with Robert's help and training he had a very good chance.

On Friday, Derek went into the office around nine in an effort to avoid running into Melissa. He felt horrible for leading her own and for letting it go as far as he had, but he did not know what else to do to get Camille out of his head. This situation was driving him crazy.

Maybe I should tell Rashad, he thought. He had no idea what that would accomplish aside from guaranteeing himself a butt kicking. The last thing he would ever want to do is cause a rift in his friend's relationship so he knew he could not do that.

Derek decided to put the thoughts out of his head and concentrate on work. He made calls to clients, potential clients, contacts, and teams on behalf of his clients. He was so focused on work that he barely realized when five o'clock had come around until he got a call from Rashad.

"What's up man?" Rashad said.

"Just working," Derek answered.

"Working? You? Get out of here."

"Shut it," Derek said.

"I'm just messing with you man. You feeling better I take it?"

"Yea, I'm in the office. Had a pretty productive day. Some of our guys are getting some looks for the pro basketball summer league and the developmental league."

"That's great," Rashad said. "I spoke to Robert about his boy and he's going to give us a chance to sit down with him to pitch our services."

"Really?"

"Yea. He said he'd fly up next week to meet with us both."

"He's gonna come see us?" Derek said surprised.

"Yea, I was a little shocked too, but he knows we're small and he said he has family up our way that he was planning to visit."

"That's great," Derek said. "I'll start putting a presentation together this weekend, and we can work on it together when you get back. When are you coming back by the way?"

"Oh, I'm taking a flight on Sunday morning. Robert arranged for me to get a tour of the Miami training facility and he's started construction on his gym so I wanted to check that out too."

"Okay, well I'll try to have something together by then."

"Alright, man. Well I'll see you Sunday," Rashad said.

"Okay, bye." Derek was actually excited about how productive he had been and about getting to make a presentation to such a high profile client.

I could learn to love this job, he thought to himself as he packed up for the evening. He was so lost in thought that he nearly forgot about potentially seeing Melissa in the elevator. At the last second he decided to walk down the seven flights of stairs instead of risking a confrontation in the elevator.

*****

RDR had completed Sean's contract with San Francisco and he was in Arizona playing in the rookie league. He and Derek talked about every other night on the phone.

"So how are things with you and Syd?" Derek asked as he plopped down on the couch and turned on the game system.

"Pretty good," Sean said. "I miss her to death, but I'm doing what I love and she really loves working with Camille."

There's that name again. Derek thought.

"Yea, she sounded pretty smooth in that radio spot they did a few months back. They still play a clip of it for the radio commercial for the club," Derek said.

"Really, she didn't tell me that. That's great," Sean said. "I am so proud of her."

"You should be. She's really got her stuff together. Have you guys talked about what happens next?"

"What do you mean?" Sean asked. He shared an apartment with a couple of his teammates from the team. He lay on his back on his bed tossing a baseball up in the air and catching it barehanded.

"Well you don't know where you're going to end up after spring training," Derek said. "You could end up in single A ball or back in the rookie league."

"Yea, I know, but I'm hoping, that with my experience from college and if I can keep hitting like I'm doing now, I can at least get up to double A. And since they just moved there double A affiliate to Richmond, I'll be an hour and a half away."

"Well what if you get called up to the bigs? I know it's a long shot, but you'll be all the way on the other side of the country. You guys talk about what happens then?"

"No, not really," Sean said, his mood changing a bit. "I've kinda been scared to bring it up."

"Why?"

"I mean, everything she, hell *we* know is on that side of the country," Sean said sitting up in the bed. "Her family, her friends, and now she's found this great job she loves. I feel like if I don't give her a reason to stay interested she might move on."

"You're crazy," Derek said as his team lined up for a field goal. "That girl loves...you." He said as the ball sailed just left of the upright.

"Yea, I love her too, but can I really ask her drop everything and move all the way to the other side of the country with me?"

"So she can stay here and keep working at the PR firm, and you can come back during the off months," Derek said. "You are going to be on the road for weeks at a time anyway."

"Yea, but what's gonna make her wait for me?" Sean asked. "I mean if she's there, then I'm all she has, but if she's here, what reason does she have to stay faithful?"

"Love you idiot," Derek said. "That girl loves you and you love her. If she comes out there and is basically alone for week long stretches, she'll start resenting you. I mean this way you can both pursue your dreams. Don't make her give up hers so you can have yours. That's what dad did remember?"

Sean was silent on the other end of the phone.

"Hello?" Derek said.

"Despite all your cynicism, you've always been a romantic at heart," Sean finally said.

"And despite all your romanticism, you've always been a cynic. You could always ask her to marry you," Derek said half jokingly.

"I've been thinking about it," Sean said.

"That's great, man," Derek said. "Syd's a great girl and I would be proud to call her my sister."

"Thanks bro," Sean said.

"When are you gonna ask her?"

"I'm not sure yet. I want to concentrate on making a good showing out here then when I get back, start talking to her about some things."

"Well, I'm proud of you little brother. And mom would be too."

Chapter 31

Derek had spent Saturday night working on the presentation for the potential client. He wanted to have something to show Rashad when he got back from Miami.

Sydney came into the living room dressed in a tight fitting pair of fashion jeans, and a three quarter length purple button up blouse. Her lease had run out at her apartment and her roommate had moved back home. So while she tried to find a new place she was staying in Sean's room.

"You sure you don't want to go out with us?" Sydney asked. "We are going to hit Jillian's at Waterside to play pool then head over to Destiny for some dancing. It's old school hip-hop night. It'll get your mind off Melissa." He had told her about breaking it off with Melissa, but had left out his true reason why. She was going out with a group of friend's from college.

"I'm cool," Derek said. "I have some work to do. You guys have fun."

"You sure? I'm sure Sean would want you to keep an eye on me. Make sure I don't get out of control."

"I'm sure you can handle yourself. Just be careful," Derek said.

"Okay, well give me a call if you change your mind." Sydney said.

"Will do," Derek said knowing that he had no intention of doing so.

Derek got quite a bit of work done on the presentation before dozing off on the couch watching a baseball game. When he awoke the next morning, there was a fleece blanket thrown over him and the television had been turned off. He figured Sydney had come home and decided to let him sleep on the couch instead of waking him. It was only about seven in the morning. Rashad had not told him when his flight was arriving, so he figured he would just wait until he heard from him.

I probably won't hear from him 'til tomorrow anyway,

Derek thought. *I'm sure he'll want to spend the day with Camille.* Despite his attempts to push them away, feelings of jealously hit him and he sighed deeply. He decided to go up to his room and lay back down.

He heard a light knock at the door and Sydney stuck her head into Derek's room around ten o'clock in the morning. "Hey, you want some breakfast?"

"Naw, I'm tired," Derek said rolling back over.

"Alright," Sydney said. "Don't sleep your life away."

*****

Camille decided to clean up the place a bit. It smelled lemon Pledge fresh in the living room. It was about 10 o'clock. She wasn't exactly sure what time Rashad would be landing because she didn't know if he had a direct flight or a layover. She was a little nervous about talking to him. The thought of moving in together threw her for a loop. Inside, her emotions were all over the place and deep down, she knew it wouldn't be fair to lead him to believe that things were moving in the direction he hoped for this quickly. She wanted to at least discuss slowing things down a bit. *What a mess all of this is.*

By the time Camille had showered and dressed, it was 11 o'clock. She headed out to Target to pick up some necessities. As usual, she took a detour on her way to the domestics department towards the book section. She read the backs of a few black fiction novels. "Mmm, maybe I'll write my own book one day." She said in a low voice to herself.

She pushed the cart around the corner towards the movies and saw Tyrone further down the back isle with a gentleman. She looked a little harder and noticed it was Phillip, the open mic host from Club Destiny.

"Tyrone?" She called out lightly but loud enough for him to hear.

Tyrone turned around holding a couple of CD's in his hand.

"Camille!" Tyrone responded. Each of them began to walk towards the other. "Getting some shopping done I see."

"Yeah, you know, I had to pick some things up." Camille said. She waited for Tyrone to finally introduce his friend. She wanted to be polite, so she took the initiative.

"Hello, I'm Camille Jacobs. I believe I've seen you at the club." She extended her hand towards the friend.

"Yes, I recall. I'm Phillip. Nice to see you again." Phillip said extending his hand to exchange a friendly shake. Tyrone stood there for a second until he broke out of his trance.

"Yes, how rude of me. I suck." Tyrone said disappointed in himself. Phillip kind of curled his lips and gave Tyrone a funky stare.

"I'll be over in electronics." Phillip said walking away.

Tyrone turned to him slightly and nodded his head to show that he had heard him. Camille just smiled.

"So are you here with your friend... Rashad, right?" Tyrone asked.

"No, he's actually on a flight back now from Miami. He had some business to take care of down there. I'll see him within the next couple of hours or so."

"Oh okay." Tyrone nodded.

"You know I've received a lot of hits on my website ever since the radio spot and the club opening. Sydney and I are pretty excited. It's all thanks to our business relationship and marketing endeavors for Club Destiny." Camille said.

"I'm happy to hear it. If there is anything I can do to help in any way, please don't hesitate." Tyrone offered.

"Thanks, I may take you up on that." Camille responded. "You know I was thinking that you should really consider creating a website. You could post an events calendar, special guests and whatever else on there. It would be great advertising."

"Yeah, that's a good idea. A really good idea." Tryone agreed. "I'll brainstorm and let you know my thoughts."

"All right then." Camille said.

"Well, I'd better go." Tyrone gave Camille a hug. "I'll talk to you soon. Enjoy your day with Rashad."

"Thanks." Camille said. Tyrone walked away towards Phillip in the electronics department.

Camille proceeded to shop. She spent about a half hour longer in the store before she headed home.

Camille had unpacked her purchased items and made herself a turkey sandwich for lunch. It was nearing 1 o'clock and she had received no contact from Rashad.

"Well, I guess I'll give it a little longer." She whispered to herself. To keep her mind occupied, she decided to catch up on some work. It would be a good time to make out a schedule for the week. Camille plugged in her laptop and got busy. She went to Pandora for some music to get her going. She requested a Jill Scott play list and A Long Walk was the first thing she heard. *Ohhh, I love this song!* She adjusted the volume louder.

Bzzzzzz. Bzzzzzz.

"Hello." Camille answered.

"Hey sis, what's up?" Shayla asked.

"Girl, I just plugged in this laptop to do some work. I'm waiting for Rashad to get back. He's supposed to be back soon so I'm just killing time. Thought I'd try to be productive."

"Oh okay. Well, I won't keep you then. I just wanted to say hey." Shayla said.

"Did you need to talk about something? Are the kids okay?" Camille asked.

"Yeah, everything is everything. I'm gone for real. I'll talk to you later." Shayla insisted.

" All right, love you." Camille said

"Love you." Shayla said and they both disconnected.

*****

Derek was awakened by his cell phone ringing. He looked at the phone and saw a 619 area code. He was unsure of who it could be.

"Hello," he said as he answered the phone.

"Hey, may I speak to Derek please?" The man on the other side of the phone asked.

"This is him," Derek answered.

"Hey, Derek this is Malcolm," he paused obviously waiting to see if Derek would remember who he was. "Rashad's older brother."

"Oh, hey Malcolm," Derek said his memory finally jogged. "How are you?"

"I...well, Derek I have to tell you something."

*****

Thump! Thump! Thump! Thump! Thump! Camille had fallen asleep on the couch. She was awakened by a knock at the door. She let out a small groan and got herself together. She rubbed her eyes and matted her hair as she raised herself from the couch and approached the door.

"Who is it?"

"It's me, Derek."

What the heck is he doing here?

She undid the deadbolt on the door and opened it. "Derek what are you doing here? How did you know where I lived? What's going on? Damn I must have dozed off. What time is it?"

"Listen, can I come in, first?" Derek said seriously. Camille noticed he looked disheveled.

"Um, sure. Have a seat on the couch." She closed the door hurriedly. Derek remained standing.

"Derek I'm confused. What are you doing here and...oh, my gosh! Did something happen to Rashad?" Camille exclaimed. Derek dropped his gaze to the floor. He took a deep breath and raised his head. A tear began to roll down his left cheek.

"There was a plane crash. There are no survivors. Camille....Rashad." He began to cry harder. "He was on the plane Camille, he was on the plane!" Derek shouted. "He's gone. Rashad is dead!" Derek fell to the couch.

Camille stood as Derek fell to the couch. She lifted both

hands to her mouth. “Oh no! No! No! No!” Camille cried out. She fell to her knees in front of Derek as he lay weak and slumped over the armrest of the couch. “This can’t be! This just can’t be!” Camille cried.

Chapter 32

The next week was a blur as Rashad's family flew in and Derek assisted with preparations for the funeral. He helped Malcolm go through Rashad's contacts to determine who and how to inform them of the situation. Derek broke down several times over the week between finding out about Rashad's death and the day of the funeral.

He spent many hours looking over the news reports about the plane crash. Apparently a flock of birds had flown into one of the engines of the plane disabling it. According to the black box recordings and the accounts of the air traffic controller the pilot and co-pilot had done everything they could to make an emergency landing, but were unable to get the plane down safely. All one hundred and seventeen people onboard were killed.

Rashad's parents decided to have the funeral at the Monumental Methodist Church on Dinwiddie Street in Portsmouth, since it was not too far away from Rashad's apartment. Derek served as a pall bearer, he felt like he did not deserve to honor his friend in that way, but did so at the request of the family. It was a beautiful service. Over a hundred people showed up including Liz and Ian, Robert, Alan and members of his family, and Daryl and Charity were also in attendance. Derek saw Camille sitting a few rows behind Rashad's family crying on another woman's shoulder. He assumed that it was her sister, Shayla.

After the minister gave his final remarks at the graveside, Derek walked back towards Sean's car. Sean had been granted permission to leave the team for a couple of weeks. There would be no gathering afterwards. Rashad's family was flying back home that evening and Derek had told Sean he did not want people gathering at the house. He avoided Camille at the funeral and had no intention of speaking to her anytime soon.

Derek's guilt was suffocating. Not only had he made advances towards his best friend's girl, his lie had sent him to die in his place.

"If I had gone to work that day I would be the one that had

died."

"That's ridiculous," Sydney said as she turned to look at Derek sitting in the back of Sean's car.

"You are out of your mind," Sean said as he merged into downtown tunnel traffic. "There's no way you can blame yourself for this."

"How can I not?"

"Because Rashad didn't have to choose that flight. You may not have chosen that flight. You might have left a day or hour earlier or later," Sydney insisted. "What happened *happened*. It was his time to go."

"Who's to say if he hadn't stayed here that he might not have gotten hit by a bus or died in a car accident? You know as well as I do that we have no say in when or how we go."

Silent tears began to roll down Derek's cheeks. He felt like crying was all he had been doing for the past week. Maybe they were right, but that did not relieve the guilt of betraying his friend's trust. Derek began to pray for the first time since he knelt at his mother's bedside the night she died. He asked for forgiveness. He prayed that Rashad would forgive him for his betrayal and that he was at peace.

It was nearly midnight. Sydney rolled over and began coughing.

"You okay?" Sean asked groggily.

"I need something to drink," Sydney said as she sat up in bed.

"I'll get it." Sean rolled, half asleep, out of bed and onto his feet. He stumbled towards the door as his eyes adjusted to the dark. "I'll get you some water."

"Thanks, honey."

Sean made his way down the stairs. The entire house was dark. The shock of turning on the kitchen light caused him to squint as his eyes readjusted. He nearly screamed when he noticed Derek sitting motionless on the couch.

"What the hell are you doing sitting in the dark?" he asked.

"Thinking. Praying."

Sean walked over and sat down beside his brother. "I know you miss him."

"I have something I need to tell you," Derek said closing his eyes.

"What?"

Sydney had decided she would rather have warm milk instead of water and had started to make her way downstairs, when she heard Sean and Derek's voices. She paused. She could only make out some of what they were saying.

"I kissed Camille," Derek stated.

"What? When?"

"The night Destiny opened and then on the night we went to happy hour."

Sydney lingered for a few moments more before turning and going back upstairs to the bedroom. She decided not to eavesdrop or interfere in the conversation.

"Did Rashad know?"

"No," Derek said quietly.

"So...she kissed you back?"

"Yes."

"That's all that happened?"

"Yes. It never went any further than a kiss."

"Did you want it to?"

Derek did not answer.

"I guess that was a stupid question. So now what? Are you going to pursue...this?"

"I can't," Derek said. "Rashad's dead and I feel like it's my fault and I betrayed his trust."

Sean put his arm around his brother's shoulder and squeezed. "You have to stop blaming yourself."

"I know man. I just can't."

****

It had been a month since Rashad's death. Camille slowly got back into the groove of work. It was around eleven Saturday morning. Camille was in bed trying to relax with a hot cup of green tea. She closed her eyes and massaged her temples. She hadn't even showered. There was a knock at the door. *Who would be coming over? Oh well.* She ignored it. The knock continued. *Okay shall I dare answer this door?* She planted her feet on the floor and made the walk to the door.

"Who is it?"

"It's me sis."

"And Sydney."

Camille was not up for company but couldn't help but feel warm and fuzzy inside when she heard it was them. She opened the door. The two ladies stood with big smiles on their faces and she returned the gesture. They all embraced in a group hug and Camille invited them in.

"What are you two doing here?" Camille asked.

"We came over here to provide you with some quality girl time." Sydney said enthusiastically.

"Yes. I wanted to spend some time with you. Plus Sydney mentioned that you've kind of been burying yourself in your work for the past couple of weeks. I thought we could just hang out, ya know, have a girls day." Shayla said.

"Oh you guys, this is so sweet." Camille said almost in tears.

The ladies were all seated on the couch with Camille in the middle.

"You know it hasn't been easy getting through these past few weeks. Sometimes I still can't believe it. He asked if I would consider us moving in together you know." Camille revealed.

"What?" The two responded in unison.

"You never mentioned that." Shayla said.

"Yeah, in our last conversation he asked me. I told him that we could talk it about it more when he returned." Camille said.

"Well what were you going to tell him?" Sydney questioned.

"That I wasn't ready." Camille answered.

“If you don’t mind me asking, what was stopping you? I mean you two seemed so happy.” Sydney said. Camille sat in silence for a few seconds.

“You know what never mind. I shouldn’t have probed. Please forgive me, Camille.” Sydney mildly pleaded.

Camille looked over at her sister. She wasn’t comfortable with telling Sydney about her feelings for Derek and the kisses they had. She blew it off quickly.

“Listen, I’m gonna get in the shower and get myself dressed. You two make yourself at home. I want to take advantage of this. Besides how often does a lady get to be pampered by her two best girls in the world?” Camille said smiling as the ladies smiled back.

After Camille got dressed, the ladies went out for a day on the town. They went window shopping at MacArthur Mall and decided to catch a movie while they were there. In Camille’s mind, this was just what the doctor ordered.

Chapter 33

Camille was starting to feel a little better each day, especially after the girls' afternoon out, which was over a month ago. Since then, she had gotten more back into the swing of things. She had picked up a few new clients and she was working out at least three days a week. In addition, her friendship with Sydney had grown stronger. It was time for her to move on. As much as she loved Rashad, she couldn't bring him back. His life was cut short but he was in a better place. She would miss him always.

The fall was nearing and the weather was getting cooler. She was staring out of the office window across the city buildings. *Mmm. I need to consider moving to Florida one of these days.*

"I love this job." Sydney cheered. Camille looked around with her arms crossed. "There's always something to learn and I enjoy meeting people and being creative. Thank you so much for giving me this opportunity Camille."

"Sydney, you've been working with me long enough now. You're my colleague and a young professional. No need to thank me. You earned the opportunity." Camille said.

"You know Sydney I really wanted to tell you how much I appreciate you being here. Not just as my colleague but as my friend. You and my sister have been such a huge support system to me since Rashad's death. I don't know how I would have made it up to this point."

"Oh girl, don't mention it. I know you would have done the same for me. We all need someone to lean on sometimes and I'm glad that you consider me your friend." Sydney said.

"Hey what do you say we go grab some lunch? My treat." Camille offered.

"Sounds great!" Sydney agreed.

"How do you feel about sushi?" Camille inquired.

"Oh, okay. I think there's a sushi bar in Waterside. Maybe we can go there." Sydney said.

"Yeah that's exactly what I was thinking." Camille said.

The ladies worked diligently until the clock read 12:15. "Oh my. It's already after twelve. You about ready to go?" Camille asked.

Sydney responded, "Yea, wow time flies. Listen I've been wanting to tell you something."

"Is it serious?" Camille said with undivided attention.

"Well, that depends. I overheard a conversation Derek and Sean were having late one night. I know what happened between you and him."

Camille's stomach dropped as if she were on a roller coaster free fall. "What?"

"Derek told Sean that you two kissed on a couple of different occasions while you were dating Rashad. Now I know this is none of my business but me knowing was on my conscious and is sometimes downright uncomfortable. You're my friend and I just wanted to let you know I knew." Sydney said nervously.

"Does Sean know you overheard the conversation?" Camille asked.

"No he doesn't. I've kept it to myself for all this time." Sydney answered.

"How long?" Camille asked.

"The night of the funeral," Sydney answered.

Camille didn't know where to begin. Sydney continued. "Listen, from the little I did hear, I gather that Derek really has deep feelings for you. He beat himself up something awful because he felt like he betrayed his best friend."

"I don't know what it was. I mean we had tea one time and then dinner. This was all in the beginning stages of me and Rashad's relationship." She continued as she paced the floor. "And then it was like we ran into one another while we were out and about. The first time we kissed was at opening night of Club Destiny and then again sometime later following a happy hour outing. Neither one of us expected to feel this much chemistry for the other. Rashad never found out about it. My plan was to ease out of my relationship with Rashad, forget about my feelings for Derek and just be on my merry way. I didn't want to be the woman to come between a lifelong friendship between two wonderful guys, especially over something like that. You must think I'm an awful person." Camille took a deep breath after she finished her rant.

"Camille, of course not. Things happen." She got up from the chair of her desk and walked over to Camille. "I know you both loved Rashad very much but maybe you two need to talk, you know to clear the air. It's not healthy to keep this bottled up inside. You guys owe it to yourselves to at least talk. Everything happens for a reason."

"Sydney it's over." Camille stated.

"Do you *really* believe that?" Sydney asked.

*****

The two months after Rashad's death were difficult for Derek. Many of RDR's clients had joined the company based on Rashad's pitch and now that he was gone Derek decided not to force any of those who chose to leave to honor their contracts with the company. Most did buy out of their contracts just out of common decency.

For those who decided to stay, Derek spoke to each one individually. His conversation with Alan was indicative of the rest.

"Hey Mr., I mean Derek," Alan said quietly. "How are you?"

"I'm making it," Derek answered. "Look Alan, I know you want to be loyal to the company, but I'm not sure there's gonna be a company for you to be loyal to much longer."

"Are you closing down?"

"I'm not sure what I'm gonna do Alan," Derek said. He looked across the office at Rashad's desk. He had only cleared it of Rashad's papers in the last week. "This company was a dream that Rashad and I had as kids and something that he always loved. I enjoy the job, but I don't know if I enjoy it enough to do it without my friend."

"So what are you going to do?"

"I don't know yet. I spoke to some friends of mine at other

companies and they are interested in buying your contract. You know I wouldn't set you up with anyone that I don't trust."

"Yea, I know," Alan said hesitantly. "I understand where you are coming from, Derek. I hope you change your mind, but I trust you to put me in good hands."

Derek sold off the majority of the contracts but decided to keep Alan's and of course he would continue to represent his brother. That left him with three contracts: Sean's, Alan's, and Robert's. Since each of their deals were finalized with there teams, and none looked like they would be getting any endorsement deals anytime soon, Derek needed to figure out what he wanted to do with his life.

One thing that he felt he needed to do was speak to Camille. Derek had no idea what he would say to her but he knew something had to be said. He had never had the type of connection he had with her. He just felt that if he could talk to her then things would be okay. He had no idea what okay would look like, if it meant they would be able to be friends or if they would just say their goodbyes, he just felt as though talking to her would make the world right.

Sean had flown back out west to complete his stint in the Rookie league and would not be returning until mid-September. Derek spent that time getting closer to his father. He helped him complete the nursery and was there when Charity's water broke. His new baby sister Diana Melody Ballard was born on August 23rd. He decided to allow Daryl and Charity to spend some time alone with the baby and did not see them for the next few weeks.

*****

"Hey Syd," Derek said as he entered the kitchen one evening a couple days after Sean had returned home.

"Hey," Sydney was preparing some turkey burgers that Sean was going to cook on the grill for dinner.

"Hey bro," Sean yelled from outside where he was attempting to light the grill.

"Hey, man." Derek sat down on the couch heavily.

"You okay?" Sydney asked.

"Yea, I think I am," Derek said.

"That's good," Sydney said.

The two had grown closer while Sean was away. Sydney had been a major support system for Derek, and he was glad that she was around.

"How's business?" Derek asked.

"Great! I love this job so much," Sydney said cheerfully. "And Camille is a great boss."

"That's good," Derek said. "How is Camille anyway? I haven't seen her since the funeral."

"She's doing better. She really threw herself into the job for a while, but I think she's coming around to being her old self again. Losing Rashad hurt us all, but life does have to eventually go on." Sydney smiled knowingly at Derek before taking the burgers out to Sean who finally had the grill ready to cook.

Derek wondered what that smile meant. *Did Sean tell her? Or did Camille?* What if Camille had told her? What would that mean? He did not want to slip back into old habits so he quickly pushed the thoughts from his head and joined his brother and Sydney in the backyard. They ate and after dinner played dominoes while Sean told stories about his teammates and the crazy fans that he had encountered.

"Oh my goodness," Sydney said looking at the clock. "It's nearly midnight and I have to work in the morning. I need to get to bed." "You coming baby?"

"Yea, I'll be up in a few minutes," Sean said.

"Okay, don't be too long."

"I won't."

Sean watched her walk away and waited until he heard the bedroom door close before he said anything to his brother. "I wanna ask Syd to marry me."

"Yea, you told me that already," Derek said wryly.

"Ha ha," Sean said. "I mean that I want to do it soon." He reached into pocket and pulled out a ring box.

"Wow. When?"

"I have a plan percolating," Sean said wiggling his fingers on either side of his head. "And when it is ready, I shall let you know."

Derek raised a concerned eyebrow at his brother. "This isn't going to be anything too cheesy, is it?"

"Me? Cheesy? Never. I, my friend, am a romantic," Sean said as he stood from the table. "And now I am going to go make love to my future wife. Sleep well."

"Yea, that thought'll help," he laughed.

Chapter 34: The Proposal

Perhaps Sydney was right. Maybe it wasn't over. Camille wanted to have a conversation with Derek but found not uttering his name around Sydney at work was more therapeutic at the time. Now, some time had passed. Circumstances were different. Camille thought. *Could there be a chance for me and Derek?* Her cell was going off on the living room table. She was delighted to see it was Sydney.

"Hey girl." Camille picked up with pep in her voice.

"Hey Camille. What you doin?" Sydney asked.

"Right now nothing. I know I left the office a little early today. Is everything all right?" Camille asked with concern.

"Everything is fine. Why don't you come out to Destiny tonight?" Sydney suggested.

"Mmm. I definitely don't have any plans. Cool. What time should I meet you there?" Camille asked.

"Around ten o'clock. " Sydney answered.

"I'll be there." Camille said. "Hey I wonder if Shayla can get out. It will be a drive for her but I think the kids may be with their dad for the weekend."

"Oh, yea. It's always a pleasure to see her. Well, I'll text you when I leave the house." Sydney said quickly.

"All right then." Camille said and disconnected. She smiled to herself thinking this was a great idea. Getting out was just what she needed. *Hmmm what am I going to wear?* She thought as she searched in the closet. Shayla's number was on speed dial in her cell. When she answered, there was commotion in the background.

"Hello!" Shayla exclaimed.

"Shayla." Camille answered

"Hello!" Shayla said again. "Put that down and get back over here!"

"Girl it's me. Sounds like a circus at your house." Camille said with a chuckle.

"Please excuse me for yelling in your ear. These kids are off the hook." Shayla came back.

"I was gonna ask if you'd be interested in coming out to Destiny tonight. I'm meeting Sydney up there in a few hours." Camille said.

"Damn! I wish I could but the kid's dad won't be here to get them until tomorrow morning. Plus I'm lookin' after my neighbor's daughter until about nine o'clock. So you'll have to count me out sis."

"Oh ok. Don't let those kids drive you crazy." Camille laughed.

"Oh no, it's gonna be all right. I'm gone. All right one....two....three....!" Shayla hung up the phone.

Camille shook her head as she hung up. *All right sexy lady, it's time go out and have some fun.*

*****

Sean and Sydney were on their way to Club Destiny. Derek was taking forever to get dressed so they left without him, plus he said he wanted to drive his own car. Sydney pulled her phone from her purse.

"Who you textin?" Sean inquired.

Sydney cleared her throat. "Camille."

"Oh!" Sean said surprised. *How would Derek react?* "Uh, did you invited her out?" Sean asked.

"Yeah. She's my friend. Besides we've worked hard all week. I thought it would be nice to chill and have a good time tonight." Sydney responded.

"Yeah of course." Sean said. He didn't want to betray his brother by telling Sydney about their conversation but he wasn't completely comfortable keeping it from her either, especially now.

Sydney felt guilty for not telling Sean that she heard what Derek said downstairs that night. It was time for her to come clean. "Babe, I got something to tell you."

"What is it?" Sean asked.

"That night of the funeral, I kind of heard some of your conversation with Derek."

"How much did you hear?" Sean asked.

"Enough." Sydney said.

"Sooo, that's why you're inviting Camille out tonight?" Sean had put it together.

"Listen, I hope you're not upset. There's more." Sydney said.

Sean braced himself.

"I told Camille." Sydney said with her eyes squinted.

"Oh my gosh Syd!" Sean exclaimed. "Exactly what did you say to her?"

"I just told her I knew that they kissed a couple of times while she was seeing Rashad." Sydney responded.

"Does she know Derek is going to be here tonight?" Sean asked.

Sydney with her eyes squinted again. "No."

"Oookay," Sean said. "So are we playing matchmaker now?"

"I don't know. I just think they need to talk. They haven't seen each other since the funeral and if they have feelings for each other they at least need to talk about it," Sydney said confidently.

"Syd, I hope you know what you're doing," he had learned to not question her when she was like this.

"Yea, me too," Sydney said under her breath. She prayed the entire way to the club that this evening did not turn into a disaster.

*****

Derek was actually dressed fifteen minutes before Sean and Sydney had left for the club. Sean had asked him to pretend to take a long time, because he knew Sydney would get impatient and want to leave.

He waited until their taillights disappeared around the corner and quickly exited the house and got into his SUV. He drove over to the DoubleTree hotel located in the Military Circle Mall. Sean had reserved a room for the weekend and had asked Derek to set it up for him. Tonight would be the night that Sean would ask Sydney to marry him.

Derek used the key that Sean had given him and let himself

into the room. There was a clear box of rose petals along with a few other items on the bed. Derek spread rose petals around the king size bed and also in the Jacuzzi style bathtub.

He also set up candles throughout the room, which Sean would light when he and Sydney arrived. Derek felt a little odd spreading rose petals on his brother's bed, but wanted to make sure that the night was perfect for his little brother and Sydney. He also placed a bottle of champagne next to the bed in a metal tin of ice. Hopefully the ice would not completely melt by the time they arrived. The final piece of the experience was the chocolate covered strawberries which were on a metal plate which he place in the middle of the bed.

Derek stepped back and admired his work. He smiled. He was proud of his little brother. He turned off the light as he left the room and headed over to Club Destiny.

*****

Sydney and Sean found a good table. They had already ordered their drinks and were there for about fifteen minutes before they saw Derek walk in. Sean raised his hand in the air to get his attention. Derek noticed and made his way over.

"Hey you two. I see you started drinking without me." Derek said.

"Well you know a girl's gotta try to get a little drink on. Especially since I'm not driving." Sydney said sipping on her cosmopolitan.

"Uh huh." Derek said.

Hell Sydney needed a drink. She didn't know how Camille was going to react to seeing Derek and vice versa. Derek sat down at the table and Sean ordered his brother a drink.

They laughed it up for five minutes. Derek excused himself to the restroom.

"Slow down, Syd." Sean said.

"I'm a little nervous." Sydney said. She looked up and saw Camille walking in looking around for Sydney.

Sydney raised both hands so she could see her. Camille smiled and made her way to the table.

"Hey girl," Camille said. "Thanks for inviting me. Sean it's nice to see you. Sydney didn't tell me you'd be out too. Not that I have a problem with that or anything. Hell, I was just amped to be going out period." Camille said.

"Sure....yea." Sean said sipping on his drink.

Camille took a seat and noticed another drink at the table. "Oh, I see someone else is here with us. A friend of yours Sean or you Sydney?" Before they could answer, Derek approached the table.

Camille was shocked. "Derek."

"Camille." Derek said back. "Have you been in here?"

"It's nice to see you, Derek." Camille said now mildly shocked and trying to get her thoughts together.

"Camille let's talk for a second. Sean, order her a drink will you?" Sydney got up from her chair and grabbed Camille's hand. She walked her to a corner of the club where the music was a little muffled.

"Sydney what is going on?" Camille demanded.

"Sean wanted to go out tonight. I told him in the car on the way here that I overhead his discussion with Derek that night. Sean didn't know I asked you to come. I thought this would be a good opportunity for you two to talk. Please don't be mad at me Camille. I just gave things a little push, that's all." Sydney explained.

Camille didn't know how to feel. She stood there for a second leaning against the wall.

Meanwhile, Sean was getting an earful from Derek. "Man what the hell? Did you know Camille was going to be here?"

"I had nothing to do with it. Sydney knows what happened between you and Camille. She heard us that night and told her about it." Sean said.

"So what is she trying to accomplish here?" Derek asked.

"What's the worst that can happen, man? You two need to talk for real, get this out in the open. Stop tap dancing around and confront this issue tonight." Sean strongly advised.

"It isn't an issue." Derek said.

"Okay." Sean said with a sarcastic tone.

The ladies made their way back over to the table. Everyone took a seat. There was a drink on the table that Camille assumed Sean ordered for her. She picked up the glass and took a small gulp. No one said a word for what seemed to be an eternity. Sydney decided to make a run for it.

"Sean let's dance." Sydney ordered. She didn't give him a chance to speak and grabbed his hand and off they were. This left Derek and Camille at the table alone. They both sipped on their drinks in silence until Camille spoke.

"This is ridiculous. We're sitting here like two kids who just got in trouble at school. We may as well be standing in a corner with our faces to the wall."

"Damn that happened to you too?" Derek joked trying to break the ice even more.

She chuckled. "First grade for talking while the teacher was talking."

Derek laughed back. "It's been a while since we've seen each other. How have you been?"

"It was hard at first but, every day got a little better. I've had a lot of support from Sydney and my sister. Work has kept me busy. And what about you?" Camille asked.

"It's been a struggle. Rashad was like a brother to me. I kind of shut down for a little while." Derek said.

Camille nodded slightly indicating that she understood. Derek continued.

"I've been doing some soul searching. Also been trying to establish a better relationship with my father. Charity had the baby by the way."

"Yeah Sydney told me, a little girl." Camille said.

"Yeah, a little sister," Derek said with a smile.

Camille was happy to see Derek smile. He had a great smile and she had missed it.

"Derek," Camille said her tone turning serious. "What are we doing?"

Derek smiled again, "We were at Destiny the last time you asked me that."

"Yea, and then you kissed me," Camille said.

"Excuse me. Actually, if memory serves that time you kissed me."

Camille smiled as she realized Derek was right.

"Look Camille, we obviously have...had some chemistry, but with Rashad's death...I'm just not sure if...." He stopped and stirred his drink with the thin straw.

"You're not sure what?" Camille asked.

Derek sighed and closed his eyes. When he opened them Camille was looking at him waiting for an answer.

"He saw you first, and me pursuing you was just wrong. I betrayed my friends trust and he never knew."

"Well, not to be contradictory, but you and I met long before I met Rashad."

Derek looked at Camille confused. He wondered if she was getting weird and talking about past lives or something.

"You don't remember do you? I didn't either until you told me you were in Chicago last summer. I had braids then and I was wearing glasses."

Derek continued to look perplexed, and then suddenly it hit him. "O'hare airport! You were at the baggage claim."

"Yea, and you gave me some lame lines," Camille said. "I thought you were cute though."

They both looked at one another like a couple of middle school kids who had just admitted to liking one another.

"I still do," she added taking another gulp of her drink.

"So have you two worked things out yet?" Sydney said as she and Sean returned to the table.

"Don't mind her she's a little tipsy," Sean added as he pulled out the chair for Sydney to sit.

"I am not drunk," Sydney said. "I just want two people that I care about very much to stop torturing themselves."

"Yes, Syd," Camille said. "We've worked a few things out. Thank you for pushing things along."

"You're welcome," Sydney said as she turned and stuck her tongue out at Sean.

"Hey ya'll we gonna slow it down for a minute," the DJ said through the speakers as the music changed from hip-hop to an instrumental jazz piece. They saw Phillip, Tyrone's friend, walk up on the stage.

"Good evening ladies and gentlemen," he said in his smooth voice. "Normally we reserve Wednesday nights for open mic poetry night, but tonight we have a special request. Please welcome Mr. Sean Ballard to the stage."

Everyone one at the table looked at Sean in shock.

"What's going on, Sean?" Sydney said sobering up and grabbing his hand.

Sean simply smiled at her and walked up on to the stage. He shook Phillip's hand and stepped to the microphone.

"Um, sorry to interrupt the party, but I'm going to try to make this quick," Sean said nervously. He reached into the back pocket of his jeans and pulled out a folded piece of paper. "I know that most of the guys that get up here go off the dome, but I need some notes." He cleared his throat.

"Derek, what the hell is he doing?" Sydney asked desperately.

"Shh," Derek said pointing up to the stage.

"This is titled *To Sydney, My Perfect Song*:

Your voice moves me
Like the soft melodies of Jazz
Your eyes pierce my soul
Like the soulful sounds of the Blues

When we kiss my heart pounds
With the rhythm of a phat Hip-hop beat
When we touch my skin tingles
With the power of a classical symphony.

When we make love
Our souls sing.

Sydney you are the music of my heart."

Sydney began to cry as Sean concluded his poem. Derek stood up and escorted Sydney to the stage where Sean took her hand and brought her up to join him.

"Sydney, through everything you have been there. You are my queen, you are my angel, you are my heart," Sean said as he got down on one knee and pulled the ring box out of the inside pocket of his sport coat. He opened it and the crowd cheered and wooed. Sydney could not control the tears and covered her mouth with her hands.

"Sydney will you-"

"Yes! Yes! Yes! Yes!" she hugged him tightly around the neck not giving him a chance to complete the question. The crowd cheered even louder and more boisterously.

Sydney pulled herself away from Sean just long enough to allow him to put the ring on her finger, before basically wrapping herself around his neck. Sean half walked half carried her back to the table.

"Did you know about this?" Camille asked Derek as Sean and Sydney arrived.

Derek smiled and nodded in response.

"Congratulations, girl," Camille said hugging Sydney when she pulled away from Sean so that they could sit down. "I'm so happy for you. Oooh look at that rock."

"Thanks. I know. Isn't it gorgeous?" Sydney said.

Derek hugged his brother and whispered, "You treat this girl good, you hear me?"

"Yes, sir," Sean said. They had always promised one another that they would never walk out on their families like their father had done to them. Each made the other swear to keep them accountable and to be a constant support in their relationships.

"So you guys need to get going," Derek said as he hugged

Sydney.

"Where are we going?" Sydney asked.

"Well, my dear the evening is not yet over, I have another surprise for you," Sean said.

"What?" Sydney nearly screamed with excitement.

"I'll have to show you. Come, my dear your destiny awaits."

The newly engaged couple made their way out of the club receiving pats on the back and handshakes from the other patrons as they passed.

"So where are they going?" Camille asked curiously.

"Sean had me set up a room he reserved for the weekend at the Double Tree," Derek explained. "Then tomorrow he has some other stuff planned."

"What kind of other stuff?"

"I think I'll let Sydney tell you about it on Monday. I know how you girls like to gossip."

Camille looked at him suspiciously. She hated it when someone knew something she did not and would not share, but she decided that maybe it would be more fun to have Sydney tell her about it and let it go.

"You know it's almost midnight," Derek said. "I missed dinner getting all the stuff for Sean and Sydney together, you want to maybe head over to IHOP and grab something?"

"Yea, let's get out of here," Camille said.

"So what do you mean my lines were lame?" Derek asked as he took another bite of his pancake.

"I was just kidding. I don't even remember what you said to me. I just knew I wasn't in the mood to be dealing with anyone right then, males in particular." Camille responded.

"Bad break up?" Derek asked.

"Remember I told you about the guy that was threatened by my career." Camille said.

"Oh yea, well, he was crazy." Derek said.

"Yeah, well, that's in the past." Camille said quickly. "So, do you feel weird or anything?"

"About what?" Derek asked.

"About here and now. Us sitting here talking." Camille said.

"No. Despite everything, I've always felt very comfortable talking to you. " Derek said with a smile.

"Oh, okay. Good." Camille said. "Life is funny."

"How do you mean?" Derek asked.

"When I saw you in that airport, I had no idea that I would see you again, let alone fall for you." Camille said without thinking.

"Excuse me. I'm sorry could you repeat that?"

Camille quickly took a sip of her tea trying to give herself a moment to think. She sighed as she placed the tea cup back on the table.

"Does it really surprise you to hear me say that?" she asked deciding to not play the coy role.

It was Derek's turn to stall for time. He took the last bite of his pancakes and washed it down with a swig of chocolate milk. "A little...well no I guess not. It's just that...I...I've been wanting to hear you say that, but at the same time afraid of hearing it."

"Why afraid?"

"I don't know," Derek lied.

From the way Camille looked at him he knew he was not going to get away with that answer. The waitress came over and placed the bill on the table. She asked if there was anything else she could do for them and they said no.

"I already felt like I did something wrong, when I fell for you," Derek said resuming the conversation. "Now that Rashad is gone, I don't have the guilt of feeling like we're sneaking around behind his back."

"But we never really snuck around," Camille argued. "We probably should have told him that we had talked and gotten to know one another. I think the lie of omission is what made it feel wrong."

"That and the fact that every time I saw you I wanted to grab you and kiss you," Derek said.

"Yea, I guess that would have made things a little awkward," Camille said with a chuckle. Derek joined her in chuckling at the absurdity of the thought. "So has that feeling passed?" Camille asked still smiling.

"Not at all," Derek said the smile disappearing from his face.

"So why haven't you done something about it?"

Derek smiled. *Nice teeth*, Camille thought.

They went to the register and paid the bill. Camille told Derek if he would pay for her tea she'd leave the tip since she had a little cash on her. They walked out into the cool late night air. Autumn had arrived in full force and it was obvious that winter was close at its heels.

Derek walked Camille to her car and as she turned, around presumably to say good bye he placed his hand gently on the small of her back and pulled her towards him. The kiss was perfect. There was no fear of being caught. No twinge of guilt. It was just Derek and Camille. Camille felt as though she fit perfectly in his arms, and Derek felt as though time had stopped.

"I want to make love to you," Derek said as they finally pulled away from one another.

Camille swallowed hard. She had not wanted anything or anyone as much as she wanted Derek in that moment. She nodded. Her breathing and heart rate increasing.

"Sydney and Sean should be gone all weekend. Follow me to my place." His words came confidently but his eyes pleaded with her.

"Okay," she said breathlessly.

Once Derek and Camille got to his place, they rushed in through the front door. They began kissing and touching each other all over. He pulled her dress off her body over her head, stopped and stared at her for a long moment.

"You're perfect," he said softly.

She looked deeply into his eyes. She began to undo his shirt. He was wearing a T-shirt underneath. She returned the favor by pulling it off. She rubbed her hands along his smooth, dark chest.

"So are you," Camille said. She unzipped his pants. He stepped out of them one foot at a time.

They started kissing again as they playfully made their way to the bedroom. Derek picked Camille up, "over the threshold" style and placed her on the bed. He walked around to the foot of the bed and stood admiring her perfect form in the moonlight which filtered in through the window. He crawled in between her legs and began to kiss her thighs lightly allowing the tip of his tongue to slip between his lips. He blew on the moist spots gently. She moaned at the cool sensation. He made his way up gently gliding his tongue across the lips of her vagina. He lingered for only a second allowing the intoxicating aroma of her juices to arouse him further.

His journey continued as he played with her belly button with his tongue again blowing it dry. As Derek reached her breasts, he lightly kissed and nibbled them. He ran his tongue around the edges of her areolas feeling the tiny bumps indicating her arousal. Derek took her left nipple in his mouth and flicked it gently with his tongue and then did the same with the right. He kissed her on the neck, behind her ears, on her cheeks, nose and forehead, before again kissing her passionately on the mouth.

Camille was outside of herself in ecstasy. She was enjoying everything Derek was doing, but felt as though she wanted to participate. She was not lazy in bed by any means. She gently pushed him away and sat herself upright and began to suck on his neck.

"Oh, I see how it is," Derek said.

She motioned for him to lie on his back. She kissed him beginning with his lips and neck. She ran her hands over his chest and kissed and sucked on each of his nipples. She paused at his belly button for a moment.

"You have an outtie," she said with a chuckle.

"Hmm-hm," Derek said completely aroused.

As she reached his waist with kisses, she wrapped her hands around his penis. He was hard as a rock. She began to stroke him with her right hand, caressing his six-pack abs with her left. He moaned with pleasure. She grabbed one of his hands and sucked on his fingers one by one. Derek lay back with his eyes closed only for a second. He wanted to watch her every move. Camille continued the foreplay by going down on him a bit, just as a tease. Derek allowed her to continue for a few minutes as he rubbed his hands along the smooth skin of her shoulders and back. He motioned for her to stop and lie on her back.

"I've gotta return the favor, right?"

"If you insist," Camille answered as she followed directions.

Derek made his way back between her legs. He lay flat on his belly propping one of her legs over each of his shoulders. He gently kissed her inner thighs allowing the perfectly trimmed pubic hairs to tickle his cheeks. Camille's body lay still until Derek worked his tongue between her lips and she released a sigh...and then a louder sigh of pleasure. She felt Derek's tongue searching her. He worked his tongue in every direction possible. He moaned and breathed deeply like a starving man eating his first meal in days. Camille began to moan louder and arch her back.

She thought he wouldn't stop until she climaxed, but just before she did he stopped. He crawled quickly up the bed and began kissing her. He slipped into her effortlessly as her juices flowed and swallowed him into her. They both moaned simultaneously. Camille climaxed quickly as Derek had already brought her to the brink with his tongue. Her orgasm was intense and long. She felt tears begin to flow from her eyes. She grabbed Derek's face with her hands and looked into his eyes. He then spoke the words that his eyes were saying.

"I love you."

Camille wrapped her arms around his neck and pulled him on top of her, relishing in the full weight of his body on top of hers. She climaxed again as Derek also finished. They lay motionless in one another's arms. Derek nuzzled his face in Camille's neck breathing heavily. She kissed him on his neck and cheek and caressed his back.

"I love you, too," she said. "There's no place I'd rather be than right here, right now, with you."

Bonus Features